BLACK FEATHERS

BLACK FEATHERS

{ *erotic Dreams* }

Cecilia Tan

*To Jake —
Can you
Believe it?
Enjoy!*

HarperPerennial
A Division of HarperCollinsPublishers

pp. 293–95 are an extension of this copyright page.

HarperCollins books may be purchased for educational, business, or sales promotional use. For information please write: Special Markets Department, HarperCollins Publishers, Inc., 10 East 53rd Street, New York, NY 10022.

FIRST EDITION

Designed by Elina D. Nudelman

Library of Congress Cataloging-in-Publication Data

Tan, Cecilia, 1967–
    Black feathers : erotic dreams / Cecilia Tan. — 1st ed.
        p.   cm.
    ISBN 0-06-098501-1
    1. Erotic stories, American.   2. Fantastic fiction, American.   3. Women—Sexual behavior—Fiction.   I. Title.
    PS370.A483B58   1998
    813' .54—dc21   97-53232

98 99 00 01 02 ❖/RRD 10 9 8 7 6 5 4 3 2 1

{ contents }

{ acknowledgments }

Thanks go to my agent at Lowenstein-Morel Associates, Eileen Cope, without whom this book wouldn't exist, and my editors Elissa Altman and Cynthia Barrett, who have nurtured it along.

I'd also like to thank the editors whose encouragements and deadlines keep me in the writer's chair, Laura Antoniou, Susie Bright, M. Christian, Michael Thomas Ford, Amelia G, Richard Kasak, Pam Keesey, Geraldine Kudaka, Carol Queen, Thomas S. Roche, Lawrence Schimel, Marcy Sheiner, and Tristan Taormino. I'd be remiss not to also thank Pamela Perka at Emerson College.

I also couldn't have done it without the loving support of my partner, Corwin; my parents; and my communities: the BASFFWG writers group, the National Writers Union, the National Leather Association, and all the prospective members of the Erotic Writers Too Busy to Have Sex club.

And Ted, Diana, Gayathri, Robert Michael, and Ian (among others), for their parts in the creative process.

Wish Fulfillment

Having one's first book published seems as
though it ought to be an auspicious occasion, with
much fanfare, but as I sit here to write this
introduction I think I'd prefer to keep it simple—
there are fireworks and crescendos aplenty in the
stories themselves. I decided to open the book with
the stories that are the shortest, and in some ways
the sharpest. Each one is the pith of a fantasy,
where the important sex takes place in the mind.
You might think that fiction would obviously imply
fantasy. But the craft of the fiction writer is judged
by how believable the story is, making it less than
trivial to remind the reader that what we are
exploring here is the world of our imaginations—
or, more specifically, the world of my particular
erotic imagination. Fantasy is important, and
something I'll talk more about again.

"Penetration" is the only story I've ever written
using the second person point of view, a form of
writing I believe works best in erotic stories, when
the narrator is speaking to an imaginary (or real)

1

partner. The second person is pure fantasy, because it is one person's vision of another entirely dreamed up. When I teach erotic writing workshops, one of the exercises I give my students is to write an erotic love letter; in a story such as this, that communication becomes prose fiction.

The other two stories in this section both have their roots in autobiography—they say you should write what you know. I won't reveal what parts here are autobiographical, but I will say these stories are a reminder of just how important fantasy and fantasizing were to me when I was young, inexperienced, and alone. If we can't be free to imagine anything our hearts desire, how will we ever know love or happiness when we find them?

Cecilia Tan

You think I'm going to tie you down and fuck you, don't you. You think I'm going to strap on a dildo, and do this intercourse thing, play butch boy for you, and let you scream and carry on, indulge your rape fantasies and all that good stuff, that stuff that gets you so hot, that makes you drip wet . . . I can see you dripping now, from the way I grabbed you by the hair and forced you into the bonds, spread-eagled on your bed. Maybe it's the bed, especially, that makes you think we're going to fuck, and maybe it's all the hints you've been dropping to me about the way you like it, the things you've done . . . you're a smooth bottom, practiced, you've been with badder bitches and butches than me. So if I'm going to give you what you want, I know, I've got to give you something you don't know you want. I'm going to start with my finger. I pull off my leather glove and toss it away, and work my index finger right between your wet lips, right into the hot spot, and into you it goes. I can see the look in your eyes—*What, no foreplay? No clit action?*—but as my finger slides as deep as it can go, your eyes close and you gasp with deep pleasure. Then two fingers. You don't need foreplay, you don't need lube, sweet thing, your cunt is hungry and I'm going to feed it. Next, I pull a dagger from my pocket. It's not a dagger, it's a letter opener, but you don't know that. I see you gasp and flinch and squirm—you think I'm going to pretend to cut you, run the tip all over your flesh, across your nipples . . . I see your eyes go wide as I dip it between your legs. Have you figured it out yet? I slide the dull metal into you, using the flat blade like a tongue depressor, to peer into the folds of your flesh. Your vagina convulses as you realize what I'm doing and you strain against your bonds, helpless to stop me. I know if you really want to stop me you'll say the word. But you're too interested, wondering what I'm going to do next, to stop now. I pull a Magic Marker out of my pocket and write my name in flowing script across your belly, then cap the thing and hold you open with the fingers of one hand while I slide the hard plastic cylinder into you. Your legs are shaking as I move it in a wide circle . . . what are you thinking, darling? Have you ever put a Magic Marker up your cunt before? Is this something you used to do when you were a kid, under the sheets at night, terrified of being caught, but unable to stop yourself—what did you turn to when your fingers weren't enough? The marker is not large, but it is hard and foreign, is that what's making you shake? The thought of this thing protruding out of your body, probing into places it was never intended to go? You almost laugh when you see the kielbasa, a thousand phallic puns half-remembered flicker across your face as your eyes take in the curve of sausage in my hand. No, I wouldn't, you think. But I will, and I do, rolling a condom onto the end for full phallic effect, and pushing the thickness against your lips until they give way and then inch it inside. You whimper, a sweet sound. It feels big, I know it, I see you clenching and relaxing, trying to take it in. Good girl. It's too soft to fuck you with so I settle for burying it a few inches deep and then lean down to bite off the end. When my nose rubs your clit I stop my nibbling and pull the meat out of you, toss it away. Too late I realize I should have made you eat some of it, should have let you taste your own juice on it. No matter, there

   Cecilia Tan

is more in store. The unlit end of a burning candle. You twitch as you feel the heat of the flame, although I'm the one who gets wax on her hands as I move it from side to side in you. A pair of black lacquer chopsticks, so thin you barely feel them at all, until I split them like a speculum and widen you side to side, top to bottom. I let you lick them when I'm done. What else can we stick into your cunt, my girl? I've used up the things that I brought with me, so I cast about your apartment looking for more. You've got dildos galore but they don't interest me, cunt girl. I roll a condom over an Idaho potato I find in your fridge, cold and fat and wide, and I push the tip of it in as far as it will go. I fuck you with it until it is sliding in up to its widest point, and you are moaning and thrashing. Have you ever been fucked with something this big, cunt girl? You probably have, I don't kid myself after all the hints you gave me. Have you ever slept with a man? The potato is getting slick and hard to hold onto, but I'm shoving it with my palm into you now. I bet you have slept with men, before, even if you haven't said anything about it to me. How could that hungry cunt resist? A pole of hard, hot flesh, that fits snug and twitches in response. I'd love to have one, myself, love to have one to ram into you and feel your wetness on every nerve ending. But there's no use wishing for things I don't have, and what I have is you, wide open before me, your cunt is my cunt, and I can put anything into it that I like. The potato slips out onto the floor and your head jerks up, your vagina gasping like a fish, so empty, so needy. A bottle of shampoo. The handle of a hairbrush. Pinking shears. Yours is the cunt that ate Tokyo. When I'm done with you there won't be a phallic object left in your apartment that doesn't smell like your desire. Everything will remind you of me. I am just beginning to wish I had a crusty baguette to go with the kielbasa when I decide maybe you've had enough. You sense the hesitation and look up, hope in your eyes. No, I'm still not going to fuck you. You realize it when I pack the harness back into my bag. You want to ask so bad, I see you holding back, you want to beg me for something but you aren't sure whether you can abase yourself that way. Silly girl, you'll let me stick anything into your slit as long as you're tied up. Maybe next time, I'll sit and watch while I order you to stick things up into yourself—a flashlight, a fake rubber dog bone, the old standby: the cucumber. Maybe I'll take photographs of each of these things sticking out of your cunt to horrify my politically correct friends with. You're biting your lip with impatience—I'm sorry, my sweet. I get this way sometimes. For now, what kind of a top do you think I am? Don't worry, I'll get you off. After all, I've brought a whole array of things to try on your clitoris—fur, sandpaper, chains, a nail file, macramé rope, a hairbrush, a braided thong—and when I run out of those I'm sure there are more things here I can try. I'm not tired, not in the least.

Things aren't that easy for a young lad coming out these days, you know. Don't believe me? Think about it: How on earth am I supposed to consider the politics of gay identity, how to tell my parents in the most painless fashion, and safe sex, not to mention getting a fake ID, redoing my wardrobe, and losing my roommate on Saturday nights, when I'm going through life in a hormone-induced, sex-deprived daze? At my desk, I stare at the phone, wondering whether I should call my father, or if I should study, or if I should work on my word processor.

Matthew, my roommate, comes home from his late-afternoon organizational behavior study section. I hear his key in the lock, the door swings open behind me, then shuts. I am alone in the room with the jock from Hell.

My eyes freeze on the Chinese history text on the desk in front of me. Perhaps I should go to the library? Depends on if he's in a monosyllabic mood . . . too late, he grunts as his heavy hand falls on my shoulder. When I don't move quickly enough, he grabs me by the throat with his other hand and lifts me right out of my chair. He pulls me onto my creaking dormitory bed, one hand in my hair, the other hand pushing at his shorts. I take a deep breath of his doughy sweat before he rams his hardening cock into my mouth, shoving my head down as far as it will go. I don't gag, because I take pride in my work, you know. His meaty hand pumps my head up and down like a piston and I eagerly await his bitter, salty come. I want to feel it shooting hot and wet down the back of my throat. I want to suck and lick every last drop of it off of his man meat.

But that's what I get for having most of my knowledge of gay sex come from one or two dog-eared magazines. In reality, Matt comes home, gives me a derisive look, and then calls one of our neighbors on the phone. The neighbor, an almost identical twin to Matt in his shorts, T-shirt, and grungy baseball cap, knocks on the door a few minutes later and the two of them take off for an early dinner before a fraternity rush party tonight. Now I know I can expect him at about three A.M., and hopefully he will have puked already before making it back here.

I go to the caf for dinner somewhat later. As I'm sitting alone with my turkey tetrazzini, I notice a blond guy walking from table to table, putting flyers on each one. He's wearing a tank top and has sunglasses perched on his head, like he's just come from the beach. As he comes closer I can see how good his tan is. Maybe he's from California, I tell myself.

Then he comes and puts a flyer onto my table. It's pink and triangular. I snatch it up right away to read it before he disappears.

Frat boys not your type?
Want to rush where lambda really means something?
Come to our meeting . . .
YOU MIGHT EVEN GET LAID.
Brothers In Gaiety
Do It, College Kids!

My mouth hangs open as I read the meeting time and place. A gay frat? Could it be?

He must notice my shock and apparent interest because he

 Cecilia Tan

circles back around toward me. My pasta is forgotten as he slides into the chair across from me.

"Um . . ." I say, trying to think of a suitably leading question. "Is anyone welcome to join?"

He smiles, but coldly. "You'll find out soon enough if you've got what it takes."

"What does that mean?"

"Follow me." He leads me out of the caf, down the hallway under our dorm toward the computer center. But before we reach the turn in the hallway, he pulls me through a door and into the steam tunnels. "Are you a virgin?" he says, suddenly.

"Uh, yes," I admit.

"Good." He pushes my face against the red painted metal of the door and pulls down my tennis shorts. I feel his bare hand slide along my ass and my cock hardens against the coldness of the door. He keeps one hand on the back of my neck, the pressure just hard enough to let me know that he's in control of me, while his other hand spreads my ass cheeks, a finger sliding between my thighs, tickling the back of my balls, and working its way into the hot center of my asshole. I gasp and begin to shudder uncontrollably as his finger works its way deeper, and then his voice is in my ear. "Quiet down, or do you want everyone in the comp center to hear you humping this door?"

The flyer is for the golf club. I leave it on the table with my uneaten turkey.

Back in the room there is a message on the answering machine from my father. "Colin? We miss you. Your mother and I would like to hear from you. Try to give us a call tomorrow, not too late." Something in the edge in his voice makes me think he's beginning to read between the lines of the letters I have been sending home. I can't quite make myself say, "Dad, I'm gay." It's not for the reason you think. Admitting it is not going to be the hard part. It's what am I going to say afterward when he says, "Are you sure? Have you . . . *ahem, ahem* . . . have you ever . . . ?" And I haven't. I erase the message and change my clothes—a polo shirt, chinos, penny loafers. I've got a fake ID in my wallet and a vague idea of where I'm going.

I've heard rumors of one gay bar in this little city, they call it the No Name because it hasn't got a sign outside. Of course not, because you have to know it is there in the first place or you can't go. Coming out would be a lot easier if someone gave me a map.

A handful of change puts me on a bus downtown. I move past two women sitting in the front, chattering in Portuguese or Italian or something, and make my way to the rear. The bus lurches away from the curb and throws me into a seat across from a large black man in a trench coat.

Here in the back the engine of the bus is so loud I can't hear what he says when his lips move. But maybe he isn't talking to me. He's rubbing his fingers together and muttering. I realize my eyes have fixated on his hand in his lap and I then recognize what he is doing. He is tugging on his penis, folding it this way and that, and it remains flaccid and dry in his hand. I want to look away but I can't, I'm fascinated by the manipulation of his flesh, how he squeezes it between his thumb and forefinger, and stretches it along his leg. His hands are large and creased, his palms pink, as if he's played with his dick so much the color wore off his hands and onto it.

And then he sees me looking. His hand does not hold still. But he stops his muttering, and looks right at me. He smiles, big white teeth in a friendly mouth, and looks at the empty seat next to me. He gives a little nod of his head to me. I nod back, not sure what I'm agreeing to, and put my own hand onto my fly. I'm hard already from watching him play with himself. I want him to continue as he had been. But he stops his hand motion then, and looks at my hand, my crotch, and nods again.

There's no one else in the back of the bus. What's the harm? I think. I unzip my fly, push my briefs down, and let my cock

10   *Cecilia Tan*

stand up. I let my fingers circle around it and look at it in the light of passing streetlamps.

And then he is next to me, like a big warm bear, and one large seamed hand encircles mine and moves over my cock. I slip my hand away and then there is my seemingly small red penis, poking out of the cage of his black fingers. His touch is firm but soft, and he lets the curve of his knuckles fit against the rim of my cock's head as he pulls on it.

In reality, I am daydreaming so intensely that I miss the stop. I get off the bus several blocks away and find myself in a mostly dead neighborhood, downtown offices dark for the weekend and unleased retail space with soaped windows all around. I am heading back toward what I think is the main drag when I notice three figures loitering on the corner ahead of me.

A car pulls past me, then slows to a stop at the corner, window rolled down. The driver is saying something to one of the guys on the corner who takes a few steps toward the car. Then the guy goes around to the passenger side and gets in. As the car pulls away, one of the men left grinds out his cigarette with his heel and walks away with his hands in his pockets and his head hanging. The other settles back against the wall and his eyes slowly turn my way. We make eye contact. I decide to ask him for directions.

"Hey there, pretty boy from up on college hill," he says before I can phrase my question. "Come and shake that ass over here."

"Um . . ."

"I mean now, kid." He snaps his sunglasses over his eyes and everything around me seems darker. His hair is jet-black and his leather jacket gleams with chrome. "Come show me what you got."

My brain is dimly coming to the late conclusion that he is a hustler, a male prostitute, waiting for a customer. "I don't have any money," I say.

He clicks his tongue like a mother hen. "No, no, sweet buns. I been sellin' my ass all night. Now I want yours." He rubs the inside of his thigh and licks his lips. I'm frozen in place as he saunters close and breathes into my ear. "Let me do you right, baby. Come to papa."

I can't even answer as his breath tickles my neck. His tongue flicks my ear and then he pulls me against him, his mouth snaking along my neck, under my chin, all over. I feel nothing but spasms of pleasure down my back and I gasp for air as the hot, wet pressure moves over my skin.

But then he lets me go. "Well, sugar pie, I think whether you want it or not, you are going to get it."

He yanks me into an alley, a crack between buildings barely wide enough for the two of us, and pulls out his cock. It is thick and veined and hot to the touch, and touch it I do, wrapping my fingers around it to learn that yes, it is as thick as it looks. He growls with pleasure as I stroke him. I have the vague hope that I'll jerk him off and he'll be satisfied—I even wonder if I should try to get him in my mouth—but he chuckles after a moment and pulls my hand away. He twists my arm behind my back and I barely can cushion my head against the rough brick with the other. He orders me to step out of my slacks and I do, if only because I hope he won't rip them. I want him so bad, it's true, I'm whimpering as I spread my legs wider for him and thrust my ass out as far as it will go. I want that huge hunk of meat spearing me. I feel it nosing around my virgin asshole and I know it is impossibly large. I want to say no, no, no, but I'm afraid he'll actually stop . . .

I realize that I've found my way to an unmarked door. Muffled sounds of dance music come through it. This must be the place.

The bouncer comes out in a blast of loud noise and tells me my ID's not valid, but he'll let me in if I ream his asshole with my tongue. When I'm done with him, to get a drink I have to let the bartender run cold beer bottles over my nipples and lie on the bar holding a bottle of chardonnay in my crotch while he uncorks it. While I'm on the dance floor, three guys surround me and strip off my shirt; two of them hold my arms above my head and lick my armpits while the third tongues my cock through my slacks.

The phone is cool and smooth in my hand. I decide that letting my father read this story would not be the most painless fashion to inform him that his son is gay. But if it comes down to the proof being in the pudding . . . I don't indulge myself in the fantasy that he reads it and likes it. I just dial the number I know best by heart.

You know what I love about masturbation and a creative imagination? There's always something new to try. Don't ask me what it is about my parents' house that makes me tremendously horny. Perhaps there's this lingering effect of my adolescence, spent poring over teen magazines, being frustrated, hours on the phone with cute but unattainable boys, more frustration, and masturbation.

I went back for a visit when I was in the area for a business trip, and one night I found myself wandering around the house alone after everyone else had gone to sleep. I was tired of the jill-off-and-zonk-out five-minute-orgasm routine. It was time to work up my willpower and top myself again. Self-bondage has been a part of my masturbating as far back as I can remember, and that's pretty far. (Age five, if you must know.)

Kneeling on my bed, I pulled my panties down to my ankles and wrapped one foot around twice, binding my ankles tightly together. Pulling my T-shirt over my head, but without removing it, I exposed my breasts, shivering. Twisting the shirt between my wrists, I bound my arms behind my back, with just enough room between my hands that I could still reach the interesting parts of my body if I tried hard enough.

Then the Top in me ordered me to shut off the

lights. It's much more effective than a blindfold—you can't peek. I nudged the wall switch with my shoulder and the room went black.

I sat that way for a few minutes, resting my buttocks on my heels and my head on my knees, letting my mind go blank. I don't know how long I sat like that, but at some point I was surprised to feel one of my heels was wet. I was dripping with anticipation.

You little bitch, you can't wait for it, can you? Well, you're going to . . . I had the sudden inspiration to try on a belt I had brought with me. Made with three large metal rings, attached to one another by two thin studded strips of leather, I wondered if there was a more creative way it could be worn than just around the waist.

Of course, I had to find it in my suitcase in the dark. I hobbled over on my knees, reaching backward into the bag to feel for it. Not very hard to find, though I mistook the leather studded dog collar for it—that gave me another idea to try later.

I kicked the panties off my ankles and threaded one leg through each set of leather straps, putting the center ring right over my vagina and clitoris. I didn't have anything else to attach the two end rings to, so I hooked them together behind my back. I praised my Top-self's cleverness—she let me turn on the light for just a moment to see how it looked. *Delicious . . .*

I danced around the room in the dark a little, feeling the leather squeeze my thighs and the hard pressure of the ring drawing more and more blood to my vulva. I threw myself down on the bed and slapped myself with the dog collar. But no matter how hard I tried, I just couldn't hit myself hard enough. Perhaps it's like tickling yourself—can't be done. I gave up on that, then, when another idea for the collar came to me.

I stood up and threaded it under the ring, so it was pressed into the crack from my anus to my clitoris. I pranced around some more, feeling the leather rub against my skin as I moved my feet. I moaned, then gagged myself with one thought: *My parents were asleep in the next room.* I wasn't about to try to explain anything, so I kept quiet. (Oh it was so hard to do, especially near the end!)

My Top decided I was going to wait some more, though. The number of minutes past the hour would be how many times I was going to pull that collar through, from one end to the other, as slowly as possible, before I could come. It was twenty-five minutes after. That meant twenty-five long, slow, agonizing strokes, each cold, round, smooth stud on the collar grinding slowly over my clit. After about twenty strokes, I lost count. What was I going to do? I couldn't get away with cheating.

You're so sensitive down there, aren't you? You couldn't count because you're thinking with your clit. So, count with it. I decided to count the number of studs on the collar as I pulled it through. For every one that I was wrong from the actual number, I would get five more extra-slow strokes. In that instant I became a prized slave, on display, to be sold. I would fetch a higher price for more stamina . . .

But before I began the test, I turned the light on once more. I looked around the room for something the right size and shape. Hmmm . . . I rolled a condom onto a sample bottle of shampoo, tied a knot in the end, and turned the light out. I took the collar out of the ring, slid the bottle into my vagina, and put the collar back. It held the bottle in place perfectly.

I counted fourteen studs on the collar, gritting my teeth and whispering the numbers to myself as each nub of metal tweaked my clit. Then I pulled the collar free, and counted again with my tongue, licking the juices from it. Sixteen studs. I counted again with my fingers. Damn. That meant ten more strokes!

I lay still for a full minute as punishment for my impatience. As the numbers flipped on the clock radio, I started the collar moving. I thought I would never get to ten, my clit throbbing, but I imagined veiled masters watching me from behind diaphanous curtains, bidding on my price, betting on my abilities. I finished the tenth stroke—which I made extra long and slow—and then moved from my back to be on my knees again.

Putting one leg through the shirt between my wrists, I got one hand in back and one hand in front. Holding on to each end of the collar, I started sawing it back and forth on my clit. As I pumped my hips, the shampoo bottle fucked me, and I couldn't have stopped myself from coming even if I had wanted to. I collapsed forward (and almost fell off the bed in the dark) in a wet heap. I never get this sweaty when someone else works me over, I thought. I slept soundly next to a small pile of damp leather and clothing and waited until my parents had left for work to wash the shampoo bottle.

$\mathcal{R}$ ituals

II

People—friends, fans, strangers in e-mail— sometimes ask me if I believe in magic. I can't answer that question because the definition of magic is so hard to pin down. What I can say is this: I believe in the importance of rituals as a part of human life, and that rituals, ceremonies, and rites of passage carry power, an unquantifiable, sometimes uncontrollable, power. I'm not a pagan and don't know anything about witchcraft or crystals or that kind of stuff, but I do know that a spell is a ritual, and so is a prayer—both are a kind of focusing, as the form of the spell or prayer forces you to define and delineate what you want, why you are going through those motions, to name your goal or your obstacles. Well, writing a story is a similar activity, following prescribed patterns, giving form to energy, and naming desire.

So here are three stories about rituals. I was going to go into some detail about each, but really the thing I should be telling you is that the first story here, "Heart's Desire," I wrote about my life-partner the day after we met. I do believe in love at first sight, and after feeling that zap of Cupid's Arrow I was too nervous to talk to him much at the party where we were introduced. I didn't know anything about him or his home situation—the story blossomed entirely out of my imagination. But when I wrote it I knew I was trying to cast a love spell, I was trying to focus my energy in his direction. Do I believe in magic? I don't know. But the story turned out to be truer than I'd guessed, and the spell worked—he and I have been together for six years, with no end in sight.

Cecilia Tan

Sometimes, looking around my bedchamber before I sleep at night, I am awed by what I have. Could I really have achieved, garnered, realized all of these desires? Around me the largeness of the house seems to grow, twenty or more empty rooms between mine and the nearest servant, filled with the silence I have hoarded. It seemed like hardly any work at all. Thinking deeper, before dreams begin to creep up under my eyes, I realize that while it may not have seemed to be such a conscious effort, subconscious desire is always at work. What was it that made me invite Glinda to that party?

She and I had never liked each other particularly. We got along well, based on our mutual respect for each other's talents, and certain shared tastes. But we differed in a few opinions and were never friends. Still, I never wanted to do anything to hurt her. Let me stop kidding myself, and you. I invited her because I secretly hoped she would bring Corwin.

The party itself was unremarkable as these things go—the usual beatings and humiliations, and a good deal of wine was spilled (much less than was consumed). As host I mostly watched that night, detached from my guests by my stature. But by the time the fire grew low, we were five women in the drawing room—myself, three others, and Glin, with Corwin. Their act had gone uninterrupted since they first arrived, late, at the front gate.

They had made a grand entrance into the main hall, her driver announcing, "The Lady Glinda Trisel, Duchess of Alaming."

She swept forward into the room, trailing a gold-and-black dress and a crinoline almost as stunning as her flaming red hair. She fanned herself gently and raised her voice. "And may I present my consort, Corwin, Prince of the Panatans." She turned back toward him as the driver shoved him into the room. He stumbled and nearly fell to his knees, chains clanking, but recovered, eyes smoldering. He was a gorgeous sight to behold, in a blue velvet tunic, the square cut of the garment exposing the gentle curve of his collarbone, his long brown hair fastened behind him in a matching ribbon and topped by a silver circlet. His hands were bound in front of him with bright polished chain. She beckoned and he followed her further into the room, his head held proudly. It was easy to forget she was a designer and he a programmer—I saw a noble lady and a prince.

They greeted me, their hostess, first. Glin and I exchanged some niceties, and I complimented her on the scenario. We had many people come in costume, enacting everything from movie characters to wild fancies of their own. But I have a soft spot for that medieval fantasy period. And Corwin, the roundness of his face, the fullness of his lips—I would have thought him beautiful even if he had been a woman. I could not take my eyes off of him.

Neither could many others. Even at that late hour, when Glin slapped him in the face (I missed what he had said to deserve it), they had an audience. As the duchess forced him to kneel and pushed his head to the ground, unbuttoning the tunic in the back, Marella turned to me and whispered, "Do you think she'll let us each have a turn?"

 Cecilia Tan

"Goodness, I hope so," piped in Dara, licking her lips.

I simply nodded, unable to take my eyes off them. She stripped away the tunic and fastened his hands behind his back, standing him up by his long hair. Now he wore only tight black leggings, his perfect chest exposed. "Cleo? Where shall we put him?"

I resisted the urge to touch him. "The drawing room archway." I led them to the gilt doorway, met Corwin's eyes as we chained him to it. I looked away. Hooks the perfect height for him. They had originally been placed for a woman my size, which is small, and Corwin was just about my height. Glin put a collar around his neck, clipping the long ends of the chains to it. He made a delicious picture like that, the fire backlighting his spread-eagled figure, the chains shining in the flames. She put a pretty black clip onto each nipple and stepped back. I could have sat and admired him for a few more minutes, but she wasted no time, going to work on him right away.

She started with a cat-o'-nine-tails, passing it deftly from hand to hand as she worked up a rhythm. She fairly danced around him as she heated his skin. The cat was too light to leave marks; his skin began to glow in the firelight. She switched to a leather paddle, and we began to hear him. His voice was as sweet and beautiful as his face. With his pride he tried to choke off the cries, but when she began using a stiff leather thong he coughed out a note with each stroke. The thong bit into his skin, raising a blue welt where it fell. I realized as I was watching his fists clench in the cuffs, I was clenching my own. She did not stop. He thrashed in the chains, his hair coming loose from the ribbon and hanging down over his chest.

"Milady," he gasped out between blows.

She did not answer him.

"Milady, please stop. Ah!" His eyes were shut tight and he sucked his breath through his teeth as he tried to keep speaking. "Milady, please!"

"He means nothing to me," she said to the rest of us, the motion of her arm continuing. "He is but a spoil of war, like a good horse. A fine possession which I will use, or misuse, as is my privilege."

His chest heaved with pain and also, I could see, anger. I suddenly wondered what their safeword was. He opened his eyes again and I looked away. Was she drawing blood?

"Come on, Glin," I said. "Let us see the rest of your prize."

She stepped back, smiling. He hung limp for a moment, resting, while she stripped the leggings down to his ankles. There was an appreciative sigh from us: The rest of him was as perfectly formed as the upper half, his strong legs lightly dusted with hair, and the family jewels hanging delectably between them. In the light I caught the glint of metal. He wore a ring around them that matched the circlet in his hair. His legs quivered as she stepped him out of the leggings and then reattached his ankles to the doorframe.

"May I?" Marella stepped forward, dangling her cat from her hand.

Glinda bowed graciously and stepped back. "Please. Make him sing."

Marella was even more graceful than Glinda, with more variation to her rhythm. My palms were sweating. I felt my teeth clench as each blow fell. He did not open his eyes now, trying to melt into the pain. Glinda tweaked the nipple clamps with her fingers and he screamed. Marella gave him no breath to go limp. My heart jumped as she gave him a final extra-hard whack. I wanted to leave the room, but at the same time, I couldn't bear to leave his presence. Dara got up next and went to work on him with clothespins. Each of the women had a turn with him, Glinda making suggestions as they went along, as though they were setting a table or making a flower arrangement. They blindfolded him. They chatted among themselves as they marked him.

Cecilia Tan

Glinda flicked the nipple clamps off and he screamed. She turned away from him, to look at me. "Would you like a turn, as well?" she was saying, but I barely heard it over Corwin's song of agony. My goosebumps sprang up and I could barely maintain the act to nod my head.

"Take him down, onto his knees." They released the collar first, then his hands, and he slumped forward into me. He tried to regain his feet, but I lowered him gently to the carpet. I could feel his back with my hand, hot, corrugated. I held his head back with my hand wound in his hair and whispered into his ear.

"You are the most beautiful creature I have ever seen." I pinched a very sore nipple and he shook in my arms. "You are truly, truly a beauty. Do you know why I do this?" I slapped him on the thigh and he gasped.

"No."

"Pain is a gift from me to you," I continued, working on the nipples more. "In exchange for your beauty. At this moment, you are the most precious thing to me on earth."

I held him to my chest then, as he broke down sobbing.

"You are a prince," I whispered. I looked up then and met Glinda's eyes. She glared, a hint of disbelief on her face. I don't think she'd heard anything I said.

She broke character for a moment. "Well, Cle', do you think he's had enough?"

I shrugged. "Ask him."

She raised an eyebrow, crossing her arms.

I spoke into his ear, "Corwin, Corwin, are you all right?"

He would not look up from where his face was buried in my chest. I waited to see what she would do.

She walked over, knelt down, her hair sliding down her shoulder to touch his. "Come on, Corwin, let's go."

He clung to me. She said again, "Let's go." This time she used her bare hand on his back. He wasn't the only one who gasped. "That is an order, princeling," she added, as if her words could reestablish the scene's rules. But it was she who had broken them.

He covered his ears and she raised her hand again.

"Wait," I said, grabbing her wrist. As our eyes met I could not tell what she was thinking. I did not want to play this wrong. "Duchess, how much do you want for him?"

She raised her eyebrow in surprise. "Oh, he's not for sale."

"I thought you said he meant nothing to you." Corwin sobbed silently in my lap, his voice spent. Perhaps it was true.

"You are right." She stood up and tapped him with her boot. "I suppose I could set a price."

"Name it." I swallowed, unable to tell where this scene was going next.

"Twenty-five lashes, hard enough that we might hear them in the next room," she said, her voice cold. She held a whip out to me, daring me. "On him. You deliver them."

I looked into his eyes.

He nodded. I began lifting him up. "Give me the whip." They put him back up in the frame and Marella went into the other room to keep count.

"I do this," I said, drawing my arm back, "because I love you."

My first stroke wasn't hard enough for Marella to hear, but it was hard enough to make Corwin scream. I pressed the whip handle to my forehead, praying. I said, "I love you," and let the second one fall. Marella shouted "One!" from the other room.

On the next blow I drew blood. Corwin was whimpering. I let another blow fall. Tears sprang to my eyes as he bit down on a cry. Sweat broke out on his skin as I struck him. We were both crying. My arm began to hurt. By the time I got to twenty I didn't know if I could give him the last five. I was panting, the whip hanging limp as I had to look away from his tortured skin. You have to do this, I told myself, or she'll finish it for you. I could not steel myself to raise my arm again.

Cecilia Tan

"Cleo!" he said, his head hanging. "Finish me!"

By the time the last one was delivered, Glinda had already gone.

I let the whip fall and sank to my knees, unsure when exactly the line had been crossed between play and reality, waiting for the scene to end. But there was Corwin in my arms, kissing me.

Now I lie here at night, before I fall asleep, admiring his hair falling over the pillow. Some nights, like tonight, I'm happy to watch the moon shining on his skin. Other nights, I'll wake him gently and make him talk to me. My prince.

In a fit of fury at me, my mistress Myrtle once said, "The only thing worse than a predicament, is knowing that your own stupidity got you into it." She was wrong. It was even worse to know she would be waiting for me when I finally got out of it.

This tidbit of superior knowledge was no consolation either, as I considered my current position (on my back) and the keen blade at my throat. Myrtle would have the last laugh if I got my gullet slit, anyway. I kept still, and waited to see what the woman would do next.

She eased herself back onto her haunches and smiled, holding the knife. She was wearing more paint than anything else, some beads, some worthless talismans. The knife, however, it had the scent of power about it. The women sat all the way back and put it on the ground, the point still toward me. "You can sit up, you know."

I did. Now I could see the markings on the ground all around me, mystical signs and sigils. She wiped the sweat from her brow and smiled again with such satisfaction I shivered.

"What do you want of me?" I asked. There was probably some ritual greeting I was supposed to give, but it had been more than a hundred years since the Summer Country had met with the mortal world, and I hadn't been long in it. No one had ever mentioned this eventuality to me. If this woman had the power to summon me from across the borderlands, she had some powerful magick indeed.

Her smile was almost maniacal. "It worked," she said.

"Pardon me?"

"It worked," she repeated. For a moment she didn't seem to know what to say, her self-assurance sagging, but then she went on. "I didn't think this would work. I've been trying it every summer since, well, my years won't matter to you. For many years."

I rested my arms on my knees, feeling my breeches growing damp from the dark loam under me. She never would have snared me if I hadn't been screwing around where I shouldn't have been.

Myrtle had been after me again; I'd heard her calling me through the woods. I hated Myrtle's touch. She claimed she'd fashioned me from the stem of a rose and a sausage, and brought me to life because of, well, because of how much she liked sausage. And she was always hungry. She was beautiful as elves go, you know the story—eyes like stars, hair like the black net of the night that holds you inescapable until the golden morn. Why she'd made me for a mate, instead of seeking out one of the highborn in Titania's court, I was not sure. I suppose none would have her, a rejection which stung her enough that she had to detest me at least as much as she loved me, perhaps more.

I had longed to escape from her. I looked at the knife on the ground. I'd hoped to avoid her for just another hour, to have just another minute to myself. I'd gone hiding in the borderlands, where her powers to find me were weak.

And this woman's were strong. I asked again, "What would you have of me?"

She picked up the knife and waved it as she spoke. "You can't leave the circle, but if the circle gets broken, you are still bound to this blade. Do you know what that means?"

"No." I admired the blade from where I sat. It looked to have a handle carven of bone, and a blade that tapered to a graceful point. "I know nothing of human magicks."

At that she laughed. "Human magicks!" She looked at the blade. "Look again, elf, sprite, pixie, whatever you are." She came forward and knelt beside me. "This dagger came from elfland with some ancestor of yours," she said. "He, or she, went back across the border with something that belonged to an ancestor of mine."

I let myself feel the spark of magick off that blade. In the golden beams of the setting sun, it was far too blue to be plain iron or steel. "Um," I said, wanting to back away from her but unable to because of the circle, "would you like me to return it?"

Her smile was half astonishment, half amusement this time. "You're not joking, are you?" She hunkered down a little bit lower, as if to tell me a secret. "Look, I don't think you get it." She held the blade closer to my face than I was comfortable with.

I kept guessing. "Were you trying to summon the elf that did the deed?" I did back away, just a hair.

"No, no, no." She examined the handle. "No, I'm supposed to be enacting the revenge of my ancestor on you."

"Oh." If that blade was what she said it was, then she could certainly spill my blood with it. So, it looked like maybe I was going to escape Myrtle after all. It wasn't fair, to have so little of life before being reduced back to a twig and a bit of meat. "Are you going to kill me, now?"

She rested the blade against her lip as she phrased her reply. "I'm not sure." She scratched a bit in the moist dirt with it. "I don't think so." This time her smile was apologetic. "You see, I've had to make this up as I went along. And it doesn't feel like killing you is the right thing to do."

She stood up and I breathed a sigh of relief. She was shaking out her hair and scratching herself where the paint was flaking off her ribs. When she had stepped out of the circle, I felt safe enough to speak again. "If you tell me more about the magick, I may be able to make a suggestion."

"Oh no you don't, elf." She spat out the word like a curse. "You're my one chance in a million to get this to work. I'm not letting you botch it up with some faerie trick."

I shrugged. "Suit yourself. I'm just curious is all."

"Curious about what?"

"About why you're trying to work a magick over something that happened before your great-great-grandmother was born. If you'll pardon my asking, why go to the trouble?"

She was gathering wood and sorting it at the circle's edge into piles of twigs, sticks, and logs. "Ah, well, it's hard to explain."

"I'm not going anywhere."

She favored me again with a smile. "Somehow, I didn't expect an elf to have such a sense of humor."

I tried to think of a witty rebuttal. I was thinking more about if the fire she was building was going to be for me. I hoped she wasn't disappointed. "Some would say I have a thorny wit."

She went on a little longer gathering wood around the clearing before speaking again. "Well, I figure this knife is some kind of onus laid on my family. No matter how we try to get rid of it, it always comes back somehow. I tried, you see, figuring the magick wasn't real. I mean, no one believes in this stuff anymore. Sure, me and the girls get together once a month and dance under the moon, but nothing special happens. But here's the blade again, and here you are." She wound her black wiry hair into a braid down her back. "And the curse is real, so maybe lifting it will be, too. For a long time I thought the knife was the source of the curse, but I think the true source is somewhere, or someone, in elfland. And the knife is going to be the tool to break it. Or, one of the tools," she said, nodding at me.

"But, what's the curse?" The last ray of sun disappeared beyond the horizon.

"It's pretty simple, really, well, it's just," she blushed, "it's hard to explain." She fell silent as she made a flame from a colorful tube in her hand. It hissed as she held it to the birch bark, and then went out with a loud click. She put the firemaker into a sack.

I watched her build the fire as the shadows deepened in the forest, adding the twigs, then bigger sticks, and finally two logs propped against each other. Then she went away. I sat without moving until she returned, the woods black outside of the fire's light.

"I know what I have to do," she said to me, the knife still in her hand, the paint still flaking from her skin. "Take off your clothes."

I shivered a bit as I took off my tunic and my breeches. The night air gave me gooseflesh.

She hesitated a moment, her eyes on my selfsame sausage hanging limp between my legs, then hardened her resolve. I saw the knife flash as she stepped forward into the circle. She stood before me, then, and using the flat of the blade, pushed aside one of the fleshy halves of her pubis, exposing the moist pink underneath. With her free hand, she beckoned me closer, and then gripping me by my hair, pulled my face close to her crotch. She pressed my lips against her. Then I felt the tip of the blade on my shoulder, "Lick me."

My tongue pressed between my lips and between the folds of flesh on her. I moved it forward and back, with a care Myrtle never appreciated. This woman did, her grip tightening and her back arching as I went on. Her hips moved as I sawed at her slit with my tongue, flicking it over the pearl hidden there, now grown hard, and tasting salt.

Then she broke away. "There must be more to it," she said.

"More to what?"

"Breaking the curse." She looked at the knife in her hand, and sounded sad. "Maybe I'll have to kill you after all. I know this damn thing has to be involved somehow . . . "

I was already on my knees, perhaps that's why the begging came so easily. "Please don't," I said. "Please. I know what you want, I can give it to you, oh please don't kill me."

She tilted my chin up with the point. "How do you know what I want?"

Indeed. Because I could feel the fire deep in her belly, almost see it flickering over her skin. Or maybe that was the real fire. It was so much like what Myrtle was like, when she was hungry, only without Myrtle's taint to it. I sensed it with every sense. "Please," I said, again, unable to explain these things to her, these things that were a part of my being, part of why I was made.

She let the tip droop. "You can't," she said. "The thing I want, the thing I need, I can't have. That's what was stolen from my ancestor long ago, a curse that has been passed down to all her daughters' daughters."

I hung my head. This curse had Myrtle's stink about it. Was this why she was shunned as a cuckolding partner by the court? Because she possessed a human woman's capacity for pleasure? Perhaps she possessed even more than one. Myrtle was voracious, insatiable. Perhaps, too, that was why this woman's magick had caught me, with Myrtle's blade, Myrtle's curse. I wanted to weep. If she spilled my blood, she spilled Myrtle's blood, and perhaps that would lift the curse. I doubted it was so simple. "I'm sorry."

She sighed. "It's not that I don't like you, don't feel so bad." She put a hand on my head, stroked my hair. "You do that very well, and I appreciate your trying, but . . . "

Her tenderness had brought me to weep.

"Look, I'll let you try it again, okay? But I'm telling you, it won't work. It's never worked." She sat down in front of me and spread her legs. "Go on, I'll command you to do it if that's what you need."

I wiped my eyes, "No," and set to with my tongue again. I could feel the blood pulsing though her as I sucked at the soft flesh, and I lapped with her heart's rhythm. She began to move again, moaning a bit, working against my tongue. And I noticed as she fell into the rhythm, that the hand that held the knife had gone limp.

I kept licking, but could feel at my chin that other mouth gasping, waiting to be filled. I pressed two fingers between her legs and they were sucked in. My tongue never stopped as I began to move my fingers.

"Ah, that's good," she said, her muscles grabbing my fingers tight. "But I just had an idea, you see." She stopped herself with a nervous laugh. "I don't usually do men, but, well," she flailed her hands a little. "I just got this feeling." She couldn't bring herself to say it.

I knew what she meant. She wanted Myrtle's favorite part in there where it belonged. I started to press forward with it, but she held the knife, unforgotten, against my chest. She forced me onto my back and pinned me in place with it as she mounted me. "Now, move."

I tried to do as she commanded, to press into her, but she was too heavy for me to do much. Then she flicked one of my nipples with the point of the knife and I jumped into her. She did the other and another jolt of magick went through me, bucking my hips. I shuddered as she drew the sharp point along the skin over my ribs, raising gooseflesh but not cutting me. "Ah," she was saying as I squirmed beneath her, inside her, "that's definitely it."

She ground her hips against me, then stopped and sat still, panting. She held the knife up. "This is nice, but it's still not lifting the curse," she said. "Maybe I am supposed to castrate you with it, keep you inside me forever?"

I couldn't answer. Though our bodies were joined, her mind was leagues away from mine. I tingled from need; now that I had started inside her I was desperate to keep going.

"Perhaps I need to kill you at the moment that you come," she went on, exulting in the heat and the power coursing through her. "Spill your blood onto me, transfer your pleasure to me?" She laughed. "This is really pretty strange for me, you know." She pressed the point of the knife against the hollow of my throat and I thrust into her, shuddering. As my body jerked, I felt the hot trickle down my skin and knew she'd pricked me.

As a drop spattered the ground by my ear, I heard her gasp and squeeze me tighter with her thighs. She was riding me and I was moving as the blade scratched across my throat, and as another drop spilled she gasped again. She returned the sharp point to my nipples, then, pricking each one again and again until I was bouncing my ass against the ground with desperate thrusts. She ran the blade down my sternum, nicked me under the chin, and again, as each drop left the knife she gasped and shuddered. She left long thin lines of red down my arms, behind my ear, the prickle of the knife and the magick making sparks off my skin as I let the spell swallow me whole. Strands of her hair hung down into my face as she licked the tiny wounds on my neck and I convulsed under that tender touch.

Then, she held herself still, and me as well with the point suddenly at my groin. She looked into my eyes and nodded, "Just a wee bit more . . ." Her hips began to grind in double time as the knife traveled up the length of my body, leaving a red trail in its wake, and then she slashed me across the cheek. I screamed as she screamed and in that especially long moment, when the magick was stretched to its limit, I saw the arc of blood droplets, my blood, Myrtle's blood, swinging through the air off the edge of the knife, the gleam of the blade like the tail of a falling star cutting the air, until the strand snapped, and she fell limp over me, panting, her dark hair obscuring my sight.

When she didn't move for a while, I began to wonder if the magick hadn't been too much for her. "Hello? Are you still there?"

She sat straight up and I winced at her weight. "Oh," she looked down. "Sorry." She rolled into a sitting position off to one side. "So that's why it's such a big deal."

"I'm sorry, what?" I guess we were both a little dazed.

"Orgasm. No wonder it's such a big deal. I mean, it felt exactly like I had hoped it would, and yet, I couldn't have really imagined it." She brushed some dirt from her hands, noticed she was still holding the blade. "I can't believe I'm saying this to an elf." She looked at the blade.

I looked, too. "Can I, uh, could I see it?"

She handed it to me, and then went and put more wood onto the fire. My blood seemed to have stained it along the edge, but the glow was brighter than ever, pulsing with a light all its own. I imagined Myrtle howling somewhere on the other side of the briars and though I smiled, I also shuddered. I had one ragged feather from the wings of hope and I clutched at it—that her desire for me would be gone, and that I might finally taste the freedom of life. That—I held the dagger tight in my fingers—I might trade this trinket for my freedom. Stranger things have happened.

She was looking at me. "Are you okay? You look a little ill."

I forced a smile. "I'm fine." The sky seemed to be turning lighter, or perhaps it was just aglow with my anxiety. "Um, what now?"

She shrugged. "Well, the curse is lifted, I feel like a new woman! Goddess, wait until I tell Felicia!" She squealed with delight. Then she knelt down by me. "What are you looking at?"

I was watching the dagger glow. As I held it, felt it warm in my hands, I became certain Myrtle would want it back. This was the key to her power now, she would neither love me nor hurt me. I felt where the scar would be along my cheek with the tips of my fingers, and looked up, wordless.

"Thank you." The woman smiled a gentle smile. "I'm probably not supposed to say that or something, but anyway." She kissed me on the cheek, just over the crusted line of the final cut. "I'm going to erase the circle now. As far as I know, you'll be free to go once it's broken. Or, maybe you need the sunrise. I'm not sure, actually . . . "

I held the dagger between my crossed legs. "Will you wait with me? For the sunrise?"

She smiled. "Sure." She kicked a hole in the circle with her bare foot, then retrieved a pack from behind a tree. She wrapped a blanket around herself and then held open a corner as she sat down. She was warm and smelled like the earth and soon I had fallen asleep, the deep sleep only the faerie know, we who walk the land adjacent to dreams and death. With the dawn I would return there, to make my bargain with my maker, and from there, to start again my life.

Magda brewed chamomile tea with a touch of comfrey in it for me. I could smell it steeping from where the cup sat on the white Formica counter of her kitchenette, familiar and meant to be comforting: chamomile to help me sleep and comfrey to help clear up any bruises she might have inadvertently introduced to my flesh in the course of the evening. But tonight it was not comforting, it was irksome. I sat with the comforter wrapped around me on her futon, watching her busy herself with spoons and saucers, and I wondered if, for once, she might not ask me whether I wanted to stay up, or if I wanted to *keep* those bruises. Magda and I had been together for a year now, a year come Solstice, a year of becoming familiar to each other, a year of settling. A year when, once a week, I would come to her place, and submit to her touches and tickles and her whips and paddles, and she would send me off into space, into that special bliss that we worshiping masochists know. Or she would at least try to. She carried the tea over to me and sank into the covers next to me. She was brownly naked, the black gloss of her hair unbound, covering her back like a short cape. My goddess in flesh.

I took the cup and breathed the steam. It wasn't like me to be so moody after a scene. PMS, I told myself, the universal paean.

She broke the silence, not noticing my mood. "Oh, I forgot to tell you. Those fire dancers from Santa Cruz aren't going to make it to the meeting."

"Why?" In the year we'd been together I'd not only become a fixture in Magda's life, I'd also become Programming Chair of Leather Pagans United, her spiritual, political, and sometimes problematic family.

She shrugged and sipped her tea. "I don't know, they just said they can't, and to tell you."

"Dammit, Magda, you should have had them talk to me."

She arched her eyebrow in that High Priestess way of hers, but the way she looked at me from under her lashes suggested Little Girl guilt. Magda could be a contradiction sometimes. "There wasn't anything you could do."

"I could have gotten them to reschedule, maybe, and swapped someone into their place. Jesus, Magda, the meeting's only two weeks away."

Her pouty look turned to a glare at my pronouncement of the *J* word.

"I'm sorry," I said automatically. I wasn't going to have another version of our long-standing argument over swear words. She was always coming out with fake-sounding stuff, like "By the goddess!" Whereas my theory was, swear by using a deity you *don't* like, not one you do. When I wanted to needle her, I could make up some pretty fake-sounding stuff, too, like "Satan take my bicycle!" But not tonight. Tonight, I was annoyed already. "I'll have to come up with something else."

She crossed her ankles and leaned against the perfect white of her apartment wall. "Maybe it's time to do another mutual respect workshop."

"But last month was the relationship roundtable."

"I know, but I think some people could use a refresher." Her dark eyes looked into her tea.

"Like who?" I blew on my tea, trying to look nonchalant.

"Like Isa," she said, puckering her lips a tiny bit. "I've been hearing some things."

I blew on my tea some more. If I waited long enough, she'd tell me. And so she did—rumors, hearsay, gossip, and dish, which amounted to a probable suspicion that Ms. Isa, a top who considered herself a mere second to the Supreme Goddess herself (hence her interest in a spiritual group like LPU) was coming down with a case of Top's disease. No one had come forward and accused her of being a lousy partner, but we hadn't been seeing as much of some folks as we used to, and rumors did get started somehow. And seeing as how Magda felt she was bucking to take the High Priestess role for herself next year, Magda wanted to know the truth. "I can't let someone who doesn't respect her tools lead the worship," she finished. "If she doesn't respect her bottoms, she's not channeling the goddess, she's just on an ego trip."

"One way to find out," I said, setting aside my cold full cup. "One way for sure."

If I thought it was going to be difficult, if I thought I was going to have to flirt with Isa and insinuate myself like a spy, I was wrong. After the meeting Magda walked up to Isa and told her she wanted her to take me on for a night, a preliminary to a public worship next month. Isa said sure, she'd e-mail me about convenient dates.

That's how I came to be riding down the Pacific Coast Highway to Swanton on a Saturday afternoon. The music of my own anxiety and nerves played inside my helmet as my reflexes led me around the curves, sometimes making a little voice: *come on girl good girl that's the way nice keep on going keep on moving that's it that's a girl* . . . and whether I was talking to myself about the ride or my destination I wasn't sure. I had a reputation with the Leather Pagans as a bottomless bottom, a tough one, I could stand up to anything. And, yeah, I

    Cecilia Tan

had been through a lot, especially since coming to the Bay Area three years ago. But maybe having a rep was worse, because I wondered if that meant people would go farther than they normally would. And tough or no, I had never outgrown that special chill of anticipation when it came to a new top, a new unknown, something new to fear.

I pulled off the highway at a tiny embankment, five parking spaces and a weather-worn picnic table. With my helmet perched solid on the sissy bar, I swung off the bike and walked to the cliff edge. Below me a living moon of tidepool craters glistened in the late-afternoon sun. I'd taken this road all the way down to Monterey many times; I'd seen the aquarium exhibits of anemones and hermit crabs and starfish. Here they lived as they had for thousands of years. If Mother Nature could create an organism that looked like a flower but could eat a fish, it didn't seem unlikely that she'd create a person like me.

And what was Isa, did she have a poison sting, too?

She lived in a surprisingly suburban ranch-style house, like one you'd see a dozen of in different colors along any housing development east of the Mississippi. Swanton was a mixture of run-down fisherman shacks and cliff-dwelling mansions with a few odd normal houses like hers. She had converted the family room into a full blown dungeon with leather-padded sawhorses, a Saint Andrew's cross, and a wall covered with nasty-looking implements and bondage gear. I had a quick peek at it when she gave me a tour of the house before dinner.

We sat down to eat on her back patio where we couldn't see the ocean but we could see the sunset. She'd grilled vegetables—zucchini and red peppers and huge portobello mushrooms, mushrooms that you eat like a steak, with a knife and fork, and juice dribbles down your chin. It was while digging in to one of those that she remarked, "God, how I miss beef sometimes."

I kept chewing. If I couldn't chime in sympathetically it didn't seem polite to say anything.

She raised an eyebrow at me. "Are you . . . vegetarian?"

She meant *Aren't you,* but I shook my head. "I know, I know, I'm the sacrifice, I should have some sympathy, some kinship for the lamb. But nature, the Goddess, whoever, made me a predator, too. And I try to . . . stay true to that nature."

She smirked, a little teriyaki sauce in the corner of her lips. "Well, you know, I didn't give up meat for spiritual reasons. I saw one too many meat-packing documentaries and decided it was time to quit." Her tongue snaked out to catch the sauce and there was no doubt in my mind she was as much a predator as I. Her hair was black, too, but not the wavy cloud that Magda's was—more like a smooth helmet that covered her head and neck and shone with bright bits of red in the sunlight. She could have been anything—Hispanic, Italian, Middle Eastern—but my guess was Filipina. Which got me thinking about Roman Catholicism and stuff (did she say "God" earlier?) and wanting to talk to her about becoming pagan, what road she had traveled to arrive at that choice . . . but whatever I might have said stayed under my tongue as she stood. I felt something change, her power come to her, the subtle shift that was the scene beginning.

"Your nature," she breathed, echoing my last words. "Your nature is to serve Her. To serve Her by serving me. To submit to Her by submitting to me. To perform with me this rite, of your own choice and will."

I felt that required an answer but I did not know which to give . . . *Amen . . . I do . . . Yes ma'am . . .* I nodded silently.

She went into the house and I followed her, trying to make my mind a blank, to make myself a vessel for whatever this priestess would pour into me. But through my mind were playing a hundred other scenes, a dozen other first times with other tops, other women I had given myself to in the name of the Goddess. There were always patterns; there were always things to be expected. So of course I was guessing. With all that equipment I wondered if she would be the type who would immobilize me, make me feel her iron grip, and then lay into me with everything she had. *Give it to me both barrels, baby.* My skin tingled. *I can do this, I can do this,* came my little voice again, the agitated music preparing me for pain. *I can do this.* In a basement off Divisadero I'd had my skin cut and set on fire. In an open field north of Muir Woods I'd been hung from a tree and whipped with freshly cut sticks. But usually I was tied to a bed, or secured with soft cuffs in a rack, while carefully crafted leather and wood was applied.

We stood outside the dungeon door. She faced me. "If you have anything to tell me that we haven't already discussed, tell me now."

I shook my head.

She looked for a moment like maybe there was something she wanted to tell me, but then it passed and she looked away, saying, "Take off your clothes and leave them here. Once we enter the chamber, we've begun."

I nodded. Some tops left the bottom alone for a few minutes while they gathered their own energy, but not Isa. She turned away from me and began shedding her clothes, draping them over the back of a chair. I folded mine neatly and placed them on the floor next to the door. As I bent low to lay them down I reminded myself one last time of my purpose for being here, to find out if Isa was . . . what? Safe, okay, worthy? The real thing, or not? To see if she'd respect me as an equal? Thus far she had been exemplary.

Inside the room, the fire of the red sky mixed with the flicker of candles she lit. She indicated the open space on the vinyl padded floor and I knelt there while my still-busy mind was cataloging details: *Black floor, soft on the feet but easy to wash up, where did she get it?*

The sound of her chuckle brought me back to the moment. She held a single candle and stared into it, then lifted it over her head and let the wax drip down over her small firm breasts. Her chuckle became a throaty laugh that sounded nothing like the Isa I knew. She looked back at me, the candle burning twin images in her eyes. She knelt in front of me, waving the candle like a magic wand. The flame burned higher as it tipped and hot white drops of wax dotted my skin. I sat still because I did not know what else to do. Unbound, uninstructed, I reminded myself it was my duty to submit.

And then she was on me, her body on top of mine, pushing me flat against the padded floor, her wax and mine pressed together, making me think of flowers in a dictionary. I hadn't realized it at first but the instant the wax had hit me I had broken out in a sweat, and now it made my skin slick against hers. I had no idea where the candle had gone and even though I told myself it wasn't my place to worry about it, not my responsibility, the thought remained. Her hands held my head in place and her mouth sucked at mine, and without thinking, I struggled. I was used to ritual beatings with numbers called out and the solemn gathering of energy before the piercing. This wrestling was so much more like . . . sex.

She reared up, hands on my shoulders, pinning me, the gleam still in her eye not from candles but from an eager madness to devour me. *This is my will,* I told myself, *this is my devotion,* but I could not make myself sink into submission. Isa raked her claws across my cheek and I resisted, my chin up in defiance. I wanted to lie still, and let her have her way. I wanted to obey, to let the Goddess ravage me if that be her will. But something in me said *fight!* I struggled to unseat her from me and found myself instead facedown on the floor, one of her hands in my hair, one drawing lines down my back with her claws. My spine arched against that rough touch, like the tide following the moon. I tried to turn my head, but her hand

 Cecilia Tan

held me fast. I felt her hot breath on my neck, her lips moved as she mouthed whatever incantations she wished into my skin, and then her teeth found purchase and a frisson of energy shot from the spot straight to my groin. I felt as if she had plucked a string in me, and the vibrations grew louder as I fought her, as the sensation strobed through my brain of her biting me and me bucking and her weight riding me . . .

Then her mouth was at my ear as my legs flailed for some leverage on the slippery floor and she spread herself over me like a blanket. "Did you wonder why you're not bound? Did you wonder what I would do?"

I didn't answer except to push harder against her. I wanted her to let go of me, to let me free. One side of me knew this was wrong, to resist like this, while the other side of me knew it could be no other way.

Her voice was loud and low in my ear, the spice of her breath surrounding me as tightly as any bonds, "Because I had to know your will. I had to know what you would let me do."

Obviously, I'll let you do anything, I wanted to say, *because I haven't been able to stop you.*

And then her weight was gone. I turned onto my back to find her standing above me, the windows behind her dark with night. "What will you let me do, eh, sister?" She knelt where she was and I pushed myself back a few inches out of instinct. "If you serve, you will not move. If you submit, you will not move."

There was power in the way she crawled toward me, jungle power, fierce and hungry. She crawled toward my cunt and licked her lips like a jaguar before she let her tongue snake out to sting my clit. She jabbed at it, parting the folds of my flesh with the sharp tip and sinking it hard against my nerves. I held still. I held my breath. I pressed my hands flat against the floor and let my head fall back, but I kept my legs as they were, knees bent, feet flat on the floor, spread wide for her, for Her. Her hands reached up for my nipples, rolling them in her fingers like two peppercorns, then pulling them like pieces of taffy. I raised my head to look and found her eyes staring at me over the horizon of my mons. Waiting, waiting. Her tongue continued to jab, the sensation building to a jolt like pain, like a shock, slow but sharp, a Chinese water torture dripping acid onto my clit, moment by moment.

I had never felt a pain quite like it in my life, so bad I ground my teeth and yet I felt a flutter in my stomach as if it might make me come. Now that I had nothing to struggle against I felt shame heating up my face. Why had I fought her? Did a year with Magda teach me nothing? How could I have failed in my devotion that way? My way is to suffer. When I go to leather bars, when I go to parties or group meetings, it's so hard to explain to some of these tops, no, I'm not a slave. I'm not a servant, only to Her. I'm not submissive, only to Her. If I obey, it is because it will lead to my suffering. If I let myself be put into bonds, it is to free me to suffer for Her. Simple, really.

The pain grew excruciating. Her tongue felt like an ice pick, stabbing the nerve cluster without mercy. But mercy was one thing I never expected. I counted the jabs to myself, grouping them in sets of ten like a weight lifter, packaging the feeling to make it manageable. I had withstood worse torture than this, and I shielded myself with that thought. The goal became to make it through, to make it to the end. How long would she go on this way?

I had lost count. My breasts were on fire; her hands grabbing at hardened wax and pinching my nipples. That little voice was there, trying to tell me to keep going, but it was fading, fading as I began to slip away, to the best place of worship of all. To that place where the mind falls aside and the body becomes the empty vessel, to that place of pure existence, pure sensation. I didn't think about it happening at the time, because if I had thought of it, it would have pulled me back to the present, back into my consciousness, and ruined it.

 Cecilia Tan

I let myself go, my whole body rigid but resisting nothing, my fingers clutching at a floor I no longer thought about. Thinking about it now, it happened as if to someone else, like some slow-motion movie. As my hands drew up to my chest, and held her hands there as my hips bucked hard, pulling her forward and dragging my cunt across the full length of her tongue. My hands holding her hands on my breasts as my legs closed over her head and my hips shook, wringing the orgasm out over my skin, the convulsion shaking us so hard that we came apart. And then I was on her, her head on the ground and my cunt grinding into her mouth, and then covering her, my cunt against her leg, lips spread wide as I rode her, my hands raking her body and my mouth sucking at her breasts. There was wax in my mouth but it didn't feel like my mouth; there was power radiating from between my legs, and I couldn't stop myself from making myself come.

Then suddenly the orgasms stopped and I was staring down at my fingers, woven into the straight silk of her hair behind each ear, staring into her eyes, which no longer gleamed with hunger but sparkled with awe. She tugged gently at my hands, pulled them down to her breasts. I found myself eager to return the torture of earlier, as I twirled her nipples in my fingers and listened to her moan and cry out. My mouth to her mouth, my legs wrapped around hers, my hand sank into her pubic hair, wanting to pinch her clit, to pull it like taffy. But my finger slipped right past it and went deep into her, and suddenly I had another handle to hold her down with. Her cries became more frantic and she thrashed, but not enough to break free of me, not enough to make me think she didn't want it. My thumb on her clit, I plunged my long fingers into her and watched her hips rise to meet me. Could I do this to her for as long as she had done that thing to me?

I didn't. It seemed only a moment before she was bucking hard, her hand locked on my wrist and driving it in faster, her head flailing and her teeth sinking into my too-convenient shoulder as she struggled to take back from me the power I had stolen.

But she could not. I still had her on my hand, and as the orgasm subsided and my fingers could move again, I shifted my weight to keep her from sitting up, pressed my free hand against her throat, and kept my hand moving. I flicked her clit with my thumbnail and felt her cunt convulse. "I want you to come again," I heard my voice saying.

She whimpered very softly but did not say no.

I ground my thumb into her and her hips rose up, her legs shaking suddenly to give her that extra boost, and again she came. Again I kept my fingers inside her, and again I made her come. I made her come until I saw her face, and saw that she too had gone off to that place of pureness, that place I always sought and sometimes found.

Thinking about that brought me back to myself at last. I withdrew my hands from her and sat back on my heels, receding from her like the tide from the cliff. She lay there a moment, taking deep breaths, and then she came back to herself, as well. I saw her eyes blink as she stared at the ceiling awash with candlelight.

She sat up slowly, her face impassive, and drew a shaky breath. She shifted, until she was kneeling, too, but her body continued forward until her head touched the floor in front of me. Her hands reached blindly for me and I caught them. Her shoulders shook and I knew she was crying. She held tight to my hands like her tears might wash her away, and I squeezed back, helpless to do anything else other than berate myself.

What did you think you were doing? How could you let yourself go like that? I didn't understand what had just happened and the only person I could ask was in tears.

Eventually, she wasn't. She composed herself, and even began to smile. She wiped back stray tears from her cheeks and grinned at me. "Thank you," she said.

 48   *Cecilia Tan*

I wasn't sure if "You're welcome" was the right thing to say at this juncture, not when I felt like an apology was on my lips. "I, uh, I didn't expect that to happen."

"No one ever does," she said, a wistful sound in her voice that reminded me I knew nothing of where she had come from. "Not many people can do that. You have a power, you know."

I shook my head. "No. That was, I don't know."

"Don't deny it. You felt it. I felt it. I was yours."

"Stop it." Empty words, loaded words, like guns. "That's not what I'm like. I'm not supposed to . . . "

Isa's eyes turned dark, confusion and disappointment registering on her face.

No. It had felt good. It felt as good as the day I had walked out of the church, and as good as the day I had first been bound to a cross five years later, as good as the day I'd discovered as a child just what it was we weren't supposed to do with our hands in our panties, as good as the day I'd had my first orgasm from being whipped alone. But good didn't make it right. "Look, Isa, it doesn't mean anything." I pulled my knees up to my chest. "I don't know what it means."

She looked hurt. "You've taken me to a place I've never been. This is the first time I've known what it was like . . . "

To be the sacrifice, I thought, *to be the one who gets no mercy.* "I know," I said, and reached for her, cradled her head against my breast. "I know."

"I never knew I needed it this much." She was warm and the room felt cold to me now. "I never knew that this was what I was looking for. But now I do."

I just nodded. I put her into her bed with promises I'd join her in a few minutes. When she was breathing deeply, I went back to the doorway of the dungeon and pulled on my clothes. In the driveway, I sat for a long moment on the bike, looking at the moonlit hills and wondering if I should leave. Maybe she was right, maybe I had touched something deep and important in myself, something new and vital, just as she had. Maybe I should stay and explore it more with her.

But I didn't want to see her gaze up at me with moonstruck eyes. I didn't want the responsibility of checking her for bruises and making her some tea. I wasn't ready to think that the same Goddess who moved me to give myself up had moved me to fight and take and dominate tonight. My world was not supposed to be so complicated.

I rolled the bike to the end of the driveway before I started it. Perhaps in the morning everything would look different. Now I had a dark and unfamiliar road under me, the curves unwinding beneath the roar of wind and the crackling of my uncertainty.

$\mathcal{I}$nto the Gap

III

So I said something earlier about fantasy and how important I think it is to let the imagination run free. In the life of a fiction writer this can be difficult only because if you let your visions run far enough, you can run yourself right into the genre ghetto of "science fiction." Personally, I've tried to ignore the boundary between what's genre fiction and what's literature. I let each story define its own place. In some ways, I think I enjoy things the most when they are in the gray area, somewhere in between clearly defined areas. In fact, if I have any kind of overarching worldview, that's probably it: that it is best to be between. That's me all over—between white and Asian, between gay and straight, between female-identified and male-identified (more on that later). Here are some of the "in between stories," contemporary American, but existing on the edge of realism and fantasy: a retelling of a fairy tale in modern terms, a dream-laden trip into something different, and an ancient myth come to life.

Brief Explanation:

This has always been a mysterious tale to me. In the original fairy tale, the nightingale is taken from the woods to please the emperor, and when a mechanical replacement for her is brought from Japan, the nightingale falls from favor and she is sent back to the woods. Despite this shoddy treatment, she returns at the end to chase the demons of death away from the emperor. It seemed to me the elements that needed full illumination were her relationship to the kitchen maid who brings her to the emperor in the first place and her feelings that brought her back to save him in the end. There are issues of loyalty here—to king and country, to something larger than oneself—of subservience and submission. There are also the tales from the romantic poets who believed that the nightingale's song could only be so beautiful, so sad and full of pain, because the nightingale pierced its breast with a thorn. Searching for a context to explore both the issues of loyalty and masochism, I found the nightingale became a performance artist and the emperor an underworld Mafia figure. (The quotes throughout are taken from *Fairy Tales by Hans Christian Andersen*, a facsimile of the 1884 edition.)

"It is my pleasure that she shall appear here this evening," said the emperor.

The knife girl writhes on a stage scuffed with boot marks and stained with wine, blood, water, and sweat. The knife is alive as it twirls in her hands, electric as it flashes under the lights, cruel as it opens her skin and the wound cries blood. A golden ululation issues from her throat as the blood flows, and she sings, entranced, transforming her pain into ecstasy, her self-destruction into sacrament.

She is jarred by the empty sound of Michael's cough echoing off the walls of the club. He is standing between Carl and Karen, Karen who the knife girl had almost forgotten was there.

"I've seen enough," he says to Carl, and rubs his eyes against the flickering of the lights. Knife girl sees him pull his coat and fine silk scarf tighter around him even though the club seems warm to her. "She's hired. Set it up." Michael, whose name she remembers because he is the owner and she knows it is important to remember it, turns away from the stage and disappears through a black door behind the bar.

Carl comes to the edge of the stage, the silver piercings around his face flashing in the lights, and says, "Well, Night, that's it. See you in a week."

And then Karen steps forward. "Night? You okay?"

The knife girl presses a hand to the cut in her arm and the bleeding stops. Now Karen will take her home, and Night will use the edge of the blade to slice Karen's clothing from her, the cold edge of it to harden her nipples, the pinpoint of it to flick her clit and the smooth pommel to fuck her until she cries. The knife girl knows this with a certainty that makes her close her eyes and press her lips together in something like a smile.

At last they met with a poor little girl in the kitchen who said "Oh yes, I know the nightingale quite well."

They had been lovers perhaps a month when Karen had

explained it all to her, the club, her bartending job, Michael's underworld ties, and Carl's idea to turn business around. Business had been bad, so bad that Karen could lose her job, Michael could lose the club. "They want a performance artist. Michael heard about that show you did at Artspace and wants to see you. I told him I could . . . introduce you." Night had kissed Karen on the lips and told her of course she would go.

The nightingale sang so sweetly the tears came into the emperor's eyes.

The knife girl stands in the darkness of the DJ booth beside the stage and breathes deep. In a few moments, she will step beyond the veil of darkness and into the glare and flash of the lights. Karen told her Michael even spent some extra money to install better lighting and a fog machine. Announcements of her performance have been made in the right publications, to the right people. Night takes deep breaths and waits for the moment to arrive.

The lights dim and she takes her place in the smoke in darkness. Faint music rises and then the lights, and the she unfolds herself before the crowd. She lets the rhythm of the music curve her spine and the faces at the edge of the stage become small whitish blurs as she spins the knife in the air.

The knife. It is warm in her hands as she begins to sing to it, and a little sweat shines on her skin as she dances. The marks on the stage are obscured by the smoke and the knife girl feels she is the moon, rising above the storm. The knife flashes like lightning and she lets her tongue taste the sharp tang of the metal. She feels the eyes of everyone in the room on the knife as she presses it to her skin.

Not yet, she thinks. More foreplay before the penetration. But though she thinks to wait, she can only keep it up so long. Her voice is getting shaky as she cuts the gauzy material from her breasts. The song changes, becomes more breathy and desperate. Night plunges the hilt of the dagger toward her crotch and hears someone nearby gasp. The knife swoops and slices open her leggings and she slowly sinks to her knees.

She hugs the blade to her cheek like a lover's hand, singing, pleading, singing, until she lets her hand fall and the knife scratches a red line along her jaw. The pain opens her eyes and makes her breath deep, her song loud. With one hand covering her bare crotch, she draws swirls with the knife tip across her breastbone, a few places the point parts the skin and blood begins to run down her belly toward her crotch. She criss-crosses the lines of old scars until the blood flows as easily as her song. Her pubic hair is sticky with her own blood and she brings her hand up to smear the blood across her eyes, the mask of war, the mark of death.

At that moment, she looks up. With those blood-stained eyes she sees Michael in the DJ booth, looking back at her with his eyes full of hunger and sadness.

"I have seen tears in an emperor's eyes," she said. *"That is my richest reward."*

He looks at her the same way when she goes to collect her pay at the end of the night. He counts out the bills and holds them in his hand for a long moment, his eyes focused past her on something only he can see.

"Michael?" She does not lean against his desk nor look away into the dim stacks of papers that crowd his office.

His gaze snaps back to her with a little shake of his overgrown hair. His small beard and mustache, she notices, are neatly trimmed. He holds the money in his hand, as if he knows when he gives it to her she will leave. "Is your name really Night?"

Her eyes, dark and placid, do not waver. "Do you want me to try the piercing thing next week?"

"I . . . sure, whatever." His fingers touch hers as he hands her the money.

 Cecilia Tan

*　*　*

Now, the whole city rang with praises of the bird.

The knife girl's tongue dances on the edge of her lover's clit. Karen is squirming, but her bonds hold her pelvis still while the knife girl uses the tender tip to torture her. The knife girl has lost track of time, lost in the sensation of Karen and the rhythm of her tongue's moving.

"Ahh! I can't take it anymore!" Karen pulls hard on her bonds, trying to shut her legs, but to no avail.

Night looks up. Something else, then. She sucks Karen's swollen clit into her mouth. Her jaw begins to tremble as she snags the flesh between her front teeth and begins to close them. Her fingers slide into Karen's cunt. As she bites down, Karen screams and Night feels the spasms around her fingers as Karen comes.

While Karen lies limp, Night loosens the bonds and tucks coils of rope like white cobras into her bag. She leans over to kiss Karen on the cheek.

Karen stops her with a hand on her shoulder. "Don't ever do that to me again."

Night's eyes close in a long blink. "Do what?"

"I didn't like it."

The knife girl considers whether her remark should cut, or not. "Your body did," she says.

Karen's hand connects with Night's cheek, a sudden but not forceful slap. Night holds her wrists then and drags her full weight on top of Karen. "Tell me what you didn't like."

Karen twists her head to the side. "I'm not like you. I don't like pain."

Night releases her suddenly, and stands up. "You're not supposed to like pain. If you did, it wouldn't hurt so much."

Karen sighs and sits up in the bed. The only light comes from the streetlamp below the window, making Night's face look blue, her lips dark. "I'm sorry I hit you," she says, watching Night for a sign of forgiveness. "I . . . you know you stir up a lot of crazy feelings . . ." Night could be a statue of herself she is so still. "And you've been getting so . . . at the club, your show is so extreme sometimes, it scares me. I mean, I know that's what gets the big crowds, the publicity and everything, it's great how we're doing, but I just get a little freaked out, okay?"

Night listens to Karen go on in this vein for some time before she changes the subject. "So what was attendance last night?"

"You mean Michael didn't tell you? It was our biggest night ever."

A big crowd, a rapt crowd, people who would not be the same today as they were yesterday. Except Karen, who is easy to distract from her apologies because she does not really mean them, and Michael, who always watches her with the same expression. The knife girl chews her lip and wonders what she will dream about tonight.

She was put into a golden cage and was allowed to fly out every day . . .

She sits in a darkened corner of the club while insistent rhythms thrum the wall around her. Carl turns a watchful eye her way as he passes through the club, a walkie-talkie by his ear. He is the one who explained it to her: that her presence draws people on the nights she is not performing, that the scenesters and curiosity-seekers alike would come to catch a glimpse of her, hoping to meet her and spin their own myths about her. This corner, up beside one of the bars, is not easily accessible from the dance floor and Michael often sits here while he surveys the crowd. Night has made her appearance here several nights this week and is not surprised when Michael takes a seat next to her.

When he turns to her with bloodshot eyes and puts his hand on hers, and then buries his face in his arms, though, she wonders. And when she takes him back to his office and he knocks the papers from his desk in a rage and then beats his fist upon it, she wonders. And when he regains his composure and apologizes and suggests that she should leave him alone, and when she takes his chin in her hand and rakes his throat with her nails, and makes him hurt, and when he falls to his knees, his eyes closed, his breath shallow, then she wonders. She makes him come with one hand on his penis and one hand around his throat. The knife girl knows better than to say anything about it.

The knife girl lets Karen make her come. She curls up small in a ball until Karen coaxes her open, soft hands and probing fingers seeking out her pleasure spots and manipulating them. Night's throat opens with soft cries as Karen's fingers saw at her slippery clit. Karen pumps her fingers in and out of Night's soft cunt, rubs her thumb over Night's clit, fast, slow, hard, soft, and still Night does not come. Her cries become longer and her breathing deeper, but she does not come. Karen, tired, takes Night's nipple in her mouth, sucking hard and letting her teeth graze across the hard flesh. Night decides to let her think that is what she needs and she lets loose a wail. Karen does not notice that as Night comes, Night's fingernails are digging into her own buttocks.

When they are both relaxed, Karen brushes Night's hair from her face and says, "You are so beautiful when you come."

"Thank you," Night says.

"Why don't you do it more often?"

"Because I don't need to," Night answers.

"But I like to make you come."

"No," Night says, and though she does not intend it, her voice is cold.

The knife girl arrives early to the club, before the doors open and the adoring public arrives. She sheds her coat and carries it to the backroom, led by voices. Carl and Karen are talking in Michael's office.

"There's seriously something wrong with him," Karen.

"No kidding." Carl.

Night pauses outside the door to listen.

"I mean, I think he needs to go to a hospital or to a therapist or something. Doesn't he have insurance?"

Carl laughs. "Yeah, the Mob. Look, he can't go to the nut-house. They'd never trust him again."

"He doesn't have to be committed. I think he just needs medication or something. Prozac. I don't know."

"I've worked for him four years and he gets like this some-times. It'll pass. Just keep it quiet or everything could fall apart around us, you hear me? Something happens to him and this place goes with him."

Night goes silently back to the main room and stands under the white houselights thinking that they look like the lights on a train as it bears down on a crossing. That night, after her perfor-mance, she tends to Michael again. He is in his office alone, his head on his desk, an empty bottle of rum at his feet. With her knife pricking the soft, lethal spot behind his ear, she tells him she knows what he needs, and with her mark carved into his skin, where it joins self-inflicted scars, some old, some new, she knows she is right.

One day the emperor received from Japan a present of a golden bird.

And so it goes for the knife girl, as her performances continue, on the stage, with Karen, with Michael, and it seems to her all will remain that way, until the day she sees the courier leaving Michael's office. A dark-haired man with Asian eyes and an impec-cable suit, he inclines his head toward her, as if acknowledging her as worthy of notice, and then disappears.

Inside the office she finds Michael with a dreamy look upon his face and a needle, not her kind of needle, upon his blotter. That night he does not come to watch her performance and when she visits him later, he responds dully, and thanks her for coming as if she'd fixed a broken sink for him or some other necessary but small task. She leaves him to find Karen swamped with customers at the bar. Carl ushers her to her secluded corner table and she waits there for the night to end.

The next night, she tries again, but Michael sends her away. "Look," he tells her, "we've got to have a little variety to keep the crowds coming down here. Why don't you take a few weeks off? It'll create a great buzz. I've got some other acts who can fill in." The knife girl knows when she is being cut loose.

The emperor and the court now fell in love with the new golden bird and the nightingale was allowed to fly out the window . . . and then a real grief came upon the land.

The knife girl is not surprised when Karen comes home early one night a month or so later, angry and fuming. "He was so fucked up tonight! Everything's going to shit at the club," she tells her. "These Japanese business types are hanging around, throwing their money around, but business is down, and Michael doesn't even seem to want to do anything about it!" Karen looks around the small apartment they have been sharing and exhales. "He's fired two other bartenders this week because we couldn't afford to pay them." Her voice edges on hysterical. "It's like he doesn't care anymore."

"He doesn't," Night whispers, but Karen hears her.

"What do you mean, 'He doesn't'? That club is all he has." Her fear makes her bitter. "And that's all we've got. Or did you forget that I'm the one with a job?"

Night has not forgotten. "I wish I could see him."

"Excuse me?" Karen takes a step closer to Night, out of the kitchenette and into the dining/living area. "How can you miss that bastard after he fired you like he did?"

Night knows she should remain silent. But she does not want her lover to think that Karen owes her nothing. "I'd thought maybe I could help him."

"Help him?" Karen's jealous streak interprets her meaning and cannot help but confirm it. "You were sleeping with him?"

"Not exactly," says Night, sounding small.

"'Not exactly'? Not *exactly*?" Karen's face fights between stricken and angry. "Night! You . . . after what you did . . ." She can't speak, she only sputters.

Night waits for a silent moment to say, "Do you think I should try to help him now?"

Karen recoils from her, eyes narrowing. "What do you mean?"

Night wishes she could explain these things, these things she can only express with tears and cut flesh and songs. "Nothing," she says. "I'm sorry."

"You cheated on me, slept with our boss behind my back, and all you can say is 'I'm sorry'?"

Night says one more thing. "Perhaps I should leave now."

"Did you love him?"

Night does not answer. Karen is irrational, no answer will satisfy her. Besides, the knife girl does not think there is only one kind of love. Karen has never thought to ask if Night loves her: She is too afraid of the answer.

Cold and pale lay the emperor in his royal bed.

The knife girl does not expect thanks. She does what she does for her own feelings, not others. It is her feeling of loyalty that propels her down the dark hallway to Michael's office. Loyalty to him, the man that built the temple for her sacrament, loyalty to Karen, who needs Michael more than she will admit, loyalty to an ideal, a way of life and living that the knife girl must prove to herself. She must prove it to Michael. She shivers with the thought of the confrontation to come—it will be a hard argument to win. Though he will likely send her away again, she has to try.

She opens the door to find him slumped over his desk, as if

he fell asleep after working late. But he is not asleep. She knows it as she lays a hand on his shoulder. He is near death.

Night pulls him from his chair, knocking papers, books, the phone from his desk as she drags him onto it. His chest barely moves, he barely breathes, as she climbs astride him. "Come on, Michael!" she whispers, urgent breath through her teeth as she shakes him. "Come back to me!"

She slaps him across the face and watches the redness of her handprint appear. It is the only reaction she gets. She slaps him across the other cheek, hoping some deadened nerve endings will fire. This is about pain, she thinks. If you can't feel pain, you can't care. People cry at my shows because they can feel the pain I am going through.

The knife, never far from her, cuts his tie from his neck and opens his shirt. She runs her fingers over old scars. I understand you, she thinks. I know why you cut yourself. Because it is better to feel pain than to feel nothing at all, the emptiness. Remember?

She finds the drawer is full of syringes, the needles in a separate package from the plungers. She discards the plungers and opens the needle pack. She fans them in her fingers, chisel points outward. Remember?

She begins with his nipples, heavy with nerve endings and so responsive in the past when she used to pinch them and make him worship with her. The metal slides through his flesh, the left, then the right, and she slaps him across the face again, a guttural growl coming from her throat. I know you felt that!

She feels electric, as if she has started a motor somewhere, connecting her to him. Her nails rake his body as she chooses another place to pierce him, and sinks the needle into his upper arm. She puts another and another through, in neat lines like stitches up his arm. Come on, Michael, feel it! Pain is life, life is pain, so live!

Night cuts open his pants and squeezes his genitals, strokes him, scratches him, until she thinks he takes a deeper breath. One hand pinches a bleeding nipple while the other yanks on his ball sac. There are more needles to go through there, and his perineum, like a ladder climbing between his legs. She drags the point of a needle along the underside of his penis, and stops with the tip poised against the cleft of the head.

If you die, the ship sinks with you, Night thinks. I do this for you, and for me, and for Karen. As she drives the needle through, Michael gasps and clutches at her, like a drowning man rescued from icy seas.

The knife girl lets the blade trail down her lover's back, as her lover arches into the knife's caress. The lights pulse red, then blue, but Night sees only one thing, the ecstasy in Karen's body as she shudders, and Night runs her teeth over her neck and shoulders. There are gasps from the audience as Night tears Karen's bra away. One hand goes to Karen's crotch while the other holds the knife between Karen's bare breasts, and as Night's teeth sink in, Karen comes.

The only people who believe in "totem animals" are those who know their own. Totem animals. A few years ago I wouldn't have either. My Caucasian side would have wanted to explain them as genetic memory or some other pseudoscience, my Chinese side to take on faith that inner animal spirits are embodied in us. Either way, it sounds mystical and distant. But really, they're very close . . . just under the skin. So close you can stumble upon them like a predator in the night.

Like that first time with Jeff. One night we were in bed, making love. We usually made love on Thursdays because he didn't have to teach until the afternoon on Fridays and my weekly department meetings were over with by Thursday. I'd been thinking we'd have a kind of quick one, though, so we could get some rest—boy, was I wrong. I was holding his back against my chest and nuzzling his neck when I had the urge to sink my teeth into his shoulder—and I did. Instead of the usual "Ow!" he snarled and arched back against me, a black panther growling and trying to twist out from under me. We wrestled then, a passionate struggle that heated us like two sticks rubbing together, until he ended up on top of my back, clinging with the claws of his hands and biting me on the back of the neck as his cock nudged at my pubic fur begging entrance. I lay still and let him enter me—he edged his way in while his shoulders and jaw and hands froze rigid like stone. Only his hips moved the first few thrusts. Then I clenched my muscles tight and he mewed, his cock taking control now and moving faster, his hands flying loose and his head thrown back. *Is this what it's like for she-panthers?* I thought as the rhythm built inside me. Our love-making had been energetic before, but this was an animal passion beyond the neatness of human words like *love* or *sex*. In fact, I stopped intellectualizing after that and melted into the flow of fucking and rhythm, and found myself growling and yowling with him as the pressure of his weight on me ground my pubis into the futon and brought me to a shudder-ing climax, and then another as he doubled his speed and came, too.

Afterward, it took him a few minutes to regain speech, to return to the reality of his graduate student apartment in Evanston, Illinois. He looked around his bedroom as if it were a strange environment, when really it was about the most normal place you can imagine, secondhand furniture, piles of books alternating with piles of laundry. He shook himself and said, "Wow. That was intense."

"You okay?" I rested my head on my arm and stroked his shoulder.

"It was like I went deep into the panther-mind, and I saw and smelled and felt everything differently. I could feel the fur and the claws."

So could I, almost. I'd done my master's thesis on mam-malian sexual behaviors and knew more about cat sex than any-one should. *Having sex like wild animals could certainly be a nice change of pace once in a while,* I thought. "It was fun," I said, thinking it sounded encouraging.

Jeff gave me that little annoying frown of his and said, "It wasn't fun, it was *transcendent*."

We didn't last long after that. He became absorbed by his search to find out more about his panther "self," reading books on Shamanism and mysticism, and he kept pushing me to "discover" my own cat. "My panther wants a mate," he'd whisper through a growl while we fucked . . . and I did feel rather feline myself sometimes, but also almost birdlike, akin to a flying creature that was brought down by the hunting cat, and other times so powerful that I could twist him onto his back. All these random things—wings, claws, teeth, a snakelike tail— they were fun, but not *transcendent.* I decided he was sex obsessed and stopped seeing him. *Maybe,* I thought, *I should just look for someone I can have a normal, intellectual conversation with . . .* When an offer from a behavior studies lab in San Francisco came, I took it as a good opportunity to move on. I'd be working with the old standby, white rats. My parents (one an orthopedist and one a general surgeon) were thrilled. I put all the baloney about totem animals in the back of my mind.

I was lonely, I'll admit, at first, but I kept to myself until I settled into my routine at the lab. I could manage being alone, I thought. But I would find myself walking down a busy street in the evening, Chinatown, the Haight, wherever, prowling, hunting, hoping to make a catch. I'd go home when I realized it, thinking to myself, *Who's sex obsessed now?* I missed the intimacy and contact of warm skin. Much as I hoped things would change, I didn't expect it when they did.

I'd spent the weekend moping around the apartment, ordering takeout and not even venturing into the hallway. Sometime Sunday evening, I mustered up the energy to check my mailbox. As I shut my door behind me, I heard the clicking of the locks in the apartment next to mine. Out came a sheaf of jet-black hair, long and straight and slightly damp, and then the head that swung it as a booted foot shooed a cat back into the apartment, and a leather-jacketed, jeans-clad body slipped into the hallway, pulling the door shut. *Must be the next-door neighbor,* I thought. I'd heard the low hum of some kind of music from his apartment, but this was the first time I'd seen him. The jacket was emblazoned with some kind of animal, and I absently wondered if he was part of some rock band or Chinatown gang, or both, or if there even were such things. He was slipping his key into the lock as I went past him to the stairs. Then I heard him curse softly and open the door again. A furry something ran under my uplifted foot and down the stairs. His cat. I ran after the little beast, hoping no one would come into the vestibule just then, and caught up to him by the mailboxes. My black-booted neighbor came tromping down after. I picked up the cat, a smoke-grey beast who looked like every inch of him had been dipped in ash, but no, he was just that color all over.

I turned toward him. "I think this is yours?"

Now I got a look into my neighbor's face, broad and brown, with dark eyes so much like mine, the dark flat lashes of an Asian face. "Thanks," he said as he transferred the cat into the crook of his leather-covered arm. The cat clawed at his sleeve but he didn't act like he noticed. "I'm Jon."

"Marilee." We were both staring at each other. He was the most attractive man I'd seen since I'd moved out here. And to think he lived right next door.

"Nice to meet you."

"Yeah." We stood there a moment longer, while my pulse rate climbed. Then he hefted the cat and smiled. "Well, gotta put the kid to bed before I can go out." And he turned back up the stairs. I got my mail and passed him locking his door again as I went back to my place. "See you around," he said as I shut the door.

I read a book for an hour and watched the news before I got into bed with nothing better to do than go to sleep. I was thinking maybe I'd get up a little earlier, get in to work sooner, but as I lay there I knew I wasn't going to sleep right away. I replayed the exchange by the mailboxes in my mind. Did I imagine that he had a slightly sweet smell? Not the alcohol tang of cologne but something else. If not for the cat I would have shaken his hand, smooth and brown, but instead I only felt the slightest touch as we handed the cat off. A mere brush that nonetheless felt alive with energy to me. I wanted to touch his face, and I wanted to feel that black waterfall of hair going down his back. Sigh. I held my pillow to my chest and my eyes tight and imagined. He was probably hairless or nearly hairless all over, skin smooth and delicious . . . and yet the image that kept popping into my mind was of those catlike eyes. He was sleek, and intelligent, and slightly hungry . . . I hugged the pillow until my arms started to go to sleep and then rolled over on my back and the rest of me went to sleep for the night.

In the morning I was still thinking about him, like I'd had a dream that I couldn't quite remember. It seemed to me now that when we had met, his eyes had a slight dark glow, like an old ember. And the sweet smell. Almost like smoke, I thought. And I'd never made love to another person of Asian descent before. I'd grown up thinking that my father was just about the only Chinese in the States as he was certainly the only one I ever saw much of until I went to college, where I dated bland white middle-class boys like Jeff. It had never occurred to me to think about the ethnic blood of my lovers, it didn't seem important. But right now everything about Jon seemed important to me, every last detail. How his fingernails were slightly overgrown, how his lips looked dark. I preoccupied myself with thoughts of him until I left work early.

He knocked on my door that evening. As I stood in the doorway looking at him, still in the same jeans and boots, a tank top, his jacket gone, I decided the interest-attraction-chemistry that I'd thought I felt last night wasn't just wishful thinking on my part.

He stood there, wordless and calm.

I went with him to his place where our courtship maneuvers commenced. We learned enough about each other to be polite, and then he put me in his bed to demonstrate some Chinese massage techniques he had mentioned.

He lit incense and candles while I took off my clothes, and then began the massage. His hands seemed cool at first, reminding me of a doctor checking for fever, and maybe I could say I was a bit feverish, melting into his touch. He was saying things but I wasn't really listening, about how ancient Chinese medicine was based solely on touching the outside of the body to fix what was wrong inside. My father was a doctor, and Chinese, I told him, but I didn't think he ever did anything like this. His laugh was musical and quiet. "What about your mother?" "American," I answered, and sighed as his fingers reached the knotted muscles in my lower back. I breathed deep as I sank into the softness of his featherbed and the warmth of his breath on my neck. This kind of closeness is what I had missed.

Nimble fingers played over my sides, enticing me to turn over as he searched my stomach and my throat and my thighs for soft places. And then the kisses began, under my chin, on my forehead, my eyelids, my lips. As he broke away I looked up into his eyes.

They seemed to glow as the candles flickered around us and turned his skin gold. I drew in another deep breath of sweet incense and felt myself buoyed like a puff of warm air, like the futon had become a cloud rising in a golden sunset sky; my hands fluttered up like birds to dart into his hair and encircle his neck as I drew myself up to him or him down to me—there was no gravity in that floating state, no up or down—and we rolled one over the other. As he wound around me and I around him I breathed smoke and we spiraled higher. My conscience nagged me once, *What's happening?* but I was eager to hear his reassurances as he hushed me with a golden finger, drawing stripes around my eyes and across my cheeks and telling me not to worry, to relax. I started tasting him, and my tongue stretched impossibly long as I searched out his secret places, and he mine.

The first growl came as one of his legs fitted between mine, our circling of each other drawing into a tighter and tighter spiral, and I sank my claws into his back. The motion of his leg pressed up against my desire. I had a flash of it then, an image I had seen somewhere before lighting up the inside of my eyelids like a slide, a sinuous twisting body rising up like a skirl of smoke . . . the dragon emblem on the back of his leather jacket. Now I saw it clearly. What had looked like a shadow when I'd hurriedly glanced at it the night before I now saw was a second dragon, entwined with the first . . .

One of his fingers slipped into the hollow between his thigh and mine and over the edge of the wet cleft of my mons. He nipped at my chin. I pulled on his generous hair and his back arched away from me and his dark nipples stared at me like icons from a Taoist temple. I used my extra-long tongue to trace up the center ridge of his breastbone, up his chin, and again found myself looking into those eyes, saw myself reflected there, and felt the spinning begin again. He closed those eyes and kissed me, and I closed my eyes, too, as I felt his other leg insinuate itself between mine as I fell into the tumble and spinning again. I hooked my legs around him and drew him into me as the spiral grew as tight as it could, and we were bonded into one animal.

With him inside me now, I thrashed freely, feeling my long spine curving and twisting as we continued through a heavenly sky. Now the vision expanded, to the black-and-gold body entwined within mine, to the feeling of the wind lifting us up as we mated, to the sound of our two wordless voices mixing, to the total sensation that we were two alike beings, long and curving like wisps of smoke, flying upon the air, dragons. I felt my awareness opening like a bud blooming as he moved in me, and the room fell away to nothing, and the city below was like one giant temple festival, with incense burning and small human voices chanting. And still we rolled on through the sky, trailing thunder clouds, as I rode him and he me, the feeling of his flesh where it went in and out of mine like the point of perfect balance, like the vortex around which the whole universe rotated. I flexed my claws and held even tighter to him then, feeling my power. When I'd played at being a cat with Jeff I'd been nosing around the edges of a primal energy, tied to the balance of nature by its raw animalism. But now I felt the surge of ancient power, of something so simple that it was science and magic and religion all at once to my ancestors, a people I had never known. They did not divide up the world the same way as the Europeans or the Native Americans, and they assigned the supreme powers of all animals—the flight of birds, the predatory strength of the tiger, the grace of the snake, and a wisdom beyond man—to one creature who was never captured, never seen for more than a glimpse beyond a distant storm cloud.

This is as it should be, came his voice rolling out of the sound of distant thunder, as he breathed sweet smoke from his nostrils into mine and we rocked together like tides cycling on the shore. Like my tongue, his penis seemed to elongate as he stretched away from me and then swooped in a long slow motion, never seeming to come fully out of me, as though separation were not possible now. And again he pulled away and I pulled him in, inch by inch, over and over in a rhythm as slow as the turning of the world, the cycle of ancient seasons.

My orgasm built in intensity, radiating from the point of balance between us, strobing and rippling through me, along my skin, through my mind. I could see the clouds but feel the tangled sheets under us, feel my wings stretching into the sky but also the clenching of his buttocks under my spread fingers as I drove him deeper and I pushed myself into the heart of my coming. The vortex seemed to spin faster and I clung to him, my loins on fire and the flickering of starlight and candles in my eyes, the taste of his sweet smoke on his lips as I shuddered and shook and felt myself begin the long fall from the peak of pleasure. I opened my eyes.

He cradled me tight against him with one arm as he propped himself up with the other and breathed another puff of sweet smoke into my nostrils. We rolled to the side and his finger again found its way between us to the balance point, to begin the rise again. My second orgasm was quick in coming and I closed my eyes again and pressed my cheek to his chest. With every throb of my clit it seemed we swooped past another cloud . . . For one moment my brain remembered that I was supposed to be at the lab in the morning, and surely two orgasms was enough? I roared as my body soared on another wave of pleasure. My plain white rats could wait. I had discovered a whole new animal inside myself. I heard him take another draw from the pipe then and clamped my mouth to his, ground my hips hard against him, and the pleasure went on.

I know a secret as old as the world, a secret as deep as the ocean and as dark as coal. I know how vampires are born. I also know what you are thinking right now: You think of the bite, the blood. But it is not blood that makes a vampire, no. It is the wanting. Vampires are forged in the heat of desperate desire; vampires are birthed in the waters of a need so intense that their very souls do drown. Have you ever wanted something so much? So much that you would die for it? Kill for it? Lose your soul for it? So it is with vampires. When the wanting becomes of fever pitch, the magic ignites and transforms one from mortal being into the pure embodiment of hunger, of need, of desire. Ah, but what about the blood? you want to know. You are so sure it must have something to do with that . . . Well, perhaps there is magic in all blood ties. And, of course, the wanting hurts. It hurts more than ever. And the blood . . . the blood is only one way to quench the fire. Perhaps the quickest, easiest way, if just for a little while. I have discovered others. What else will you ask? Holy water, the sign of the cross . . . I have not found them deadly. However, the Christians have good reason to call us enemies, for their faith is founded on denying one's desires, delaying one's gratification. For us, that is our life. We live for desire, eternally.

 74 *Cecilia Tan*

I thought I might say something like that to Christina, if ever the time was right for it. She would be thrilled by dramatic flourish and poetic turns of phrase. I passed the time imagining my delivery of such a speech and the circumstances under which it would come. I looked at my silver pocket watch. She was late for our second date. With measured steps I paced the tiles of cracked marble in the vestibule of her building and resisted the urge to ring her buzzer again. If she had been there, I would have known. That is one thing about the magic: Want something enough and you know where it is. I wanted Christina. Tonight I thought I might have her.

Our first date had been a chance meeting a week ago. I'd gone out to a new club to see what there was to be seen. It satisfied my sense of irony to attend what was billed as Vampire Theme Night. For some time now I'd become aware of a fashion called Goth, mixing all the sublimated fears and beliefs of an earlier age with the trappings and trimmings of same: white lace, red roses, black hearts. Shelley's and Stoker's misunderstood monsters—icons for these young ones—melded to modern demons, industrial, postmodern, cynical . . . Dear, dear children . . . they realize that Hell *is* this Earth, and allow themselves to exult in it. When all life is pain, then from the pain must come joy.

In one of the myriad bookstores near Harvard, I had found homemade magazines filled with their dark poetry, blurred photocopies of musicians they idolized, letters and essays and more, all revealing their essence to me. That is where I found the flyer inviting me to enter their world—held one night a week—Vampire Theme Night. I looked forward to seeing these new children, to see if they were everything I had hoped they would be.

I paid the cover charge and entered the place. A few heads turned as I stepped into the main room. I had gone back to the clothes I liked best for the occasion: an off-white lace cravat, black waistcoat, silver cufflinks—accoutrements that had suited me so well in the past century. Only at Vampire Theme Night could I wear such things without seeming out of place. I noted a few others about in ruffled shirts, fine brocade; still others were in black leather, or neck to ankle in black satin. My eye was even more pleased to note that there was one—and then another, and another—whose gender was obscured by light, by makeup, by mannerism. I might find prey here, I thought. Even better, I might find kin.

The room pulsated with want. I tasted loneliness, alienation, isolation. There was the tang of lust, especially from the dance floor, and the sharp spice of a sudden, mad desire from a white-haired girl seized with the urge to kill herself, which then faded when a black-maned boy (I think) took her by the hand and led her out of my sight. It was then I caught sight of her, of Christina, wearing what could have been a wedding dress if it hadn't been night black, and carrying a bouquet of black silk flowers. Her hair, which was flamingo pink, seemed too bright for her monochrome demeanor. She settled herself at a small table by the dance floor, a few friends shedding their leather jackets around her as they went to join the others gyrating and swaying to the beat of the music.

I did not approach her. I took up a spot at the bar and asked for ice water, amusing myself by watching the androgynes sliding from posture to posture. The music was heavy and moving, like a Gregorian chant set to a rhythm. In fact, I think that is exactly what it was.

In my time, it was much easier for a woman to pass as a man, because no woman would be seen with such short cropped hair, in trousers, and smoking. Now women did these things with such regularity that it would not twist anyone's perception to see a woman thus. Now it has turned to the men to put on makeup, heels, maybe even a dress, to cross the barrier.

 Cecilia Tan

Here the point did not seem to be to pass as a member of the opposite sex, but rather to seek a maddeningly erotic mixture, to disguise whatever gender one had while at the same time radiate a unique kind of sexual allure. I found it heady and encouraging, a touch of fishnet or velvet here, lipstick or eye-liner there.

Yet of them all, the one I wanted was Christina. Christina, so dearly femme, clutching her funereal bouquet.

Eventually I went near her, near enough to taste the want coming from her—the taste of something she wanted so dearly that it was buried deep inside, under layers and layers of affectations and peer pressures so dense I couldn't sense it clearly. Yet I wanted her. I wanted her, and I sat there wanting her until it worked the magic so that she came to me. And I did what any civilized person would do. I took her out for coffee.

She agreed to meet me again, to go out for dinner at my expense and to go again to the club, this time arm in arm. Yet where was she? I rang her buzzer again, just in case. Maybe she was in the shower, but no one answered. No, I would have known if she was there. My connection to her was strong. I sat down on the cracked marble steps to wait.

Our coffee that night had been dark and rich and just a bit bitter, like the taste of her soul as she told me about her parents and her sorry adolescence. She was not as young as I had first thought. Regardless of how many years she had lived, there was still a great deal of that confusion that infects the young, a search for who she was, who she wanted to be.

It was a pain I had never understood very well. I had always known what I wanted to be, had always striven for it, despite the fact that it would always be unattainable. I hadn't listened to my parents' guidance, or even my society's disapproval. And I told her this.

The next word caught in her throat, I thought I had it—what she wanted, what she wanted to be. Something hidden under her fear, a spark of wanting something outside of the mundane. Something with a taste of the forbidden. A lesbian. A woman's woman. Yet she wanted to remain the frail flower that she was. It did not match her picture of lesbianism, but I thought her perfect for it. What she wanted was a woman's love, and that was one thing I could give her. I wanted her so much I could no longer taste the coffee at all. Perhaps the Christians and I had something in common at last as I, too, delayed my gratification. I spoke to her of the future that awaited us and made the date for dinner with her.

Where was she?

I looked at my watch again. Something must have gone wrong. I thought of how her wrist bent as she reached to pick up her ragged bouquet, of how her fingers had slid off mine as she slipped into the cab, of the delicate curve of her collarbone above the satin trim of her dress . . . and I let the wanting take me. The wanting poured from me in invisible waves, seeking her.

It was some minutes before I sensed her—to the north, probably across the river, in the direction of the club. I couldn't just hail a cab and then tell the driver to drive "Thataway." I set out, my head pounding as I made my way from the brownstones and trees that lined her street toward the boulevard.

I told you the wanting hurts. It always has, but it becomes bearable after being dormant so many years. Now I had awakened the wanting in me, and it would have to be slaked soon, even if just for a little while. *When you find her,* I thought to myself, *she will be mad with desire for you.* I knew of two ways besides the blood to quench the wanting: To satisfy someone else's want was one, to exhaust oneself with the friction and fusion of sex was another. With Christina, perhaps I would have both and sleep soundly for many nights to come. The anticipation made my head pound all the more.

A man on a bicycle whizzed past me, then came to an abrupt

stop at the corner. A sudden ragged sob tore loose from him. The heavy cottony blanket that was homesickness descended. I shook my head, trying to contain the wanting, to reel it in. I had been careless. In his proximity to me he'd caught a whiff of it. He wiped his eyes on his sleeve, shaking his head in puzzlement, and went on his way. I hugged myself as if that might help to keep the wanting in, and focused myself on her and her alone.

By the time I was halfway across the bridge, I could sense Christina more clearly. She was nearby. I came to a neighborhood full of three-decker houses and postage-stamp-size yards. She was here, in one of these houses.

I stopped in front of a house that had once been painted blue, showing underneath a flaking beige that had been hastily or lazily applied. The only decoration was a handwritten FOR RENT sign in the front window. There were lights on in the upstairs apartment, and it was there that I sensed her.

A few seconds passed and the aroma of her changed. Then I heard her scream.

I tried the door, found it open, and took the stairs two at a time. The door to the second-floor apartment was locked, but old and flimsy. The hasp gave way on my second push and I found myself in a kitchen and homing in on the eastern corner of the house—a bedroom, heavy with the scent of cheap incense. At first I wasn't sure if that's really what the scent was, or if it was the stink of the man I was facing when I pushed open the bedroom door. A man who wanted things I did not want to know about. He was naked and his black hair hung around his eyes like weeds.

"Who are you?" he said. In his hand was a knife stained with that unmistakable red. All I could think was what an irrelevant question . . . of course I was the one here to stop him. I didn't answer. Instead, I walked past him to where Christina lay crumpled upon the bed, her shock of pink hair hiding her face.

I tried to take her in my arms, but she pushed me away without looking up.

"Hey I'm talking to you." I looked back to see he was licking the knife. "You her mother or something?"

"My name is Jillian," I said, hoping that Christina would recognize my voice. He was running the knife blade along the outside of his arm, drawing long thin lines in his flesh. Now it was my turn to ask the stupid question. "What are you doing?"

"Aw," he said, "I wasn't going to hurt her." I could smell the rotten stench of a lie coming off him. It was his own blood on the knife. If I had arrived later, it would not have been—of this, I was sure. I wanted to take her out of there, away from him. Seeing her curled up, naked and defenseless, had made the want a screaming nightmare in my head.

"Christina, honey, are you all right?" She was crying. I turned to pick her up, as if I could just carry her, unclothed, to safety.

He gave himself away. I turned to face him—not because of the electric change in him I sensed when his need for violence erupted—but because he muttered "Bitch" as he lunged at me with the knife.

The knife sank deep into me, in the hollow between my right shoulder and collarbone. His eyes were still on the hilt when I took him by the throat. Now I had pain beyond pain. The magic shrieked the damage to my perfect shell, and this idiot was bleeding from several places where he had cut himself. He was gasping as I pulled him to me to lick at the wounds he had inflicted. But there was only a trickle, and a river was pouring out of me.

"Christina . . ." I said, my voice a deep rasp, "pull out the knife." I could not do it and hold on to him at the same time. "Please . . ." She was on her feet, a sheet wrapped over her shoulders, her eyes wide. She reached a hand toward the hilt. He flailed a bit and she pulled back. I tightened my grip on him. "He can't hurt you." She grasped the hilt with one hand

and it slid out of me, slick and wet and dark. Her stare never left my face. I forced out the words, "Turn away." I knew she wouldn't—she was pulled into the vortex of the wanting, the magic. The wanting coursed through me, and it seemed his neck came to my mouth of its own accord.

I drank until he was dead. It had been a long, long time since I had done that. I had taken blood before, but the wanting was so severe that I needed to drink deeper and deeper until the blackness of death ran through me, too. My own death was one thing that I could not have. I drank until we both fell back upon the bed like lovers, his fingers pushing feebly at me as he slipped away to whatever afterlife there might be. I lay back, a heaviness in my limbs making it hard to do else.

I saw Christina still standing there, as she had been through the whole feeding, the knife in her hands and the sheet held tight around her like a shroud. Perhaps I would be giving my vampire speech sooner than I had planned. She looked for a moment like she wanted to say something. As the words came to her lips, tears came to her eyes, and she began to sway. I stood up to catch her as she fell sobbing into my arms, and the knife fell to the floor.

My speech didn't go at all the way I thought it would. There was no other explanation for what she had seen. The knife wound was completely healed by the time we returned to her apartment. She had seen me exhibit a strength that was unhuman. Not to mention that I drank him dry. Now that I was full, my senses were dulled and I had to listen with care to what she said or risk missing the nuances of what she really meant. She had turned to me as soon as the door to her sanctuary, a single-room studio with an alcove hung with black curtains, was closed.

"You're a vampire," she said, breathless as if we'd just run up the stairs instead of riding the elevator like civilized people. Her eyes were not narrowed in accusation but wide with wonder.

"Yes."

She faltered a bit as she lowered herself onto the bed. In a long black T-shirt and jeans, she seemed more frail than she had in lace and satin. Her eyes went far away, and her lip trembled. I knelt by her feet and took her hand.

"It's all right. I'm here. He's gone." She looked at her little white hand in mine and mustered half a smile from her overworked lip.

"I didn't know he would be like that," she said. "I'd seen him once before, at the club. And when I ran into him today and he asked me . . . "

When she didn't go on after a moment I asked, in the gentlest voice I had, "What did he do?" She shook her head, whether to remember or forget I don't know, and squeezed my hand harder.

"With the knife, he wanted to . . . it was too much . . ." She pressed her legs together. I didn't need to hear any more. He'd lured her with the promise of sex and given her violence. I held her against my breast and rocked her like the child she was inside. And when she broke away, she kissed me like the woman she was.

I know there was still the taste of blood on my lips, but she didn't seem to care. Even though my senses were deadened from satiation, every nerve in my body told me of her need. I remembered my original plan for the evening: to make love with her, to give her what she wanted. She welcomed me into her bed. I shed my bloody clothes and luxuriated in the feeling of skin against skin.

"You're so soft," she remarked. *Let her enjoy it*, I thought, *at least someone will*. Her fingers slid over the place where the knife had been in me and she sighed a deep, luscious breath. I took my time with her. As I came to touch or kiss each unexplored patch of flesh, I gave her a moment to follow with me in assent. Her shoulder, the hollow of her bosom, the soft skin beneath her navel. While my tongue was searching at the parting between her legs, as I listened to her sigh and moan, the wanting began to seep back into me. I prayed to myself, *Let it not be as strong this time.* But I knew the prayer would be in vain, for I could sense the oldest, most familiar tingle in it, the feeling of everything I had tried to suppress all these years. Christina was alive in my mouth now, with frantic jerks and cries. I wanted to reach out with my senses and find out how much more she wanted, but I didn't dare let the power loose, not when memories and old, old desires were beginning to brim up. Not now . . . *Why now?* I could keep it in check. I kept my mind at the task at hand, licking her, tasting her salt. She held on to my short hair and kept me in place as her pleasure rose up and she rubbed herself against me. *Christina, my sweet, my dear one* . . . When at last she went limp I stopped and pulled back to look at her.

She was looking up at me with dreamy eyes and smiling. Yet I realized her wanting was still there, and it was beginning to rage back stronger than ever in me. Wasn't she sated? She seemed to be waiting for something. She put her arms around my neck and whispered, "Take me . . ." I pushed her away, reeling from the deepest stab of the wanting that I knew.

"I can't." Wasn't that obvious? How could she taunt me so, when she could see my body . . . perhaps I was doomed to live out this scene again and again. Isn't that what it is to be a vampire? To embody the desire that made me this way?

I cursed myself for a fool. She wanted something I could not give her, something this woman's body would never have, though I walk the Earth for eternity wanting it. I pulled away from Christina then, as if she were too hot to touch. She seemed to be transforming into Selene before my very eyes . . . Selene, the lover I had kept as well as I could in my mortal life, with my hunting rifles and my hounds, my trousers and pipe.

We could have married, I think, and no one would have thought it odd or out of place because by that time no one knew I was a woman . . . except her. And it grew to grate on her. She hated me in the end, when, drunk with passion, she had insisted over and over "Take me, take me!" and I couldn't. Not the way she wanted, not the way *I* wanted. I was consumed with frustration and desire. She shoved me aside and told me she had been sleeping with one of my stablehands, that I would never satisfy her. I flew into a jealous rage and she fled, never to return to that cursed life. And so I thought, neither would I.

I took up one of my hunting knives and thought to end my miserable sham of a life. I slashed at my wrists and knelt by the fire thinking on and on how unfair it was . . . I had lived as a man, succeeded as a man, but I could never be a man. My mind whirled from the sex, the pain, the violence. When the magic began to take me I did not recognize it for what it was. The surging of fire through me—perhaps that was what dying felt like. Then I saw the cuts healing. I felt my consciousness expanding . . .

And here I was with Christina, not Selene. She held me by the hands and said, "Please . . ." There was none of the cruelty in it that had made Selene's voice so cutting. She pulled me down onto the bed again, and nuzzled against me. *This is not Selene,* I reminded myself, and tried to look into Christina's eyes. Finally, in confusion and desperation, I let my senses out again, reaching deep into her now, and found her defenses gone. She was completely ready to bare her hidden desire to me.

"Make me a vampire," she whispered.

I held her for long moments as I let that sink in. Her desire for the forbidden, to step outside society. Her poor judgment about the blood-fetishist-turned-rapist. Her wonder, joyous wonder, at my performance with him. The idolization of my kind by these children, who already knew that life was about wanting and pain. And now, as the primal wanting coursed through me anew, I realized I would find no relief from it here. Because I could not give her what she wanted. If I had a way to make her a vampire, it would quench her desire to become one. Without the burning of an unfulfillable desire, she could not cross over.

The pain seemed to hiss through my chest and into my head as I took a deep breath, so tempted to take the quick, easy way out of the mess I had created. But killing her was not something I wanted.

"I can't," I said again, as she tried to show her neck to me. "But . . . ?"

"Shhh." I held her head against me again. She was so small, so beautiful. So young. She would outgrow this fascination, wouldn't she? No, not having met me, seen me, living with the knowledge that she now had. I had known other mortals in my years who had known the truth, but none who had sought to join us, not knowing what it was to exist only to live forever unrequited. I thought of the others I had seen at the club. They were, in their own way, all vampires.

That is what I told her as I tried to explain the essence of wanting, the pain of an unfulfillable desire that consumes one, body and soul. She cried clear-eyed tears of revelation, as if I had spoken a truth she had always known but never voiced. She did not believe in God or Heaven, but she believed in the pain of living. Her faith, I had affirmed.

We are all accursed to walk this Earth with our unfulfilled desires, both you and I. May your walk be a short one, my friend, as short as mine is long.

$\mathcal{F}$araway Worlds

IV

Here's what happens when I let myself go all the way over into other worlds and imaginary places: For erotic purposes, it often means that I get to scratch itches I didn't know I had; for artistic purposes, it means I can create relationships and situations that would be meaningless in the so-called real world. I can cut loose from late–twentieth-century sexual politics, AIDS-phobia, and other contemporary baggage.

With "Pearl Diver," I wanted to write a story that celebrated the power of female sexuality, where womanhood was absolutely central and vital to life, culture, tradition, and the future. The story came about when a small-press editor I knew called me up and said the press needed a story of woman-centered erotica, preferably with a non-Western cultural milieu, where the moon figured prominently as a symbol, and by the way, one that was also science fiction/fantasy. Rather than constrict my vision, the many requirements gave me the form in which to pour my desire to write the celebratory work I wanted, and the story came out in one highly polished, near-perfect rush. Only after writing it did I come to think that it was really necessary to create a whole new world to express what I wanted. That's when science fiction becomes something more than just a genre. In "In Silver A," I had the urge to write a story about two equal individuals who have an erotic, interdependent love relationship that isn't anything akin to conventional. The editor of the magazine that published it said in his acceptance that I'd finally done what no other writer for his magazine had, which was to make the sex and eroticism so integral to a science fiction story that they couldn't be cut out. Of course, sometimes the genre is just fun, a tasty backdrop for way-out what-ifs that give me a chance to indulge things like my fur fetish.

I breathe. As I lie still in the bottom of the boat, the sea breathes with me, rising and falling. There is just enough room for me in my little wooden shell, the oars tucked against each side. Droplets of seawater glisten on my bare skin, and I watch my own chest as I breathe, touch my stomach with my hands. The time is coming, and I am almost ready. The moon is still climbing up the sky, and I wait for it to reach its peak. It must, because that is the way things are and have always been, the moon and the sun circling forever above without cease, just as the waves must rise and fall, and the rains must follow the dry time. Tonight is not just any moonrise, though, not just any night upon the water. Tonight is the night of the pearls.

I sit up in the boat and peer over the edge. The water is dark, but the sand and the stones are almost white. Below me the silvery flash of fish in the moonlight catches my eye—but I know it is just fish, not pearls. I will know the pearls when I see them. When the moon is at its height. I have been prepared for this moment since my breasts first began to swell; for years I have prepared my body for this, to be a pearl diver.

The elders in the village say the pearls fell down from the skies; some say they are stars out of the heavens; some say *we* came down from the heavens, that we came long ago from another place where we were not the only people, where there were people with pink skin and yellow hair, that we traveled on the water in boats like my little shell; some say that when we die we will go back to that place and others say that when we are born that is where we come from; and in any case the only thing we all do agree on is that the pearls are magic and precious, and if there is a link to our ancestors, gods, or afterlife, it is through them.

I lie back down in the boat. The moon is taking its time. I let my feet hang over the edge on either side, warm water touching my toes as the shell rocks into a small swell. The night breeze rustles the dark cluster of hair between my legs and the lips sigh open. As they taught me, I lick my finger and let it rest there, rocking my hips as each wave passes, slow as a sleeper's breath. Just as I had been taught, I gather the magic around me, and I can almost see myself beginning to glow as I resist the urge to press my finger harder and let the energy burst and dissipate. It surges through me as I go on touching what we call the "woman's pearl," the nub of flesh now grown hard like the treasures I will be seeking.

My eyes have slipped closed, but I must keep watching the moon. I open them to find it is almost above me, looking down on me like an eager lover, who will now finally be allowed into my virgin flesh. I slip over the side of the boat and into the warm embrace of the sea. Bubbles rise up and catch between my legs, and I want to keep my hand there but I will need both of them to swim. I lower myself under the surface of the water, and as sounds grow dim, my vision grows sharp. I am a pearl diver and I know how to see through the shadows and murk. But there is nothing to see, yet. I let go of the boat and float facedown on the surface, my legs hanging free below me and open. I tense the muscles inside me and feel the energy shoot through me again. Soon those muscles will do what I have practiced so long to do. The elders chose me out of all the others to do this task. All the girls my age had been taken aside and trained, the old women rubbing our women's pearls with oil until we learned to do it ourselves, reaching fingers inside of us, first one, then two, then three, as they exercised us until we had the strength that was needed, and holding our breaths until sometimes it seemed we did not need to breathe at all . . .

And now I see why. The moon must be over my head as the shadows have all shrunk as small as they can be, and I see at first faint but then as bright as the nighttime stars, the pearls. Glowing from the bottom. They are invisible and dead as rocks at any other time, but now they glow. *Maybe,* I think to myself, *they fell not from the stars but from the moon itself, and they glow only when the moon draws so near.* I take the last breath that I will ever draw as a girl and with wide strokes I dive toward my womanhood.

The first pearl I find is small, no bigger than the end of my thumb, and I lift it from its bed of sand and turn it in my fingers to convince myself that what they told me is true, it is smoother than anything I have ever felt, much smoother than the wooden beads we used for practice. Curling myself into a ball with my head between my knees, I open myself with one hand and slide the pearl inside me, using my muscles to draw it as far up inside as it will go . . .

The shock of the first vision almost makes me lose my air, a tiny silver bubble rises toward the moon as I see in my mind's eye the moon, the stars, not spread out above me like a roof but hanging all around me like a school of fish in the water, and I know that I feel my place among them.

My legs together, I stroke with my arms to the next glowing spot, and lift out of the sand a pearl the size of my eye. It feels warm, warmer than the blood-warm seawater, and with one hand I slip it inside.

This time I am ready when the vision comes: I am moving through space like a swimmer, circling down toward a planet blue with oceans, and thinking, *Home! Home!* and already I am spiraling toward the next pearl, this one bright as it protrudes above the sand, almost too large to fit in my closed hand. I press it against my opening, but it does not slide in like the others. I cannot breathe to help me relax, and I do not have time to waste with only one breath of air inside me. While I take the time to do this I float toward the surface and it will be more work to get back to the bottom. As my hands work at my opening, they brush my woman's pearl and I feel something inside me blossom open like a flower, and take the white orb in.

I am swimming, turning and tumbling, as the planet below revolves in its dance around the sun, the moon its partner swinging 'round, and all the close family of others moving stately through the sky, and beyond, and beyond, and beyond . . . and a voice, not my own, in my head, saying, *The seeds of life, scattered* . . .

I realize my vision is getting darker and my air is almost done, but I make for one more pearl nearby. This one I lift in two hands; it is the size of my fist. Some part of me thinks I cannot hope to take it in, but one hand is already rubbing hard at my own pearl while the other is pushing the huge thing against me. It goes partway in and then slips back out, and if I could I would be gasping for breath but there is only water all around me as I thrash. I need this last pearl more than all the others, I am hungry for it, the energy and magic flowing in and out of it as I push my fingers inside myself, trying to open the way wide enough; and then it is going in, it moves in my hand into me bit by bit, up to its widest point, and then, as my other hand presses hard on my woman's pearl, I swallow it whole.

The universe breathes like giant wings beating. I see people infinitely small in a band across the face of the stars, I see white glowing star stuff spread like webs across the void, I see embryos bursting into life inside mothers' wombs, I see the "man's pearl" dripping from the tip of his finger, I see all of creation. I cry out as the magic bursts through me and my bubbles race out of me like a flight of startled birds. My hands are between my legs, one keeping the pearls in place and the other holding my own pearl, which throbs and ebbs, and my head breaks the surface . . .

. . . and I breathe . . .

I lie on my back in the water with the moon shining upon my breasts and I cannot take my hands from between my legs as I burst the bubble again and again, fingers furiously working as the sensations wash over me, and under the moon's watchful eye I know I will return to the shore, bearing the wisdom of ages.

In Silver A there is no crime, no pollution, no strife, no domestic violence, no trouble. That's what they told us at that recruitment rally seven years ago, and again when Marco and I got our silver badges of citizenship two months ago. So then, how would you explain the fact that I was sitting in someone's kitchen covered in blood? A baby was crying, there was an empty bulb of glucose in my hand, and all was not right with the world. The sugar was making it hard to think, overloading parts of my brain and trying hard to erase my short-term memory.

And who wouldn't want to forget? I remember the cops standing over me, roughing me up, I remember taking a hard hit in the face while one of them spat, "Fringe trash!" And I remember grabbing the bottle of glucose formula from the counter—my escape hatch from reality. Once my eyes rolled back into my head they stopped questioning me, stopped hitting me.

A woman's voice said: "Remove him!" I couldn't really feel it, but part of me knew they were dragging my rag-doll body down the stairs, across an immaculate lawn of prickly green irrigated grass, and stuffing me into one of those little electric vans all the police in Silver America drive. The van began to move, the woman driving, two men sandwiching me in the backseat. We pulled away from the upscale residential sector toward the rectilinear SA Center skyline, toward the seats of government and power, and somewhere on the outside of me, I began to babble.

The voice again, speaking crisp Civil tongue. "Can't you quiet him down?" Such perfect diction and syntax even in the face of a crisis. My own conditioning was not as good—try as I might to protest it came out in Fringlish: "Fuck-all, jeezus, I got rights!" which elicited sneers from the bruisers at my sides. One of them pointed at my citizenship badge and the two of them laughed.

"He's like a talking animal," the first one said.

"Yes," the other agreed. "You can train them but they always revert to their wild state."

"That's better," the first one said, smacking his knuckles into his meaty hand. "I like it better that way."

I wished I could move away from him. I'd never seen them but there was always a rumor that men from SA would come into the Fringe, "hunting parties," hunting us. Fear started to creep through my sugar-induced haze. I didn't want to face what was going to happen to me because I knew it wouldn't be good. I slipped into the wonder of auditory hallucination and swirling wormholes behind my eyes. The cascade of molecules over my receptors tweaked something in my long-term memory and the past swallowed me up.

It's seven years ago and I am meeting Marco's eyes across the crowd at the ration station. The Science jerks are on the Fringe recruiting for live bodies, ours. They're handing out food and it's all a tangle of arms and curses in broken Fringlish, but I see Marco at the center of a calm area and make my way toward him as Science's pitch begins.

We all know better than to go with the Arm. They just want cannon fodder for the border skirmishes between Silver A and Texico. But Science could be something different. Sure they're spouting words like *indenture contracts* and *eventual citizen-ship*—things we don't have words for in Fringlish. They are projecting images on the cracked wall of nice, safe, clean, shiny, warm Silver America . . . Science is looking pretty good. Marco thinks so, too. Science wants kids like us, they want converts. We want food, warm places to sleep, maybe a little clean water, too.

I look into Marco's unscarred face and think: He looks good at staying out of trouble. I can't say the same, squinting at him through an eye swollen half shut from a fight the night before. They had wanted my coat and didn't get it. Even so, I sat awake all night scared and sure that I was as good as dead.

You going? Marco says. His hair is long and black, the ends frayed, not cropped and soldered like mine.

Fuck-all. I tell him: *I go if you go.*

I felt the pressure on my shoulders from the cops on either side of me, and I was back in real time. Damn simple sugars, burn bright but quick. I opened my eyes to see we were pulling up to the glittery tower that housed the offices of Science. Not Civil, where there's a hospital, not the Arm, where there's a detention tank and where they'd execute capital offenders, surely, if they ever had any. Big Momma Science didn't own me anymore, I reminded myself, not for two whole months. The shiny badge on my chest said I was a free man. But I didn't feel like one when they grabbed me by the arms. If the glucose had run its course, I had no refuge from them. I was beginning to wonder about things like whose blood it was soaking my shirt, how it got there, and why Science wanted to know, when they hauled me upright, my brain did flip-flops, and I swirled away again.

It's six years ago, very early in the dark morning, and I can't sleep. I'm in my dorm cell and thinking about how it will be my turn to go under the knife soon. I know it, Sugar Test Series—

Cecilia Tan

Subject #11, or so it says on my indent card. They took #10 from the next cell over last week and he never came back.

Marco's in the next wing over; he hasn't been taking to the special diet very well, so they've moved him to another project. The special diet is I don't know what, but it makes me hungry all the time and gives me headaches. Dawn light makes the ceiling gray where the thin strip of window runs along the top of the high outer wall. I hear the footsteps in the hall.

They aren't coming for me. It's only one pair of footsteps, just a guard or a caretaker, not an escort contingent. I hear the door being opened across the hall, a low voice, then a scream is cut off.

I decide maybe if they come for me soon it might not be such a bad thing. And then there is a sound at my door and I hold my breath.

Hey, hey you. Marco is in the hallway.

I slip from the bed and kneel at the door. *Whatta you here?*

I had to know if they took you away yet, he says. His Civil tongue programming has taken root and it barely sounds like him. *Are you all right?*

I tell him my time will be soon, and that I don't know if I'll be coming back.

You won't, he says. *You'll be moved to another facility where you'll be isolated from the other indents for a while. So you won't see me for a couple of months.*

I wish I could see him through the door, but all I can see is the shadow at the crack. I want to tell him something more, but fuck-all, what else is there to say?

The next thing I hear is the sound of the door across the way opening, and a voice, Breton, this sector's caretaker, our legal guardian, saying to Marco: *Oh my, my, my, what could you be doing here?*

Marco starts to stammer that he has clearance, and I think he really does, but Breton isn't listening. He's pushed Marco up against the door; I hear the thump of Marco's head on the hard metal. Don't fight him, I'm thinking, just take it and he'll let you go . . . but I'm too scared to make a sound. Breton likes pushing his weight around, and on this wing we've all learned to take it. But Marco fights back. He pushes Breton off, I hear the scuffling, another bang on the door. And then Breton laughing and explaining that Marco's violent tendencies make him a likely candidate for hormone reduction. Something bad is happening; I hear Marco screaming, and then Breton saying that he'd better take care of it right away. Then they're gone.

I cry myself to sleep. Breton wakes me up later with my special diet breakfast and a tablet for me to sign. He tells me to cheer up as he looks at the bags under my eyes. He pats me on the head as he tells me my whole life will be different as of tomorrow. They come for me the next day.

They didn't kill me. That was my first thought as I started to come to. Before I thought about the cops who dragged me here or where I was, I just thought, *They didn't kill me,* and who "they" was didn't matter. All that matters on the Fringe is that you've lived another day, no one killed you for your blanket or you didn't die of the night desert cold. I used to struggle awake, quick, before anything bad could happen. When I'd signed up with Science I had seen enough life to know I wanted more, and that I could be dead the next day if I stayed in the Fringe. I wanted to be able to wake up without reaching for the broken screwdriver hidden in my shirt, without feeling like the axe was about to fall at any moment.

But, as I'd learned, that's exactly what it was like waking up in a room in Science, too.

So this time, after I came to, it took me a while to convince myself I wasn't fifteen years old and waiting for Science's next invasive procedure. A couple of things helped, like the fact that I came to alone. No Scientist waiting with a needle and electro-probe ("I'm sorry you have to be awake for this"); no escort with heavy restraints or nerve cuffs ("I'm sorry, but we can't have you damaging SA property banging your head against a wall like that"); no guardians with a grudge or wanting something personal. I could feel the hardness of my silver badge digging into my ribs where I lay on top of it, and with one small motion of my finger I felt the hard place behind my ear where my machine connection sat. I told myself a couple of times, I'm a Machine Maintenance Engineer, a citizen, I am Civil's business . . . then I tried to convince myself that I wasn't even in Science, that seeing the Science tower was just one of my bad sugar-induced flashbacks. They had been much more intense than I'd expected. So maybe . . .

I looked around the room. I lay on a hospital gurney, with a tube in my arm. Someone had cleaned up the blood and put me in soft medical whites. The room did not look like labs nor infirmary, more like an office with the furniture removed—recently, from the look of the dents in the carpeting. Science Executive Wing. Damn. The slow drip was some blue shit I didn't recognize, but whatever it was, it was making me feel pretty good. Alert. No dizziness. No hunger. Of course these jerkoffs would know what to feed me. I sat up.

My movement must have triggered something, or maybe they had cams on me, because two executives immediately came in. Both blond, in suits. One of them was smiling and I almost didn't recognize Breton. My indent officer for the seven years Science had owned me and my body and my brain, and they'd done what they liked with that brain. I wasn't glad to see him. He'd grown a beard and lost some weight. My guess was he'd been promoted as a result of how well I'd served society— up until today, that is.

He walked right up to the bed, no handshake or anything, and said, "You're in a lot of trouble, Tato." Using my name like a punctuation mark. Treating me like an indent.

The other guy, some big wig's assistant I would guess from the shine on his shoes and conservative, solid-color tie, did shake my hand. "I'm pleased to meet you, Mr. Smith." I almost laughed at that. I couldn't get used to this last name thing, but I'd had to pick one to get my citizenship. "I'm Henry Billings."

I did what they taught us to do in Civil training. "Pleased to make your acquaintance, Mr. Billings." Polite manners were mandatory for all citizens. Then I said to Breton, not quite in Fringlish, "What the fuck-all am I doing here?"

Breton could talk the talk and didn't stand on ceremony. I knew it was an insult for him to talk to me like this, but I found it weirdly comforting. "Don't give me any lip. Your ass should be over at the Arm getting fried right now. Murder, you know?"

"So why isn't it?"

"*Mis*-ter Breton, Mr. Smith, please." Sweat broke out on Henry's scalp where he was losing his hair. "I believe we have a proposal to discuss."

Breton: "Proposal, my ass. Let's just rip the fuck-all out of his head and find out for ourselves."

"You're not scaring me." I said. Which was a lie.

Henry looked shocked at Breton's language. *Fuck-all* was pure Fringe profanity. Citizens had neater things to fall back on like: *Goddam.* But he smoothed his facial expression and said in an equally smooth voice, "Mr. Breton, may I remind you that would be a violation of Mr. Smith's civil rights? As you know . . ." He was about to launch into a canned speech about what made Silver America great, and better than New Japan's meritocracy on the coast or Middle West's hagiarchy, citizen's protection, civil liberties, equality . . . but Breton headed it off waving his hand and nodding.

"Just kidding, here." Breton clapped me on the shoulder, and I suppressed the urge to bite his hand. "Me and Tato go way back, Billings, don't you worry."

"So what's this proposal?" If it was anything other than exile or killing me, I was interested to hear it.

Breton took a step away from the gurney and Henry looked unhappy and spoke. "It's very delicate, this situation, Mr. Smith. We need to know what happened, back at the Martin's place."

"And you propose . . . ?"

"Tell us what we want to know and we'll clear your ass," Breton snapped. "What's so hard to figure about that? You go back to your nice place and no more trouble. Otherwise, we dump your ass over at the Arm as murder suspect number one and only."

I didn't have any choice, but something told me it wasn't wise to give myself back to the people I'd spent so long trying to get away from. Of course the Arm could be worse. They'd just kill me, capital. Right? Still, I didn't answer.

My pal Henry went on. "We are especially concerned about what may have happened to your friend, Mr. Columbus."

Marco. "Me, too, Mr. Billings, me, too." A creeping cold climbed up my spine as I thought about the blood, and the dose of sugar, and I realized I didn't have the slightest idea what had happened back at the Martins' house, whether Marco was alive or dead, or why any of it would matter to Science. They wouldn't hand me over to the Arm too quick, I thought, not if there was something they thought I could tell them. And, why the Arm, not Civil? Everyone thought that Civil ran SA, and in a way they did, regulating all the parts of day-to-day life that made SA such a happy place, like garbage pickup, mail delivery, media entertainment, etcetera. But be a part of Science for enough years, you pick up ideas, like the one that the Security Arm and Science are really struggling for control of the country, and that it *wasn't* the Arm that put down the Hoover Dam rebellion. If this was about Arm versus Science . . . I supposed I would have to play along if I wanted to find anything out, not the least of which being whether Marco was alive. Marco . . .

I didn't want to think about it. I didn't need a med monitor to know my heart rate doubled and my epinephrine level peaked.

"Goddam, he's going off." Breton sped up the drip on my I.V. and Billings called for a woman in a lab coat, med-tech, Scientist, whatever . . . the sight of her was probably enough to send my neuro imbalance right off the edge and they slipped away in the blackness.

It's two years ago. I'm limping down the street toward Marco's place in the indent sector, hoping nobody stops me. Any teenage asshole born in SA outranks an indent—they'll stop us and quiz us on the Ninety-first Amendment just for kicks, give us orders, and make us do tricks, and if you get it wrong or disobey them it lengthens your indenture, don't you know. I don't even know if Marco's there. I only run into him once every couple of weeks, when our shift rotations coincide. I have a headache. I've just finished a job, interfacing with the internal security at Science, synching up their facial recognition eyes . . . and I feel like the inside of my skull has been scrubbed with steel wool. I ache all over and I need something I can metabolize without going to pieces.

Marco opens the door. I'm too glad to see him to remark how weird it is that he doesn't look first to see who it is. Maybe I haven't outgrown my paranoia like he has. He sets me down in front of the window and goes to get me something. I don't have to say a word, Marco just understands. He always has.

He brings me a squeeze bottle full of something smooth and greasy. He knows what sugar would do to me.

Marco tells me I look like shit. *I am shit,* I say. Science wishes I'd died like all the others, but I didn't. I'm left in the human shit pile.

You nuts, he tells me in soft Fringlish. He says I'd feel better, about everything, if I took better care of myself.

What for? I never say it out loud, but I know I've already passed the life span of the other guinea pigs. And if I last another two years, I get to inherit Utopia. Maybe I will say it . . .

But he's already kneading the palm of my hand with his knuckles. Breathe deep, he says. The empty squeeze bottle falls from my fingers as he bends the flesh of my hand, until even the bones feel soft and warm. I am a rag doll that he slips out of its silly clothes and warms its skin all over. His hands turn my spine to jelly and eventually even the weight of my skull is gone. He rolls me back and forth and makes me glad to have muscles and bones and skin. *Why should I take care of myself,* I murmur, *when you do it so well?* We moan together and move together and when I ejaculate I feel his relief more keenly than my own.

We don't do this often, because neither of us likes to be reminded too much of some of the more drastic modifications Science has made to Marco's body. The removal of violent tendencies.

I feel the slight tug as he removes the plug from my right socket. He rolls the cord neatly up to his own ear, and then pulls it from his jack. It's a one-way connection. I was never wired for a secondary sensory input the way he was. And if he wasn't, I wonder if he wouldn't have killed himself long ago or what. *Thanks,* he says.

You welcome. I feel like I ought to be thanking him, really, But we've known each other long enough that maybe I don't have to say it. Or if I did, it wouldn't go down right. My dick probably would have shriveled away by now if it weren't for him. We talked about it once. I told him that I'd gladly donate mine to him if it could be done. But it's his nerves, too, deteriorated connections. He needs me to read the climax from. But for some reason it's always me who lands on his doorstep like a lost dog.

He serves me another squeeze bulb and we drink in silence. He's right, I do feel much better.

I opened my eyes to a bright light and a voice said that my pupils were starting to contract. The woman took the light out of my eyes and stepped back. Billings and Breton were still there, looking useless standing off to the side with their hands in their pockets. She moved to the other side of the gurney and stuck some kind of monitor onto my forehead. "This will alert you if a relapse looks likely, but his system should be pretty well clean by now." She started fiddling with something in a shrink-wrapped package.

Billings—Smiling Henry—stepped forward looking down on me with concern. "Are you feeling better now? I'm sorry if this is hard for you, Mr. Smith. Have you had any other blackouts like this one? And the one you had in the car?"

"Not until today," I said. But then I'd never chug-a-lugged a whole bottle of infant glucose solution until today when the cops had started asking about the blood . . .

Breton leaned in close to us both. "I'll leave him to you, Henry. I'm sure he'll cooperate, won't you, Tato? Be a good boy, all right?"

I almost said "Yessir" out of habit, but got it out as "All right," and then my ex-guardian went out the door without incident.

The med-tech finished her fiddling and handed me a glass of a bluish solution, maybe the same stuff as was going into my arm. "Drink this, Mr. Smith," she said. "It'll help to stabilize your condition." And then she left, too.

I took a small sip. Tasted like . . . nothing much. I was expecting something salty, like broth or blood plasma. "What's in it?"

He shrugged. "I do not know, Mr. Smith. I am not very familiar with your modifications."

That was probably a lie. The sugar test series had been a big one here at Science, in their never-ending quest for building a brain-machine interface that would work worth a damn. I had been under the impression that I was one of their special cases, being one of the few who could interface successfully *and* survive. Surely he'd been briefed specially, too, for this meeting. But I was playing along. "Ah, well, it's good," I lied.

He went on to ask if I was comfortable, wanted anything else, etcetera. The whole good-cop routine. I knew as long as I said what he wanted to hear, he'd stay that way, nice and accommodating, like I was a good citizen assisting my country. But as soon as things got tough, Breton, in the sanctioned role of bad cop, was going to come back in and tear me a new eye socket trying to get the truth out of me. My goal was to put that off as long as possible.

Which wasn't that long. Because I couldn't remember a goddam thing about what had happened. Henry hemmed and hawed, and I tried to act like I really wanted to cooperate . . . "Really. Marco asked if I'd go with him to work on their kitchen system. When I arrived he was already there and at work on it. I plugged in and was deep in trance with the machine when something jostled my foot. I opened my eyes and it was Mr. Martin, slumped over and bleeding . . . where your security had just pushed him . . . that's all there is!"

"What about the glucose?"

"What about it? Your security people scared me . . . I did it without thinking. It was in the kitchen in bottles, for the baby, and I downed one. And they dragged me away." I saw his eyes narrowing, his mouth tightening with distaste as he made his decision to turn me over to Breton. "That's all of it! I don't know any more!"

"I'm very sorry, Mr. Smith, but I'm afraid that you *do* know more."

Breton came in then with a pair of nerve cuffs in his hands. "Time to go, Tato. We gave you your chance."

I'd be damned if I was just going to let him put those things on me. I was a citizen, wasn't I? I suppose I wasn't acting much like one when I tried to kick him in the nose. The gurney tipped under me and my foot only hit him hard enough to make him mad. I threw the glass at him then and backed up as he batted it aside. No surprise that it was unbreakable and rolled away silently on the carpet. The windows were probably the same stuff, sealed, and we were probably fifty floors up, no escape there. Henry wasn't smiling anymore as he called for help with his lapel com. Breton tried to tackle me but I dodged him and made for the door, which was opening.

And then my ankle was on fire as one of the nerve cuffs wrapped around it. Breton had flung them, open, on full power, and I went down, grabbing at it and the dead limb of my lower leg. He sat on my chest then and smacked me hard across the face. There was a trickle of blood coming from his nose.

"Precious goddam brains, I'll rattle your goddam brains!" he shouted.

It wasn't the first time I'd seen him like this. He hit me again, back of the fist, but he was so pissed the swing went wild and glanced off my cheek. I thought maybe he'd choke me then, but I'd stopped struggling and he moved the cuffs to my elbows, where they belonged, and my arms went dead.

"And you can goddam well walk the rest of the way." He was standing up and I wasn't even sure he was talking to me anymore, but I guess he was since the two techs who'd come in response to Henry's call stood me up and pushed me toward the door.

Before I'd gotten ten feet my arms were starting to hurt, bad pins and needles and that bone ache so cold it burned. "Where the fuck-all we going?" Two security men fell into step behind us.

Breton's hand was around my numb bicep, hurrying me along. "Nowhere you'll like. Back to the Brain Lab."

The lab wasn't in this building, not if it was where it used to be. It was out on the edge of the city, where they'd reclaimed some badlands on the other side of the warehouse sector that nobody would miss if something really *really* bad happened. They'd have to take me outside for this, into another van or rotorfoil or something to get me there. I couldn't be lucky enough to think he'd try to walk me the whole way. "I told you I don't know anything."

"You know plenty, and I'm going to enjoy getting every word out of you." He tightened his grip forgetting that I couldn't feel it. Okay. Let him have his fun. The more this was between him and me, the better. All of Science I couldn't handle, but Breton alone, maybe. Especially if I could get him agitated enough that maybe we didn't go straight to the brain-sucking lab. "Every goddam word," he muttered.

"I guess that means you missed me." I smiled, felt where my cheek was swelling up from one of his earlier blows. We got into an elevator, the four of us.

"I hope I never have to see your miserable face again," he said, his teeth gritted.

No good. He was getting cold and calculating, and any minute now he was going to remember that his job wasn't to settle a score with me, but to find out whatever precious information they thought I knew. I had to keep him hooked. My arms were killing me, the backwash from the nerve cuffs starting up an ache in my motor cortex that was going to have me trying to gnaw my arms off in a little while. I closed my eyes, grimaced, and made a whimper as if I was really in deep shit. Which of course, I was, so that was no fake, but I wouldn't have whimpered if I didn't think it'd push his buttons.

Breton yanked my head back, winding his fingers into the coarse black hair and working me like a puppet. "You're pathetic." He pushed me out at the transport level and held me while he gave the nod to the two security men. "I can take him from here, no problem."

They hesitated, then moved off.

He led me by the head to another one of those electric vans, entered through the passenger-side door, and dragged me in after him. The door swung shut. I gave another one of those little whimpers. He pressed the ignition and rolled us toward the exit with one hand on the wheel, the other at the back of my neck like it was soldered there, holding my head down against the cool, smooth seat. As he told Billings, we go way back.

Like three years ago, he showed me the apartment where I'd be living until I made the full "transition" to citizenship. He went into full asshole mode, commenting that I probably wouldn't live that long anyway, maybe this would be a comfortable bed to die in, I better not break anything . . . trying to provoke me into saying something or doing something. But my favorite word was *yessir*—I had gotten very good at giving him and any other citizen I came in contact with their way. I'd seen indents spit on, kicked, our labor disturbed or work destroyed as if we weren't working for the good of SA. I thought constantly of Marco . . . what made Marco a good candidate for hormone redux but Breton a good indent guardian? Violent tendencies. So what was the difference? Privilege of citizenship. Eventually Breton had got tired of baiting me and went away, probably to blacken the eyes of some new indent who'd only live for two years anyway.

But he didn't always act like that. I had to try to play both sides of him if I was going to get out of this. My flashbacks were still fresh in my mind and I thought about the way he'd looked into my face years ago, and asked me if I was all right, told me to cheer up. The car moved out into traffic—I could hear courier scooters zipping by us and the hum of other vans. "Breton," I said, in a low voice.

"What."

"What's going to happen to me?"

He narrowed his eyes at the road. "Dunno. If it goes the way we think, and we get the proof out of that thick skull of yours, you're clear. But maybe we find out you offed Martin and his wife, and we have to turn you over for capital."

"I didn't kill them."

"I don't think that you did."

"Then why . . . ?"

Both his hands clenched harder, on the steering wheel, on my hair. "Because someone thinks that you did, someone would *like* to think that you did. Someone would like very much for a so-called Son of Science to go berserk and kill a few innocent citizens."

The Arm. Without the indent corps, Science couldn't maintain the infrastructure, and power would swing the Arm's way. Make Science's work horses look like a threat to security, a threat to the American Dream itself . . . Civil would have to step in under public demand and cut back Science's programs. Meanwhile, proof of a conspiracy to discredit Science on the part of the Arm could result in Civil curtailing the Arm's reach instead . . . and I was that proof, maybe. "And you really think you can get the truth out of me."

Breton sneered. "I know it. How much of your brains we have to rip out to do it, that I don't know."

I shivered. Now that I had him away from the bosses, I hoped for an option that wouldn't make him look bad. "You're just saying that to scare me. Look, if you want me to testify a certain way, I will. You don't have to do this intimidation bullshit with me."

He was shaking his head and laughing to himself.

"Come on, Breton! Don't take me back to Brain. You know . . ."

He pressed hard on me, and I stopped talking. The nerve cuff feedback was giving me a facial tic where my cheek was mashed against the seat. His voice got low. "You don't get it, do you. I'd like to help you, you know, Tato? But the truth is you were always street trash."

"But you don't believe I killed . . . "

"You think I'm going to make a deal with you? That everybody'd be happy then? Nobody's going to take your word, *Citizen Smith*." He chuckled like my name and title were a joke, which I guess they were. "Especially me. No, I don't believe you killed anybody, but I do believe you're inferior scum and should be treated as such."

Bastard. "Fuck-*all* I wish I'd broken your nose."

"Shut up." He ground my face into the seat harder. From the sound of things outside, we were on the outskirts, possibly getting near the lab. My teeth were aching now, too.

I kept talking. "You know what? I hope I did kill those people. And I hope they blame you for the way I turned out . . . "

"I said shut up, you little fuck-all!" He yanked on the back of my head but couldn't hurt me any more than that without letting go of the wheel. Profanity was good, a sign he was losing control. "Shut up!"

"Oh yeah, if I go down you're coming with me, Breton." He looked at me like he was trying to figure out what to do next, stop the car and beat me to death or see if he could just ram my head into the dashboard right here. I looked him in the eye, and changed my tack. "Hey, Bret, does it give you a hard-on to push me around like this?"

He let go. He actually let go like he couldn't stand to touch me anymore. I twisted to look him in the face better. My voice shook but I kept on. "Haven't you missed me? This could be your last chance."

He stopped the car. We were traveling along the edge of the manufacturing sector. He turned in the seat and grabbed me by the neck. "You perverted little fuck-all. You sick little fuck. I know what you and your lover boy do, you know. I know what you did every moment of your life from when you first entered Silver A up until two months ago."

I went cold. I hadn't thought of that. I knew that we were monitored on the job, and in the dorms a lot of the time, but I didn't think we were actively observed in private residences. In fact, I was pretty sure that was completely against Civil rights . . . but of course, I didn't have any rights until two months ago.

"In fact, if I'd had my way, I'd already know what you did every moment right up through whatever fuck-all just happened at the Martins', right down to the holes in your goddam socks." His grip tightened and I braced for a blow. But he kept talking. "But no, we've got no live record. Just what's in your goddam head . . ." He cut off abruptly, like he just came awake. And he pushed me away like I was filthy.

What had he just told me? He started the car again and placed both hands on the wheel with a fierce determination. *Every moment of my life* . . . I thought about the way the glucose triggered those near-living memories in the blackouts. Was that what they were going to suck out of me at the lab? Could I have an unconscious record of everything that went on around me, even when I was in machine trance? *No matter how much of my brains they had to rip out* . . . I thought he'd meant they'd pump me full of drug analogues, or beat the shit out of me until they were satisfied I didn't know any more than I'd told. We really were going to the Brain Lab; that wasn't just a threat to get me to cooperate. I'd played my cards wrong, then. I had to hope that we were both right, that I didn't kill them, and that there would be enough of me left after they were done to let me go back to work . . .

And what had happened to Marco?

Breton was driving with a single-mindedness that bordered on manic. He wasn't going to let me sidetrack him again. And the ache in my arms and in my head was making it tough to do much of anything but grind my teeth. I willed my fists to clench but no signal was getting through the restraints. I kept trying to think of some way to turn this around. I was a citizen . . . I should be able to go to Civil and testify by some other means. If only I could get away, get to a Civil station ... I must have squirmed around or something because Breton reached over and turned up the power on the cuffs. Something in my brain started screaming, and I banged my head against the window, once, twice, then a long succession of bangs.

"Stop that."

I was succeeding in getting blood on the window and my face.

"Stop it! Should have sedated you ..." He tried to grab for me with one hand but couldn't get any leverage. As I threw myself at the window, we lurched to the side. Breton slammed on the brake and grabbed me with both hands. I sank my teeth as deep as I could into his wrist, bones and flesh giving way slightly although I did not break the skin. Now he was maimed *and* pissed. He tried to get me by the hair again, but couldn't maneuver in the tight space of the van. I got my feet up and kicked him away, a good hard one to the stomach, and he retched. Then another kick, in the eye.

It was then that my door opened. I didn't stop to think how, I just pushed myself through head first, hit the ground badly with my shoulder, and staggered as I tried to run. The street was all warehouses, no traffic, no people.

"Sssst!"

I made for the whisper as I heard Breton coughing and gasping in the car behind me. The doorway of a warehouse. I almost tripped over a courier scooter lying on its side in the dark. A shadow in the shadows.

Marco. He pulled me through the door and closed it behind him. "This way." There are no locks on doors in Silver A, because there is no crime. He urged me through the static and haze the cuffs were making of my vision, past rows of knee-high warehouse caretakers recharging, oblivious to our presence. Through another doorway and into another cavernous space, stacked high with sealed bins. I stumbled into the first row and stayed where I fell. "Marco . . ." Now my arms were shaking, the fingers flopping at the ends.

He turned back and seemed to see the cuffs for the first time. "Fuck-all . . . you had these on long?"

"Too . . . long." I could hardly speak, my jaw was clenched so tight. He turned the power down and then popped the release. I cried out as the sensation flooded in, pain first. It was going to hurt for a long time, I knew, and my grip would probably be weak for a couple of hours, but the first few minutes would be the worst. Marco supported my upper body as I convulsed. Fuck-*all* that hurt. I was glad Breton wasn't here to see it.

The pain was backing down to a dull ebb and I wanted to lie there in his arms, but Marco was urging me up. "Come on, Tato, gotta go." Breton. He'd be blind with murderous rage about now and coming after me . . . if he knew where I'd gone. But he didn't.

"Where?" My legs seemed to work okay as I stood. "Where can we go?"

Marco's eyes glittered black in the dim light. "New Japan?"

"What?"

"No extradition treaty with SA. We're wanted. Leastways, I am." He took my hand and led me toward the far back wall of the warehouse. "They want to kill us, you know."

"No, no, I don't know. I don't know anything!" My fingers were still smarting and tingling where he held them. "I didn't even know if you were . . ."

Marco stopped and spoke, his voice hushed in the largeness of the room as he switched back to the clear enunciation of Civil talk. "The Arm. The Martins were supposed to kill us both and make it look like we two outsider peons couldn't handle the freedoms of citizenship and fought with each other. I killed them, instead."

But not the baby. I remembered the baby crying. I let out my breath like I'd been holding it.

It wasn't fair. We'd played by the rules and everything we ever wanted should have been entitled to us. I could still go back, turn myself in to Civil and get cleared. Of course, I had to make it there before Science caught up with me. But Marco was standing there, still bloody in places, and I was shivering with the aftereffects of the nerve cuffs, the blue juice, epinephrine, and a bad, bad sugar craving. "Then you're wanted. Why are you still here?"

"Tato." He was rubbing my fingers softly and they hardly hurt anymore. He raised my hand to his lips and brushed the tips, passed the back along his cheek, then took my thumb into the warmth of his mouth. The pins and needles turned to liquid fire, but it didn't feel like pain. "If you don't come with me, I don't know what I'll do." He touched my swollen cheek. "You followed me into this place. Will you follow me out of it?"

I swayed in place. "Tell it like it is."

He touched my swollen cheek. "You all I got."

"Ain't much," I mumbled, but I took a shuffling step forward. New Japan was a long way north and west, and between there and here was the Fringe. But the Fringe might not be so bad with someone to watch my back. I leaned on him and we went out the backdoor of the place, under the old fence into the grassy, rocky emptiness on the other side.

There is something erotic about the feeling of fur, admit it. Especially when under the fur there is taut muscle, the warmth of blood beating under it. I ran my hand over her back, smiling as her tail lifted just a twitch as I reached the base of her spine. The fur was thickest on her back, but thinned down her sides and her front, just a downy covering on her stomach. I scratched her under the chin and rolled her over gently, letting my hand slide down between her breasts and over her stomach. She rubbed her head against my knee while I beheld her. Such a gorgeous creature, she had all the outlines of a woman but for the tail, her brown eyes bright against the blackness of her fur.

I wondered if I looked as fine to her, in my canvas and boots and gauntlets and shirt of cotton. She took my hand in her mouth carefully. As I did every night when she awoke, I let her rake the skin with her sharp teeth, drawing just a little blood, and then drew back from her, trying to measure how much time had passed, trying to guess how long I could continue to tarry in the woods, my Keep possibly languishing without me. Well, they could wait a week or two, perhaps even more if that is what it would take. Dara could hold things together until I returned, or so I hoped. I rested my hand on the lovely she-cat's head and was amazed and gratified to hear something unmistakably like a purr.

Some of my men had brought her out of the forest—it had been a hectic time. I had ordered them on ahead with the hunt while I stayed behind at the Keep to administrate some lordly matter. I never dreamed they would succeed in snaring something before I arrived.

When I rode into the camp, I could already tell something had happened. They were a dozen men altogether. Danton took my horse by the reins as I dismounted and headed for the first trailer. I did not have to enter it to find them, for the rest were circled around something on the ground. They were making a lot more noise than I would have expected. Then someone shrieked in pain, and I charged forward, breaking their circle.

Guilty-sounding explanations of innocence barraged me as I surveyed the scene. One man was on the ground bleeding from an eye. Another, Hillard, was nursing a crudely bandaged arm. I held out my hands for silence, opening my mouth to demand what had happened . . .

. . . and I left it open as I saw her. She was crouched low, but I could see her hands and feet were bound together and a chain hung from her neck to a stake in the ground. She was growling low in her throat, her eyes burning as she flexed her claws. We stared at each other for an age and a half. Then I remembered to ask, "What the hell is going on here!"

Hillard told me one thing, about how they'd hunted her down that morning and were just trying to tame her before I got there. But later Danton told me the truth: that they had kept her there for two days.

"Why didn't you radio me!" I was shouting, pacing in the dark cramped space of the trailer. It wasn't Danton I should be angry with, but I shouted just the same.

He did not explain. His eyes said what I knew, that Hillard had the true answers.

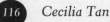

I burst out of the tiny trailer to find Hillard pissing against its wall. He backed away from me, dripping, not lifting his hands to brush the strings of dirty blond hair from his eyes.

"I take it you heard, then, what our friend Danton has said."

"That's true, milord Calidare." He stopped backing to talk, but kept rocking from one foot to the other. "We just didn't want to upset you."

"Upset me!" I slapped my leather gauntlets into my left palm. "Lying to me upsets me, Hillard, as does withholding information from me."

He was looking behind me, as if searching for some rescue, his eyes falling on Danton from time to time, finding no pity there. All the others seemed to have disappeared. "We didn't mean any harm, sir, really. We just thought you'd be angry if you found out you missed the hunt . . . "

"Do you think I'm out here to hunt? Is that what you think?" *Of course,* said a small voice in my head, *you've kept them all ignorant of your real reason for coming out here . . .* but I silenced it with the business at hand. I stepped up to him, my nose hanging just over his forehead. "If I had known you had accomplished what you set out to do I would have ordered you back yesterday. I wouldn't have left the Keep at such a crucial time." I cracked my favorite cruel smile. "But I'm truly astonished that you bumbling idiots managed to succeed." I don't think he was listening to me anymore, just trembling. I suppose I was glad he had already run out of piss. "You've done your job. Now get back to the Keep and tell Dara we're on our way back."

I did not move as he stepped back, bowing his head once, meeting my eyes as he did so. I noted the lopsided twist of his mouth. So, he wasn't entirely cowed, after all. Still, at least I got rid of him.

I turned back to Danton, who had watched the whole thing with his arms crossed. A little smile came onto his face, and then he turned away, too. In that way, he reminded me of myself ten years ago. No, not even that long ago. Young, his straight dark hair cresting his shoulders, he spoke very little. There was a time when I didn't speak so much, when I didn't have so many questions to answer, when I didn't have as much to say.

Our prize hissed at me when I went to check on her and bring her some meat. She eyed me suspiciously, but eventually took the mutton I offered. Then she slept curled up upon herself, peacefully, which is more than I can say for the fellow whose eye she scratched out. That night he broke into a raging fever. By the time it became light enough for Danton and two others to travel with him back to the Keep, he could no longer speak but for incoherent jumbles, and would not answer his own name. Later, while I was watching the she-cat pacing in the clearing, Danton arrived back to inform me that the man was dead. I bit my lip and wondered how Hillard fared. She batted an insect out of the air.

By the end of that week, she would accept meat straight from my hand, always well encased in leather to prevent her scratching me. Soon after she would let me touch her, gentle strokes on her shoulders and the back of her head. The hair on her head was long and straight like Dara's, only black as midnight. Of course, it was my own impatience that did me in. Unable to resist the feel of her fur any longer, I pulled off my right gauntlet and luxuriated in that hair, so much finer than any I'd felt before. Then she'd batted down my hand and bit it. I knew better than to pull back and enlarge the wound. She regarded me as she sank her teeth a little deeper, and then her jaws relaxed. She seemed almost to approve as I drew my hand away and she turned to grooming her hair herself, combing it out with her claws in a wholly womanly gesture. I regarded the red lines and punctures on my skin, and called for some hot water.

Within hours I was feverish, my inflamed skin tender to the touch. I imagined the water would steam off of me as Aston plied it on with a cloth, but it did not, only sent me into fits of shivering. Danton sat by me, muttering and occasionally saying "Calidare" to see if I would respond. Then he began ranting about a damn fool's errand for a man's pride. I tried to stop him, tried to explain why I'd taken the risk, but my words began to slip from me. It seemed to me I slept after that and dreamed of cats and goddesses.

In the morning I was still alive, dehydrated, queasy, unsteady on my feet. But I pulled on my clothes, and marched out to the center of the wagons. She was still awake, waiting for me. I crouched down at her level and held out my hand. She smelled it cautiously, and then, assured it was me, bit down just a millimeter into the skin. I withdrew my hand with a nod, "I thank you, milady, and now may I fetch your breakfast?" She sat back on her feet, tucking her tail around them.

I was half delirious most of the next few days, unable to keep much food down, and sleeping only between fragments of dreams. Aston began tearing out his hair every time I went close to her. I went near her more and more, until I began to spend every evening sitting on a stump by her, singing to her and telling her the stories of my childhood, waiting for her to wake up from her diurnal sleepiness. After all, what else was there to do out in the middle of nowhere? The men were beginning to question my sanity, I think, but men are often more like wolves than cats. A few well-placed arm-wrestling bouts and some biting commentary kept the pecking order straight. The time wasn't right, not yet. I wasn't even sure what it was I had to wait for, I only hoped it wouldn't be too long. I watched the moon rising over the tops of the trees.

She was still purring. I rested my hand on her head and realized she had wrapped her tail around my ankle. I knelt down next to her and began scratching the base of her neck, under her long mane, and the purring became a mewling in her throat and she began to rub against me. Without thinking, I cooed back some sweet nothing, the kind of babble Dara called baby talk, even though it hadn't produced any babies for her yet.

As she ran her head up my thigh, I realized she'd put my boot between her legs. Her tail waved from one side to the other as she continued rubbing against me, her head on my thigh, her stomach on my shin, and the tender part between her legs against my boot. I turned her chin up with a finger, and looked into her eyes. There was a flicker there, an intensity I hadn't seen before. I might have imagined it, but I could swear she gave the slightest nod. Dara will tell you, at great length even, about how I never let an invitation go unanswered.

I took her shoulders in my hands and gently rolled her onto her back, the chain on her neck clanking. As I lowered my weight on top of her I felt my erection press between us. She growled, but did not fight me. I hesitated a moment, not sure what kissing her would do. I rubbed my nose against her nose—she writhed and the purring began again. I licked her lips and let my tongue into her mouth. I felt the extra sharpness of her teeth, but other than that it was like any other woman's mouth, wet, warm, inviting. I felt her claws through the cotton of my shirt, the points grazing my skin, digging a bit deeper when I took to nuzzling her neck. *Am I going to have any back left?* I wondered. I hadn't built up a perfect tolerance to her scratches yet, and I knew she could seriously injure me. For just a moment I considered whether this was some ploy on her part to get rid of me. Deeper down I could not even think that. Lifting myself up on my arms, I nudged her to roll over.

I settled into place on her back and she writhed even more.

   Cecilia Tan

Perhaps, I thought, *this is the way cats do it.* I buried my face in her thick black fur, surprised at the sweetness of it, but that's pheromones for you, I guess. I drank her in. Now, with her legs spread, I could smell her desire as strong as my own. I stroked her underside with one hand while the other fumbled with my pants. My erection was almost painful as I sought to free it. She bumped me with her hips again and again, pushing her tail up into the air.

The night air was cool against me as I slid my pants down to my ankles. She purred and mewled and thrashed and would not stay still enough for me to enter her. I had to use both arms to hold her under me, and then I did not have a hand to guide myself. She bucked and nearly threw me off as I reached back with one hand. I dug my teeth into the fur of her neck, waiting for her to thrash, but it seemed to paralyze her. In her throat she whimpered, shivering, her hips still moving slightly. I fingered where she was wettest and led my penis there, pressed it against her. She moved a little and I bit down harder. She froze again and I slipped inside her, falling against her as I did so, gasping.

Inside her was a heaven I had only dreamed of. We moved together, stroke after stroke, until I could no longer tell where her growls ended and my grunts began. I could see nothing but flashes of black by the moonlight, yet I felt every curve of her body, every muscle responding to my every motion. For all her thrashing, I had expected it to be rough, but it was smooth, now slow, now rapid, but smooth. I do not know how long we were like that, I never wanted it to end and I prolonged it as long as I could. Then she was beginning to thrash again; she cried out and arched against me—I felt contraction after contraction ripple through her, squeezing me from deep inside and pushing me closer to climax myself. Now she cried out with each thrust, throwing her head back in a frenzy—I feared I would slip out of her as she bucked. I clamped my teeth down on the back of her neck once more and held her still as I drove the five long hard strokes into her. That was all I could stand before I began to fly in and out, unable to control my own hips, until at last I matched her cry and emptied myself into her, holding her furred frame against my chest as I shuddered with the last waves of it.

She rolled out from under me immediately. She licked a little sweat from my upper lip and shivered, yawning. I swear she almost smiled. And then, after making sure I was watching, she undid the clip on her collar with her deft fingers, and let it fall to the ground. While I blinked, aghast, she curled up against my stomach and went back to sleep. I had no doubt I would return to the Keep with her. But I wondered, now, whether she was still mine, or if the tables had been turned. With her fur filling my senses, I decided it didn't make a difference. And I slept, too.

$\mathcal{U}$topia

V

Of course, writing outside the real world isn't always about leaving politics or problems behind. On the flip side, stepping outside of reality is one way to explore it. One of the earliest works of science fiction, in my opinion, was Sir Thomas More's *Utopia*, and what writer has not tried to imagine the perfect world? But there are two problems with Utopia: (1) one person's Utopia is another person's Hell, and (2) if everything were perfect, now there'd be one damn boring story.

In my Utopian daydreams I imagine a world where dominance and submission play an important role in people's happiness and social order. Although the world is built on ideals, the execution is riddled with human error. The Kylar, as my not-so-perfect people are called, are a troubled but ascendant race, spreading their ideals of loyalty, service, and the passion of the master/slave pair bond throughout the galaxy. In "Telepaths Don't Need Safewords," we find a Kylaran master and his slave in exile, visiting among those who merely play at such roles. And in "The Game" and "The Velderet, Chapter One," we find Kylaran culture being assimilated differently on two colonized worlds. The clash of cultures, the divergence of points of view: I am fascinated by what the friction reveals about these characters, these societies, and my own beliefs.

Arshan tugged on the leash and gave me a bare-toothed smile, insistent and yet as catty as if he had winked. I replied with a sullen look, half a sneer really, saying with the look what I thought: *You know how much I hate this leash and you know how much I love this scene.* He dangled the leash over his shoulder, leading me across an open plaza toward the Hall. I kept my eyes down, not out of submission but to watch his feet. Arshan stands about six-four. With the leash over his shoulder, I didn't have much room to avoid his long legs. I may have been playing the slave, but the last thing I wanted was to look like a klutz. I could feel him smiling.

At the door we exchanged looks again, and he thought, *It's been a while.*

I know. But I'm up for it if you are, I assured him, making a last mental check on our costumes. He carried no weapon, no instrument, no tool, save pieces of his costume that had more than one use. We'd worked hard perfecting it, the belts, the waist-length cape, the boots. His colors, as always, were black and dark green. My own costume had fewer elements, just a basic black halter stretched over my breasts and black midcalf dance tights, bare feet. Oh, and the leash. I draped myself against him as he presented our pass to the doorman. We donned simple eyemasks, and proceeded down the carpeted hallway. *Think people will remember us?*

The ceiling of the Hall is at least fifty feet high, perhaps higher, with one long wall made entirely of glass, overlooking the Galdarin River. Echoes of laughter came down from balconies on the opposite wall, and crystals and lights and chandeliers flickered everywhere. Arshan made his way straight for Cleopatra, one of our old friends.

She dripped with black beads, completely covered, yet not covered at all by a complex network of beaded strands, hanging in long wings from her arms, and cascading down her back from her black hair. She turned from the conversation when she saw us, throwing up her hands and kissing Arshan on the cheek. "Arshan! You've arrived! We've missed you, you know. And you, Mriah," she added, turning to me. "It got very dull here for a while." She sighed, fluttering her eyelids. I love Cleo's act. And she loves ours.

Arshan smiled. "It's good to be back."

"Easy for you to say," I said, tossing my head.

He turned on me, shortening up the leash and speaking harshly. "I am trying to converse with the Lady Cleopatra. Now, will you be quiet or will I have to cut your tongue out?"

I gave no answer at all except to nod my head toward Cleo.

She smiled. "As I said, it was getting very dull around here."

We were lounging by the pool later, with some people we knew and some we didn't, when Arshan slapped me at last. Maidi and Bivon had been taking turns whipping Danielle, and when they were done, she thanked them for it on her knees. Gallen, a blond fop that Cleo favored, started in with "She's a proper pretty one. All slaves should behave so well, don't you think, Arshan?"

"She's very beautiful," Arshan said to Cleopatra.

Cleo swallowed a bit of plum. "I believe she's for sale."

"Oh?" Gallen sat up a bit in his lounge chair. "Maidi, how much?"

Maidi and Bivon sat on the grass, coddling Danni between them. "No, she's not for sale," Maidi said.

"I'd say she's worth forty thousand," Gallen continued. "Whereas I wouldn't pay more than five thousand for one like yours, Arshan."

"Not that I would go with you, anyway." I replied from where I sat at Arshan's feet. Arshan jerked on the leash.

"You haven't broken her, yet?"

Cleo laughed. "Arshan likes them with their teeth intact."

Gallen was unfazed. "Imagine that. I think she needs a lesson."

I sneered. "From you? I'd rather put out my own eyes."

Arshan jerked the chain so hard I pitched forward onto my hands. "That will be quite enough, slave." He sat up in the lounge chair a little, then settled back, shortening the chain so I remained on all fours. "I can handle her myself, thank you." He smiled obsequiously at Gallen.

"Oh, it's no fault of yours, I'm sure." Gallen picked up a plum from the bowl between Cleopatra and him. "Still, I can see why she's talking back. You don't even have a bat for her."

"I've never needed one."

Cleo applauded the point by tapping her own crop in her gloved palm. "Arshan has many methods."

"Still, I wonder how she would respond to some of my own." Gallen stood, placed himself in front of me, snapped his fingers. "Look at me, slave."

I drew my eyes up his leg, stopped at his crotch. I let half a smile onto my face.

"I said, look at me."

"I am."

He lifted my chin with his boot. I held his gaze for a moment, then dropped back down to admire his groin again.

There wasn't much to see really, at first. But as he grew more angry, he grew. I watched the bulge thicken as he made a fist. "You have to put fear into her, Arshan. Like this." He drew back his foot to kick me.

Arshan was up in an instant, between us. "Think again."

Cleo laughed, tugging on Gallen's velvet sleeve. "No one strikes her but Arshan, dear, and she obeys no one but him."

"Well, what good is she, then." Gallen said sullenly, sinking back down into the chair at Cleo's side. I was already holding on to Arshan's leg. I let my hands run up and down his thigh. I closed my eyes and rubbed against him with my cheek. *That was close.*

He's obviously an asshole. I'd let you bait him more except I think he's dangerous.

I don't know . . . I drew my hand between his legs to caress his crotch, letting the heat from his stiffening penis flow into my fingers. *Shall I show him what good am I?*

Arshan made some meaningless small talk with Cleo as I came around his leg to kneel in front of him. The loose-fitting pants he wore didn't end in seams on the inside. And Arshan never wore underwear. I had his cock in my mouth then. "You see," he was explaining, "she is extremely loyal. And always grateful." I would have added something of my own, but my mouth was full. Using my lips, I squeezed some pre-come into my mouth and swallowed. I let my tongue work the underside, the tender cleft just at the base of the head until he was having trouble keeping up the conversation. I felt him start to go, his hips began to buck, and then I ducked.

Semen shot out over the grass, a fair bit spattered the golden edge of Gallen's green waistcoat. Arshan recovered immediately. He grabbed me by the chin and scolded me harshly. He gripped the halter at the center and pulled it over my head; with two knots he tied my hands behind my back, using the halter instead of rope. Then he knelt in front of me, holding

 Cecilia Tan

my head still by the hair at the base of my neck, and slapped me with his right hand across my cheek.

Do it again, I thought.

He raised his hand high this time, and I tried to flinch, but his other hand held me still. "Don't you move, now," he said, almost growling, as he brought the slapping hand down to fondle my bare breasts instead. He squeezed the nipples between the knuckles of his first and middle fingers, then forced my head down to the grass. The blades prickled against my chest, cool and rough. "Are you ready to apologize?"

"I'm sorry, Master."

"You needn't apologize to me. Apologize to this gentleman, whose finery you've ruined."

I kept my mouth shut. Gallen was on his feet now, towering above us. Arshan stood, picking up the end of the leash again. "Slave." He gave it a jerk and I sat up, but I kept my head down. "Slave," he repeated.

"Screw you," I said.

You're pushing it. "Maybe I haven't made myself clear," he said, wrapping the leash around his hand, until he held me fast by the neck. "I think you owe this man something, and I intend to see he gets it." He lay me on my back in the grass, leading me by the neck. "Gallen, may I borrow your knife?"

"Certainly."

He handed down his pearl-handled dagger. Arshan slipped it deftly under the waistband of my tights, and with one stroke, ripped them open from my bellybutton downward. Uncoiling the leash, he wrapped the other end around my right ankle, binding my foot near my head. The left leg he bound with one of the belts from around his own waist, by wrapping my knee to my shoulder. I felt my own wetness drip down the crack of my ass as my pussy was now open to the wind. "Gallen, I believe this slave owes you something. So long as you do not strike her, you may do as you will."

What? I started to object. Arshan didn't answer me. Gallen opened a cockslit in his own tights and brandished his penis. "With pleasure," he said, as he motioned for two male slaves to lift me up onto the table. He pressed the head of his cock against my ass. "I will gladly spill some seed in return." he said, and with that he rammed into me. He got about an inch in, holding me by my thighs. His cock was so dry it burned as he thrust deeper in. I saw his face twist and wondered if it was unpleasant for him, too. Then I felt his balls against my ass, and he started pumping. I clenched my teeth tightly, staring him in the eye as he worked. I don't think he liked that, but it didn't matter because soon his eyes were shut. The motion became smoother as pre-come leaked out of him, but I kept my teeth bared and didn't relax. As he began panting, I growled, and he came inside me, shooting hot white blood up into my insides. I looked away while waiting for him to recover. He opened his eyes, and nodded to Arshan. "Well," he said, his dick still inside me. "She is good for one thing." I opened my mouth to speak, but he clamped a hand over it. He pulled his leather gauntlet off the other with his teeth, and began stroking my pussy. His index finger probed down between our stomachs. He brought it out from my vagina, moistening my labia with the juices there, then stroked my clit upward a few times, smiling as I shivered involuntarily.

He worked his large rough thumb back and forth. I tried to fight him, but struggling only increased the contact. My hips began moving with him as I hungrily sought my release. I bucked forward, trying to increase the pressure, when I felt his shrunken penis slip from my ass. "Ohh, looks like I'm done," he said, stepping back from me. "I hate you," I whispered between clenched teeth. With my hands behind my back, there was no way I could finish the job he started. He was laughing. "The poor little thing, look at her struggling. Ha!"

Arshan released my legs and made me stand up. I trembled,

tried to rub up against his leg, but he slapped me, again. "Down. You're a mess. I think you need a walk through the pool." As he led me to the edge of the water, he asked me, *How are you doing?*

Loving every minute. I still don't like Gallen, though.

He winked. *Yeah, but at least I got the knife away from him.*

We mingled near the buffet for a while. Arshan picked at bits of bread and fruit. Occasionally he would drop something into my mouth as he made his point or changed the tide of a conversation—when he wanted me shut up. My thighs hummed with the energy Gallen had built up. It made me quieter than usual; all I could think about was Arshan's penis, which I had held in my mouth not so long ago. From time to time, as we circulated though the crowd, I met the eyes of guests, willing them to touch me. *Look at me, how can you resist me? My breasts bared for you, my hands tied, the gaping rent exposing my mound, how can you not bring your hands to me?* They only touched with their eyes, some with curiosity ("Wish I'd seen that scene") or disdain. Very few were masked like us, I realized. Perhaps we were outdated. Finally, bored, I began nuzzling Arshan's shoulder. I rubbed my breasts against the woven fabric of the short cape, feeling the nipples contract to become rock hard.

"I think the civil unrest will resolve itself," he was saying to a man I didn't know, who also had a slave on a leash. The slave, a male, was wearing nothing at all, and posed and pranced after his master like a show horse. Arshan held me still with his gaze. "Haven't you had enough? No favors for you until I'm finished eating."

The other man chuckled. "Poor thing, she looks like a hungry one."

I tried to rub my head on Arshan's chest, but he backed up a bit. I lowered my head then, and went for the man, pressing my chest against his side and begging silently with my eyes.

"Oho! Arshan, I do believe you have been depriving the girl."

"Ah, she gets like this sometimes, uncontrollable. But she hasn't deserved me yet. What shall I do?"

The man stroked his mustache. "Slave," he said to his own, "kneel." The slave obeyed. To Arshan, as his eyes examined me still pressing against him: "I believe we might have some amusement?"

"By all means."

Arshan handed the leash to the man, who held me from behind by my shoulders. He untied my hands as he moved me forward, until I was less than an inch from his kneeling slave's face. The slave licked my stomach. "Lie down," he said, pushing me down as he said it. He held my wrists fast above my head, and called for two other men to hold my ankles. Two other guests gladly did, spreading my legs in front of the slave. "Now slave," he said, speaking to his own, "follow my instructions very carefully."

"First, run the back of your fingers up the inside of her legs, but stop about halfway up the thigh. Good. Again. Keep that up. Now move forward on your knees, run your hands up her stomach, cup her breasts. Take each nipple into your teeth, the right one first."

I twisted as he bit, not hard enough to draw blood but enough to send goosebumps down my whole right side. I moaned when he took the left.

"Now pinch them both with your fingers, keep your thumbs over the tips of the nipples, rub as you would a lucky coin. Ah, she's moving now. Fetch ice from the table. Good. Now take one cube in either hand, and hold it against her breasts. Rub. Good. Now with the ice, down the center of her sternum, down to the bellybutton, slowly now, slowly down the center of her abdomen, stop. Leave the ice there."

I felt the cold water melting down over my pubic hair.

"Now take some ice cubes in your mouth. With a cube in

your right hand, slowly draw a line from the floor, up past her anus (I shivered again), up to her vagina, stop. Can you push it in? It has melted already? Get another, now up, up, press it to her clitoris, slave. Do not rub, simply press."

I gasped. The rubbing Gallen had given me seemed to flood back into me. I felt my labia swelling and my clit begin to throb under the ice.

"Now, keeping the ice in your mouth, extend your tongue, touch her clitoris."

The rough surface of the tongue, but as cold as ice, made me jump. The slave began a circular motion with the tongue, then switched to a straightforward lapping. I couldn't stop moving my hips. I tried to pull my legs free—I wanted to wrap them around his head and keep his icy tongue there forever, but the men held me fast. I began moaning.

"Now, slave, please immerse your penis in the ice. After this." He pulled a cockring from the pocket of his brocaded jacket. The slave had trouble at first, but finally succeeded in putting it in place. Good. I wanted him long and hard and inside me. Even if it would be ice cold.

The long frozen shaft penetrated my throbbing cunt one millimeter at a time. I moaned, trying to move up further on his pole, but he kept the distance where he, or rather, his master, wanted it. When he was all the way in, they held more ice to my nipples, and then he pulled just as slowly out, and iced his cock some more. Then he came back in, slowly, and out. More ice. Then slowly in . . . I thought I would go insane. He tickled my clit with the icy tip then and a spasm ran up my spine. So close! Then he plunged into me, and began grinding in a wide circle. I moaned loudly, but kept my eyes on the man holding my wrists. After all, it was really him fucking me, through his slave. I imagined it was Arshan inside me then and I gasped, the slave began pumping in and out of me so fast I was just beginning to wonder how long he could keep that up when I came and came and came. One leg shot free as I spasmed and they all let go and I clung to the slave with all my limbs, holding him deep inside me. I rolled him over onto his back, and sat up, riding him. I threw my head back and began rocking, pushing immediately for that second explosive orgasm I knew I could have. It blossomed quickly, the energy traveling out my limbs and up through the top of my head as I cried out.

I slumped forward and Arshan lifted me off the slave's still-stiff penis. There were people applauding politely, I think. He bound my hands in front of me then, and let me lean, eyes closed against him, covering my shoulder with the corner of his cape. "There now, much more docile, you see."

"So I do see," the man was saying. Then to his slave, "Well done." He removed the cockring. "He has been instructed not to have an orgasm or ejaculate until I say he may," he explained. "I am pleased."

We moved off into the crowd then. *Thank you,* I thought dreamily.

You're welcome. But you're not done yet, are you?

I sent him the image in my mind of his penis probing the very dark corners of my soul, of the fire spreading up my limbs and back through him with a kiss, building and spreading through every pore in both our bodies. *In time,* he replied. *But I think I am going to let one more scene pass.*

He rarely gave me hints about what he was planning, unless that was a part of it all.

Yes, I think I'll trade you for someone else for a while.

What?

Trade you.

Arshan, I don't like the sound of that.

You can tell me to stop anytime. We'll go home.

I bit my lip. *Not yet. Not yet.* Even through his thoughts I was unsure if he was serious. Aftershocks from orgasm were making things jump in and out of focus. He held me tight as he led me to a place to sit, a chaise longue along one wall.

When I looked up he was smiling. *It's just I have a few interests,* he thought.

Oh? I haven't seen much worth fishing for . . .

He shared with me the image of Cleo, black beads covering them both. *Hah. How do you think you're going to maneuver that? Cleo doesn't DO public displays anymore.*

Who said it would be public? But not just now, I'm thinking of more ready game. You remember Mor?

How could I forget him? Mor was an old party-goer who had played with us a few times. He had luscious dark brown skin and long black straight hair. *But, he's . . .*

He's here tonight, as a slave. I don't think I'll have to trade you for him, but I do want him.

I returned the smile. *Let's go for it.*

I had to admit Mor was stunning. I had always seen him heavily adorned in black leather. Tonight he wore only body paint, in elaborate and colorful designs. His hair drawn back in a long top knot, he seemed a bird out of a jungle paradise, alien and irresistible. His master, Martin, whom we also knew, had once been a student of Mor's. I suspected this was a sort of graduation gift. Mor's and my eyes met while our masters talked. If I hadn't known better I would have thought he had me hypnotized. I admitted to myself I wanted him, but he was Arshan's choice. The thought of his body and Arshan's together warmed me all over. A crowd was gathering.

Suddenly Arshan dropped the leash. Martin picked it up and I was pulled outside of the circle that was forming. I resisted the urge to call out to Arsh. I couldn't see him, and a knot of panic started growing in my stomach. I looked at Martin. He smiled, remembering me, and it calmed me. Arshan could take care of himself. But, I still wished I could watch. Martin shrugged and let go the leash then, and pushed his way back into the crowd. Free, lost, I circled the knot of onlookers.

I'm not sure when it happened. At one point I could sense, even though I could not see, Arshan approaching orgasm. Perhaps it was at that moment, when the leather-gloved hands covered my mouth and nose, a strange smell invaded my brain, and try as I could to think, to send a message, I could only slip down into the darkness.

I awoke what couldn't have been more than a few minutes later. Gallen leered as he finished closing the last binding on my ankle. I was spread-eagled on a cross in one of the small playrooms. I sensed other people behind me, three? four? From their breathing they sounded like men. Gallen straightened his gauntlets and crossed his arms.

Arsh? Arshan! There was no response. I could sense him fuzzily—no telling if it was the drug that made me weak, or if he was just too busy to hear it, or both. Like me, he was always weakest after an orgasm. I looked Gallen in the face. "What do you think you're doing?"

He didn't answer, except to pick up a short whip and to come to lean against my side. I was at about a forty-five degree angle to the floor. He caressed my breasts with his leather-covered hands, and my nipples stood up defiantly. I didn't have a shred of costume left now, even the collar was gone.

Arshan, did you plan this? Arshan! But there was still nothing. I cursed at Gallen in Ardric, now only half acting.

"Screw you," he replied, but mildly, as he tickled my nipples with the tip of the whip. He ran the leather under my chin, bringing up goosebumps, tickling the inside of my ear, making me shudder. "There now." He used the tip like a feather, searching me all over for ticklish spots, until he ended tweaking my clit upward with it, not quite hard enough . . . I moaned. I was becoming wet. I hoped Arshan had set this up earlier . . .

Gallen lifted the end of the X and it locked in place with me parallel to the floor. Twisting my head I could see the others, three men I didn't know. I was going to hiss at them, when I felt the handle of the whip enter my cunt.

I looked up at Gallen. The handle was rough, and though I was wet, it did not go in and out smoothly. He smiled as he fucked me with it. It was the smile that frightened me. I tried to read him more closely, but his mind was sealed tighter than shrink-wrap.

"You like that, don't you?" He twisted it back and forth, never pushing it far enough in to touch my cervix, just enough to make me moan again. "You like the whip," he said more to himself than to me. He pulled it out then, and tasted the wet end of it. Then his tone changed and his smile disappeared. "I promised you a lesson, didn't I?"

"You've had your fun," I spat. "Let me out of here."

"Such a feisty act you two have. Let's see how long you can keep it up." He cracked the whip and I, and the spectators, jumped.

"If you lay that whip on me, I'll kill you," I said matter-of-factly. "Believe me, Gallen, if I don't, then Arshan will."

He raised his eyebrows at the use of his name, and cracked the whip again.

"Gallen," I repeated, "Stop it, now."

He circled me, rotated the X again so that I was upright. The blood was rushing from my head as I tried again. *Arsh, get your ass in here!* I struggled against the bindings, but they were as real as they looked. "I am going to kill you!"

And he struck me. The whip lashed me on the chest, just above my left breast. Pain and adrenaline flooded me. *Arshan!!*
  Yes?

I tried to tell him what was happening, but all that came through to him was a white hot burst of pain as I was struck for only the second time in ten years by anyone other than he. Perhaps that got the message through more clearly than anything. I was panting. "You will die," I said. Gallen lashed out again, and again. Sweat broke out all over my body as I fought to contain the pain. I tried to breathe deeply, but I shook too hard, he gave me no respite between strokes. He tricked me, cracking the whip into the air sometimes, or raising his arm, and then stopping. I did not scream.

And then Arshan's voice in my head. *The door's bolted. Hang on!*

"Please, stop," I was saying. I looked at the three spectators. "Someone, make him stop!" One of them started forward, but Gallen cracked the whip in front of them. He struck me again, on the cheek. I think tears ran down my cheeks with the blood. "Gallen! Stop!"

He was laughing. He let a few more strokes fall, each one seeming harder than the last, and then he threw the whip down and unsheathed his penis. He pushed the table back flat and stood between my legs, rubbing his penis against the inside of my thighs with his hand. I mustered up the strength to spit at him and he thrust into me. "Still warm, I see," he said as he fucked me vigorously. Trembling, I tried to pretend he wasn't there. I closed my eyes this time, *Arshan . . . ?*

We're almost through . . . he answered. I could almost feel the clenching of his teeth.

Gallen must have heard the door beginning to give, for he redoubled his efforts and was exploding into me just about the time Arshan came exploding through the entrance. Arshan leapt straight over the table and knocked Gallen flat on his back. One of the spectators pressed the release and tipped the table forward. I stumbled to my knees, shaking life back into my arms. The two of them struggled. I saw Arshan thrown backward and Gallen stand up.

I tackled him in the midsection, forcing him back against the wall, and swept his feet out from under him. Once on top of him, I smashed my fist into his face. And again. "I could just drive your nose up into your brain and kill you instantly," I heard myself say, "but I'd rather beat you like this." I held on to his collar, lifting him up with my left hand and then beating him down with the right. His face felt fleshy, crunchy, knobbly all at once. I pulled him up to a sitting position and switched to back-fisting him, then round-housing him, then backfisting him . . . the resounding smack of meat was all I could hear.

Mriah! Mriah! Stop it! Arshan finally grabbed my wrist and I wondered how long he had been trying to get my attention. He pulled me off of Gallen, and I collapsed, sobbing. Gallen just lay there.

He picked me up gently, wrapping me in his cape. I couldn't think at all, I just cried for a while, and he rocked me in his lap, humming a song softly in his throat. He kissed my bruised cheek, smoothing my hair with his hand and holding me. At some point I realized we were in the car, the smallness of the space comforting me. I kept my eyes closed as he caressed my face. I kissed him, drawing his energy deep into my chest as I inhaled. *I love you* was the first thing I could think. I drew him down on top of me then, kissing him and kissing him, not open-ing my eyes even once. He seemed to touch every part of my body then, the whole and the sore, warm and soft. I felt his skin, the long smooth plane of his back under his shirt, and the bony curve of his hip against mine. *Come inside me, heal me,* I said. He held me tightly, arms circling my ribcage completely. He came into me gently, probing as I opened for him. I tucked my legs behind his back, bonding us together, one animal. *You make me whole.* I felt the energy building in my womb. Our minds open, I shared it, felt the waves of blood-warm pleasure feeding back to me. Up and up we went, until shuddering and shaking as one, we passed the peak and slipped back down into oblivion. As I was drifting into sleep I heard him say, *Now I remember why we stopped party-going.*

In his arms I smiled. I answered, *But now I remember why we started . . .*

I met Marik during the last six months of my sentence, when I was assigned to a work pod at the
space port to finish my indentured servitude. All a
part of paying my debt to Malakaian society. There
was Marik, Boolin, and me. Our official title was
Mechanical Service Worker, mech techs, the people you see from your little round porthole running
about on the tarmac, tightening all the screws on
the bucket you're trusting your life to, to take you
up to light speed and beyond. We were all good at
it, efficient, hardworking, maybe because we three
enjoyed it. Marik and Boolin wore dark blue coveralls, I wore ash grey; because they were free and I
wasn't. Among the three of us, it almost didn't matter. It never made a difference in our work. It only
mattered in The Game.

Maybe it was my difference in status that sparked
The Game in the first place. Being a convict on
Malakai wasn't anything like being a legendary
Kylaran sex slave, but ever since Malakai joined the
Kylaran Federation, Kylish ways had been infiltrat-
ing our culture. The Kylar kept pleasure slaves in an
ancient and respected tradition, everyone knew
that. They called them *caitan*.

Marik had initiated it that first time. We were
required to be at the port whether there was any
traffic or not, even when the stratostorms kept the

skies closed for days. And Marik hated being bored. The three of us had nothing to do that afternoon but gab. We sat on a low bench in the workshop, talking about what life must be like for Kylaran overlords. "You could have a separate slave to wash each toe," Boolin was saying. "Every finger."

I added, somewhat wistfully: "Yeah, or a different lay for every night of the week." Sex was forbidden for convicts, even after we'd been moved to the halfway dorms, which I had been. In prison, every night we were knocked out with sleep-induction beds to keep us out of trouble. Now that I was in my transition period, I was rubbing myself half raw every night, thinking about Boolin and Marik, Marik especially, who was quite my type. Boolin had midnight hair that he kept shoulder length like a lot of the city youths; made them look tough, like maybe they were ex-convicts. But he had a roundness to his face and an open, friendly smile. Marik had the kind of harshness in his face that I found more than handsome. I stretched a little. "Just imagine, a different lay for every night of the year!"

Marik leaned his tough, small and wiry body against mine. "Or you could have just one who had to follow you everywhere, and give it up to you if you wanted it, whenever you wanted it."

I was grimy with machine lube and sweaty from the heat in the shop, my coveralls half open. I looked into his bird-of-prey eyes and couldn't quite breathe.

"They give you all your shots and immunizations when you get convicted, don't they?"

I nodded.

"But you don't get the benefits, do you? You're not allowed." He reached for my hand and slid it toward the warmness of his crotch. I felt for his erection of my own accord and touching its spring steel hardness through the cloth—I wanted it. His voice dropped to a whisper. "How long has it been?"

"Two years," I whispered in return. "I'm not allowed . . . "

He hushed me with a hand to my lips. "Let's just say I'm not giving you a choice. Are you going to put up a struggle?"

I didn't want to. I wanted him to fuck me silly. But I wasn't sure what he wanted me to do. "Should I?"

"Boolin," he said in a quiet voice. "Hold her arms."

Boolin came around to the other side of me and took hold of my wrists. He lay me down on the bench and held them above my head, while Marik opened the quick-seams of his coveralls and mine. His fingers dipped in to my crotch and he whistled. "You really are ready for it, aren't you."

I nodded and closed my eyes, hardly believing that we were going to go through with this, but my only real fear was that he would stop.

He positioned himself over me and whispered into my ear. "Now remember, if anyone were to ever find out, we forced you to do this, right?"

"Right."

And he sank home.

That was as explicit as we ever got with words. From then on it was a delicate balance of things unspoken, even the attraction, the affection. We were buddies, we worked together, I could crank a turbine as fast as he could, he could spot a hairline in the ceramic as quick as me. We would have been equals, if I had been free. But I wasn't. And I never let myself think we were lovers, no matter how many times he plunged into me. It went on that way; every few weeks there would be a break in the work and we'd indulge.

It got real serious one of those days when there was zero to do and traffic had been nil since the beginning of the week. From somewhere, Boolin had picked up a second-hand particle gun, and was cleaning it. Marik and I were hanging around, watching. Boolin began to brag, pointing the gun at the wall and sighting along his arm.

Cecilia Tan

"Now this is what I call power," he said. "This thing'll rip the flesh off a human at over fifty lengths when it's powered up." It seemed so small, barely the size of his hand.

"Let me see it?" Marik held out a hand and Boolin tossed it across the workbench to him. "Nice." He made as if to pass it to me, then pulled back, remembering my status. "Uh uh, regulations say you're not supposed to come in contact with weapons," he said, a look of mock admonishment on his face.

"Yeah, and there's not supposed to be any weapons allowed in the port, either," I said, smiling sweetly.

"Oh, ho, ho, talking back. I think that's a punishable offense for a caitan under Kylish law, isn't it?" He hefted the gun in his hand and pointed at the floor at his feet. "Kneel."

"No." I said it with enough fire in my eyes that he knew I meant no to his command, not no to The Game. It was a look that said *Make me do it.*

He grabbed me and I tried to spin away, but he held the gun to my throat, bending my head back. Out of the corner of my eye I could see Boolin, watching as he always did. Sometimes, under Marik's orders, I did favors for him, too. His face had gone pale as he watched his gun plied against my throat.

"Down," Marik said, pushing the muzzle against the soft place under my chin. I went down inch by inch, as he held my hands behind my back with his other hand, bending backward until I felt my knees touch the floor. He drew a line down my body then with the gun, straight down the center, ending at my crotch. He rubbed the muzzle in the space between my legs and I moaned.

"Marik, you bastard . . ." I couldn't say any more as the sensation swept over me and I closed my eyes. My whole pubic area began to ache and I felt the wetness starting to drip under my loose coveralls.

He grabbed me by my hair and settled the gun against my forehead as he worked himself into a chair. He let go of my hair to unclasp his coveralls from his neck down to his crotch and pulled his erection free. Keeping the gun against my skin, he fiddled with his free hand.

Boolin spoke in a whisper. "Don't! You're taking the safety off . . . "

"I know," Marik said; then to me, "You see this? I'm setting this open," he unlatched something, "so if my finger slips off this lever, or squeezes too hard, the weapon will fire. So it's your job to see that I don't go off half cocked, right?"

I'm sure he was feeling the same rush I was; the fear was making me want him more than I'd ever wanted him before. This was more than breaking regulations. It was all I could do to keep from whimpering. I didn't answer.

"Suck me." He kept the gun on my forehead as I took him into my mouth. He leaned back in the chair, closing his eyes. I went at him with such zeal you would have thought sucking cock was my favorite thing. I had never liked it before I met Marik. But once we started playing The Game, I discovered I liked being forced to do it. And I was good at it, too. So Marik was happy to force me. I took him deep in, and let my tongue work his underside, all the time trembling under the hard pressure of the muzzle against my skull.

I felt him trembling, too, and gave second thoughts to the relish with which I was swallowing him. If he came too hard, he could slip . . . I almost stopped and told him to quit, but I kept on, more afraid of being called chicken, I guess, than of getting my head blown off.

When he came, his hand shook but his fingers stayed rigid. I spat out his semen onto the workshop floor. Even after all that, he couldn't get me to swallow. I sagged against the chair as he used his free hand to put the safety back on, and laid the gun down on the workbench. He hugged my head against his crotch, muttering an oath to himself. "That was . . ." he inhaled a huge gulp of air. "That was the best blowjob of my life," he concluded.

I nodded, my clit throbbing so hard now I could hardly stay sitting on my knees like that. "Yeah . . . "

"Are you okay?" His eyes searched mine, and the corners of his mouth twitched. "Hot?"

"Yeah," I rubbed myself against his leg like a hungry pet.

He pulled me up into his lap and unclasped my coveralls as he had his own. Now I could see Boolin sitting on a bench against the wall. From the state of his clothes it looked like he'd jerked himself off already. Marik held me in his lap and let his arms circle around me, his hands burrowing down into my suit and between my legs. The first touch was like an electric shock. I gasped as he spread my lips with one hand and began tweaking my hard clit with the other. Then he slipped a finger inside me and began jiggling it furiously. He alternated between those two actions until I thought I would go mad. "Ah, come on, Marik, don't . . . "

"Don't what? Aren't you enjoying the torture? You forget you're not supposed to have a choice about this." He fingered my clit then, sawing his finger back and forth slowly.

I couldn't answer.

"I could stop, you know." He let his fingers rest.

"No! No, keep going . . . "

"Say please . . . "

"Please, oh please," Inspiration hit me then. "Please *caishen*," I used the Kylish word for master. "Please."

"Very well," he said, and resumed the sawing motion, but faster this time. He'd learned by now that it was a good way to get an orgasm out of me.

He pushed me higher and higher. I clung to the arms of the chair, moving my hips as much as I could to help speed up the process. And then the Landing Signal blew. I cursed and started to move. Boolin jumped up and fastened his suit.

Marik held me fast. "Uh uh, I'm not letting you go 'til you're done." I tried to get up anyway, but his grip was too strong.

We had to get out there or the monitors would get suspicious. He redoubled his efforts. "Come on, now, give yourself to me . . ." I leaned against him, letting him do the work. He whispered in my ear, "Come for me, come for me, my little caitan . . ." and I did, shaking the whole chair while his fingers didn't let up. And as the last tremor shook me he whispered, "You're mine."

It was a Kylish interstellar transport coming in. Some kind of VIP. It had to be, for them to let it land during all the stratoference. Not that it made any difference to us. From the underside, all ships look about the same. The chatter came over the link later; it was the overlord Bhujan, one of the high-ranking Kylar, come to oversee the latest phase of transition to Kylish law.

"What does that mean?" Boolin asked. "I mean, for you." He meant me, as an indentured.

"I haven't the slightest. You think they tell us anything?"

"Maybe," Marik said from where he sat on the worktable, tossing a dirty rag toward me, "it means they'll let indentureds start having sex. To get them in shape for shipping off to the Kyl system and a life of sexual servitude."

I winged the rag back at him and it wrapped around his face. "Not bloody likely," I snorted.

That evening when I reported back to the dorm where I and fifty or so other female indentureds were kept until our terms ran out, I did find out a bit more. At the end of our meal period, an announcement came from the viewscreens that connected us to the warden's office. She, or rather what was probably just a graphic animation of her, came on and announced that tonight we would each find a sleep-induction pad in place of our pillows. A routine psychiatric evaluation would take place while we slept.

"Wait a minute," I said when the screen had gone blank. "All of us at once?"

Harla, the big woman sitting next to me, agreed. "Yeah. I know I'm not due for my next psych eval for another two months. I just had one last week!" She cursed and muttered. "It's violating our rights."

Jenna laughed from across the table. "Didja forget? While we're here, we don't have any rights."

"Maybe it has something to do with the new rules coming down," I said, more to myself than to any of the others. That had to be the explanation.

"What new rules?"

"There's a new Kylish overlord coming in." None of the others knew anything about it but me. "They're supposed to institute new laws. Kylish laws." We weren't allowed to speculate much more after that as they ushered us off to our rooms and locked us in for the night.

The next morning, there was a warden waiting for me. My first thought was, *Oh shit, I'm busted. Someone found out about me and Marik.* I tried to play it cool. "What's this about?"

"Job interview," was all she said, and indicated a clean set of clothes at my feet. "Wash up as usual, get dressed, and present yourself downstairs."

Job interview? Well, the whole point of the indenture program was supposed to be to get convicts like me back into society, reformed and no longer a burden. Maybe they had found me something better, but I doubted it. The space port job was pretty good as it was, plus what I had with Marik was better than anything I'd ever had before.

Downstairs there was a transport waiting to take me and six others somewhere. None of us spoke, just looked at one another with glances that said *I don't know either.* We were driven to one of the palatial houses in the diplomatic sector. I swore under my breath. Maybe Marik was, perversely, correct when he said we were going to be shipped off. The others looked at me, but I said nothing.

They separated us into different rooms in the house and then I was alone with my speculations. I was in a bedroom, an unoccupied one from the look of it. The table by the bed was bare and so was the clothes chest. There were two chairs by the window and I sat in one. Judging by the sun, hours went by while I sat there, wondering what Marik and Boolin were doing, and whether the wardens sent someone else in my place.

I had dozed off near midday when the sound of the door opening made me jerk awake. A man with soft blond hair and broad shoulders came in. Since he was alone, I thought at first that he must be someone sent to fetch me. Then I saw the way he carried himself, and the way he was looking at me. I would have thought an overlord would be followed by servants everywhere.

He sat down in the other chair and his breath sounded a little weary. "So you are Syn."

"Yes."

"Say 'Yes, my lord' and you'll please me."

"Yes, my lord," I said, without feeling.

"Your file says you were a nonviolent offender, and that in two months you'll be free."

It didn't seem like that required an answer, so I didn't give one.

"Are you looking forward to being free, Syn? To being your own woman again?"

"It beats prison," I joked. "My lord."

He smiled a droll smile. "Is there something else you'd prefer?"

I knew where this had to be leading. There could be no other explanation for the way his eyes roved over me in my soft grey tunic and leggings. But I played dumb. "I'm not sure what you mean, my lord."

He stood, walked until he was behind me, and began to stroke my hair. "I think you do." I sat without moving while he ran his hands through the cropped short mass of hair and over the back of my neck. "I'll be very direct with you now, Syn. I am Bhujan, an overlord of the first order of the Kylar, and I want you for a caitan."

I hate it when I'm right, sometimes.

"I need a Malakaian caitan. It sets an example for your people. And I think you could be, oh, such a prime example."

"Why me, my lord?" He couldn't know about me and Marik. He couldn't. He only arrived yesterday.

"Because of your deep potential. You have depths of submission that only a true master can bring out."

The psych scan. Last night was no ordinary psych scan. "I don't know what you mean," I said again, my lip trembling a little bit.

"I shall have to show you, then." He pulled my head back with firm fingers against my chin, so that now I looked him in the eye. Something told me he could be very convincing. "I know your true nature."

I trembled a little as he pulled me to my feet and carried me to the bed. The psych scan was Kylish technology in the first place, and common rumor was that it had been developed for evaluating the suitability of slave stock. They could tell who would turn disloyal and in how many years, who was lazy, who would harbor secret resentment. If Bhujan really knew that I had it in me to be a caitan, who was I to question?

The Game, I thought, as he began discarding my prison grey clothing. The Game was only a taste of it. Maybe I was destined for this, to live the real thing.

"A caitan is not permitted to cover her body in the presence of her caishen," he said as he stripped away the last of what I wore. "She, or he, is expected to be, at all times, ready for service."

That sounded like a cue to me. What was I supposed to do now? Tell him how ready I was? I didn't feel particularly ready. I felt mostly scared, my mind awhirl with possibilities and wondering how this would be different from The Game. If it were Marik, he would have already manipulated me into a state of such desire that I would be begging him to use me already. Bhujan said he was going to show me the depths of my submission, was he not? Prove it to me, I thought. Prove to me that there's something even deeper and better than The Game. "And what if the caitan isn't?" I asked, in what I hoped was a timid and inquisitive voice.

"Then he or she pays the price of not being ready," he said, as he turned me over onto my stomach and forced my legs apart. I felt his cock pressing against the far-too-dry cleft of my labia and then, holding me still by my shoulders and neck, he thrust up into me.

I made an injured sound into the pillow where my head pressed. His weight was full upon me now, and his arms snaked around and held me to him as he pushed in and out. "You have the flesh of the Kylar inside you now. A great honor."

I gritted my teeth and spat, "It hurts."

"Honor usually does," he said as he pulled out, and I sighed with relief.

One of his hands was on my back now, pressing me down, and I could feel the soft loose cloth of his sleeve. The other caressed my buttocks. "You see," he explained, his voice still as calm as ever, "you will serve me today whether you choose to or not. You are the state's property and I am the state, now."

And then he gave me a hard smack across the buttocks. I gasped but did not cry out. "You are mine to do with as I will. Whether I hurt you," another hard blow landed, "or whether I force you to pleasure because it pleases me." He began to hit me harder, although I hadn't thought that possible, blow after blow sending shock up my spine and making me want to scream out the pain, although I didn't.

I don't know how long that went on. I lost track of the blows and the sensation of my whole body becoming disconnected from the pain began to grow. And then I felt his fingers sliding down the hotness of my ass, between my legs again.

He was pleased and I was surprised to find I was dripping wet now. Maybe Bhujan did know more about how I worked than I did. No one had ever hit me like that before and I'd no idea that it would get me wet. I was puzzling out how that might work; what was it in spanking that caused me to lubricate like that? Especially since I wasn't hungering for his cock the whole time? Marik would have been running the cock up and down my leg during the affair, making sure I knew just what was coming next and how he was making me wait for it.

Bhujan turned me onto my back again. I could see how his robes opened to free his groin without making him seem naked or vulnerable. "Do you understand," he said, "that I did not have to stop before. I could have just gone on until I was satisfied. But sometimes the master must be sure that his slave enjoys the honor of his cock inside her. If she does not, she must be trained to enjoy it. She must be punished if she does not. Do you understand, now?"

I didn't. Did he mean he spanked me to punish me for not being wet enough for him? How did he know that would have the right effect though? He was waiting for some kind of answer. I avoided his question. "I am ready for you now, my lord." As ready as I'd ever be, I suppose.

This time he slid in slowly, letting my cunt suck him in bit by bit as if it knew what it wanted. As my hips moved of their own accord to let him sink deep to the hilt, I wondered again, perhaps he did know me better than I seemed to know myself.

It felt good to have him inside me, though, that much I had

to admit. The soreness of before was barely noticeable as he dragged himself in and out with slow, deliberate strokes.

"Do you know why the tradition of keeping caitan was begun?" he asked me as he stroked in, then out, his eyes closed.

"No, my lord."

"I will tell you then. When the Kylar were first beginning their conquests of the other lands on our home world, ages and ages ago, the overlords were a special breed of men and women. We were raised and bred to have a certain temperament, attitude, and aptitude, that suited us to conquering our neighbors."

One might say rapacious, I thought.

"Part and parcel with the inborn zeal for conquest came other desires and needs so overwhelming that they could, in some, be a detriment. Over the generations, it came to be known that the overlords' physical needs for combat and for sexual satiation were inseparable. Likewise, their psychological needs to own, annex, and dominate."

It made a great deal of sense. I wondered how he could go on that way, his voice still and calm, even cold, as it had been when we were sitting by the window. His rhythm never broke, in his speaking nor in the way he was rocking in and out of me.

"In the caitan, there is a very special task, then; to serve the overlord is to support the greater glory of the Kylar. To quench the fires that burn in him, to contain his energy, to be the receptacle of his emotions, whether that means to suffer through pain, use, or even pleasure."

With the long strokes the way he was making them there was no way I could come, although I was pushed constantly closer and closer to the edge. Each time he sank in there would be a brief moment of pressure on my clit, and then just the stoking of the fire deep inside.

"The best caitan come to realize their place and their importance and they give up everything, even their own will, to serve

 152   *Cecilia Tan*

the greater end. They know without fail that it is their mission to serve, because there is no other time, no other place when they feel that power flowing through them, no other time when they have touched God."

For all his pompous words, I could not picture Bhujan as the embodiment of a god, not even Kyl, the God of Dominance and Submission. His words put me back to thinking about Marik. Marik, who didn't seem to need all these words to make his point.

Bhujan took a small device out of his robe and placed it against my forehead. "All your choices have been taken away. Now I choose when you come and how many times." He pressed it and the orgasm that had been building so very slowly over all this time exploded through me, making my legs shake, my eyes roll back, and my throat hoarse as I cried out wordlessly.

When I went limp he was still stroking in and out as if nothing had happened. I had never come like that in all my life.

"You have pleasure only because it pleases your master that you do." He hit the button again, and again I was rocketed through a bone-shaking orgasm. His hand sought out my clit, which by now was so hypersensitive I couldn't bear him to touch it, but of course I had to bear it, I could not move or pull away from him, impaled on him like that.

"No, don't . . ." I said, before I could stop myself.

"Ah, my little caitan," he said, and my spine went cold at how that phrase reminded me of Marik, "now you begin to learn." And he hit the button again.

It was like electric shock coming through my clit, and I screamed. And yet, it was pleasure, so much pleasure that it burned as I never knew nerves could burn. Incredible, it was, but I wasn't sure if I could take any more of it. "You see how it is," he breathed, "when you have no choices. You know I can force you to do anything, anything at all, even betray your own body with pleasure."

"Yes, yes!" I said, not because I agreed but because I hoped I'd get a little rest if he went off on another little lecture. I thought of Marik, the way Marik had forced me to come just yesterday when the landing signal went off. And the way, once I had come, he had whispered, "You're mine" just as if it was an irrefutable truth. Bhujan buried himself in me now, no longer moving, and I could feel him holding himself back from orgasm. *Marik,* I thought, *Marik, did you mean it when you said that?* Marik did not need any Kylish technogadget to bend my body to his will. And it came to me that surrender was not something truly forced. It was, ultimately, a choice that had to be made.

Bhujan was speaking to me still. "Now you have had a taste of it. You know I can force you to do anything. Now I will ask you to make one final choice in your lifetime."

"What is that, my lord?"

"Will you be my caitan? Do you understand the choice you make?"

I did. If I surrendered to him, then he had truly cowed me, whereas if I continued to resist, although he could force me to do anything he wanted, he could not truly own me. It was true, he *had* shown me how deep my submission could go.

And despite all his manipulations, I was not cowed. The only questions that remained in my mind were, *What would he do to me if I said no? Kill me? Put me back into prison?* I could feel his exalted Kylish flesh throbbing inside mine, but I knew I could not betray Marik. Marik, to whom I truly belonged, I could not betray him by giving myself to this pompous ass. I was not my own to give.

"I understand the choice I make." I said. "I will not be yours."

Bhujan's calmness cracked like an egg leaking poison. He gripped me by the shoulders and with an animal cry of fury he began to come. He pistoned in anger and frustration until he pinioned me with his arms, his weight, and his coming, his precious

Kylish seed filling me and overflowing from me as he jerked away.

As I lay there, feeling as if I might never move again, he said, "I am almost tempted to keep you anyway, to see if I couldn't break you." He fastened up his robes and picked the little orgasm inducer off my forehead. "But I haven't the time." He left shaking his head, as if he still could not figure out where he had gone wrong.

He was a spiteful bastard after all that. When I returned to the dorm they informed me I was being transferred to a higher-security facility up the coast in another district, for three months of "observation." After that was over, I would have my six months of indentures, no chance I would be at the space port again now that I was in another geographic jurisdiction, and then, I would be free.

I prayed at night that Marik and Boolin were just as I'd left them, tinkering in the overheated little shop and jerking each other off when things got dull, and that when I was given back my citizenship I could find them there, and join them, and things would be as they had been. It was less than a year, what could change in a year? I prayed, and prayed, to Kyl, the God of Slaves, that I was not wrong about this, that I would never be free again.

"I want to be a slave," Kobi said, from where he lay on the living room floor with his long black hair spread out like a carpet. "The erotic plaything of a powerful, indomitable owner." He sat up enough to take another swig of the wine and passed the bottle back to Merin where she sat on the couch, watching the light from the fireplace image on the media wall flicker.

Merin sat still with shock. She and Kobi had been sharing the apartment for several months, ever since the last housing lottery assigned them into this standard, two-occupant place. It was nice but not fancy, and she and Kobi got along better than well, sometimes sharing beds as well as friendship. But this was the first time they'd ever gotten drunk and bared their secrets to each other. "Say that again," she said, almost a whisper.

"I want to be a slave!" Kobi's voice rang off the ceiling.

A thrill ran through Merin's blood when he said it—the taboo spoken aloud, at last, and the words stirred something in her. "Me, too," she said.

Kobi sat up, the wine forgotten. "What?"

"I said, 'Me, too.'"

Kobi was as shocked to hear her admission as she had been to hear his. "Really?" She was nodding to him, slow, serious nods. He took her hand as though he needed assurance that she was real. "I thought—I thought I was the only one."

Merin held tight to his fingers and breathed a deep breath. Her mind, which minutes ago had been fuzzy and sleepy with wine, now buzzed with giddy possibilities and long-repressed memories coming to the surface. "Do you remember the stories they told us as children, about the cruelty of our ancestors toward the Gerrish, how they subjugated them and forced them to work . . . "

Kobi nodded, his eyes fever bright. "Yes, yes, and how the mistreatment led to the destruction of the Gerrish race. That's why we have the Age of Equality now."

Merin curled her legs under her on the couch and went on. "Even when I was a little girl, I used to wonder what it had been like for the Gerrish, to be bought and sold, to be used . . . "

Kobi shivered. Every Bellonian child had been taught in school that the enslavement of the Gerrish was the greatest crime committed in history, and it was only in the aftermath of the Gerrish extinction by a genetic plague that Bellonians began to build the peaceful, free society that exists today. It took hundreds of years to eliminate warring tendencies and inequality in their society. *And here I am,* Kobi thought, *going against it.* "I used to daydream about the Gerrish, too." he said. "I used to imagine I was the servant of an ailing lord who needed to be comforted in his final days."

"Comforted?"

Kobi blushed at the memory and let Merin's hand go. "In my fantasy he was dying of a rare sexual disease that required him to have sex almost constantly during all his waking hours, so he had a whole bunch of slaves who served him to ease his affliction." He laughed out loud. "I always had a vivid imagination."

"I guess so!" Merin let herself laugh a little, too, but she was still thinking about the ethics of their admission to each other.

"But the Gerrish enslavement *was* a great crime," she said.

Kobi's eyebrows came down, as did his voice, in serious thought. "Yes. But think about it. It's wrong to subjugate someone. But there's no crime in wanting to be subjugated, is there?"

She pursed her lips. "There's no law against killing yourself, either, I suppose."

Kobi frowned. "That's a distasteful comparison, don't you think? Or do you think we're self-destructive for thinking this?"

Merin touched him on the cheek. "I don't know. Do you think the Kylar are going to destroy us the way we destroyed the Gerrish?" Since the establishment of the Kylaran embassy last year, rumors were flying thick through the legislature where Merin worked.

Kobi shook his head. "We don't even know if the Kylar are going to colonize here, or just trade with us." Kobi felt his cheeks getting warm. "If they did colonize, though . . . you know what they say about the Kylar."

Merin nodded her head and smiled. "So that's what's got you thinking about becoming a . . ." she rolled her tongue over the words: "love slave."

"They say their overlords keep a dozen or more slaves to satisfy their libido! Imagine it, Merin! It could be my dream come true!"

Merin slid down to the floor to look Kobi in the eye. "If the Kylar do colonize here, it won't be for several years. If they do, they'll probably bring their own slaves with them. And if they wanted to take on Bellonian slaves, they won't find anyone suitable because we've been conditioned out of thinking that way."

Kobi smiled and stroked her short curls. "Merin, don't you see? That's why we have a chance. You and me, we're not like the others. We want this. When the Kylar come, we'll be ready!"

 Cecilia Tan

"What do you mean, 'ready'?"

"We'll have to have practice. We can practice with each other!"

She laughed out loud. "Doing what?"

Kobi was shaking his hands in excitement. "Just like when we were kids, did you play at being parents, teachers, legislators? Let's pretend. Like this." He cleared his throat and growled, "Slave! Are you ready for me? I need some service!" And he pressed her back into the floor, pinning her by the shoulders and kissing her neck.

Merin had slept with Kobi plenty of times since they had been assigned to share this apartment. They often fucked to blow off steam or relieve boredom. She'd expected they probably were going to end up in bed tonight since neither of them had plans. But she hadn't expected anything like this. Kobi had never been so intense before, she'd never felt his yearning need like this. She squirmed under him and enjoyed the buzz of sexual tension building between her legs. She said, falsetto, like a long-ago depiction of a helpless Gerrish maidservant she vaguely remembered seeing, "Oh master, anything to please you. Take me!"

Kobi let her go for a moment as he began to slip out of his clothes. "Um, strip!" he commanded. He had trouble getting his waistband over his erection.

She was wet when he slipped into her, there on the floor, pressing her down with his body. In his mind, their roles had reversed, as he dreamed the fantasy again of being a slave, serving his master's needs. Or, in this case, his mistress's. And then they were both lost in the mindless lust of heat and sex.

Merin spoke first after they were done. She wasn't sure what to say, so she settled for stating the obvious: "That was intense."

"Yes." He rolled onto his side and propped his head up with his elbow, his hair curtaining down around him.

This could be fun, she thought. "Next time, do you want me to be the one in command?"

"Yes! Sure!" He held her hand. "We can take turns."

They lay like that for a while, among their scattered clothes at the foot of the couch. Merin's mind was busy as she relaxed. We can't be the only ones, either, she thought. How could we find more? "Hey, Kobi?"

"Hm?"

"When is your next session at the Velderet?"

"I'm bartending there tomorrow."

"No, I mean, when is your next sexual encounter due?"

He blushed. "I already used one this month. So, ten days at least. What are you thinking?"

"Nothing," she said. She knew she'd tell him her idea as soon as she convinced herself it could work.

The following week passed with Merin spending her days at the legislator's cooperative where she worked and Kobi spending nights tending bar at the Velderet. They hardly saw each other, and there was no opportunity to play 'Let's Pretend.' Merin's mind kept returning to her ideas about Kobi and the Velderet.

The Velderet was a sex house, an Age of Equality institution begun on the theory that all citizens should have equal access to some basic sexual freedoms. Any Bellonian could walk into the Velderet, or one of the many other places like it, once a month and request sexual satisfaction, or save up currency and transfer it there for extra time or sessions. Merin looked up the legislation ruling sex houses and transferred them to her home system to peruse later. Was there such a thing as fraudulent use? She'd find out. While she was poking through the data banks she also found some graphics of the latest in "sensual fashions." Could be interesting, she decided, and transferred them, also.

Kobi, in the meantime, made a friend at the Velderet—a customer named Mica who had started coming in recently, and usually hung around to talk and have a drink. One night Mica began griping that he wasn't getting his usual satisfaction anymore. "Maybe I just don't know what to ask for," he said as he rested in the lounge after one of his sessions. "Or maybe I'm in here too often, getting jaded."

Mica tended to come in once a week or more. "Could be," Kobi said, as he poured Mica some iced water. "Have you been seeing the same people again and again? You could try cybersex instead. Then you could have the pick of partners from all over."

"No, it's not that. I try to come on different days. But they all seem the same. Maybe as I get older my tastes are changing."

Something in Mica's voice made Kobi listen more closely. "Like how?" he asked, pretending to busy himself behind the bar.

"Like . . . more quick? I had one woman last month who was great, really physical, rough almost. That . . . got me going." Mica stared into his glass, his dark eyebrows casting his face in shadow. "It's probably just a phase I'm going through."

Kobi looked around. The lounge was mostly empty. "I know what you mean," he said.

Mica's eyes flickered for a moment before he looked pointedly away.

"I do," Kobi insisted, and pressed his hand to his chest.

Mica also took a look around to confirm they were mostly alone and unobserved. He wrote something down on a napkin and passed it to Kobi as he stood up. "I'll see you around." And then he left.

Kobi read what was printed in damp letters on the throwaway. It was an access code for a retrievable data file. He slipped the paper into his pocket.

* * *

Merin had fallen asleep in front of the media wall that night. When Kobi came home, he found her curled up on the couch with a video of some fashion show looping on the screen. He sat down next to her and touched her shoulder. "Merin, wake up."

She woke with a yawn. "Did I fall asleep? What time is it?"

He took the control board out of her lap and entered the code Mica had given him. "Someone told me something interesting today, I think."

Merin yawned again. "What?"

"We'll see what it is." The screen went dark while the system retrieved whatever it was. On the screen appeared the words:

The Kylaran Desire

They both watched, rapt, as the letters dissolved into the image of a naked, kneeling woman, her hands bound behind her back. She wore a suit of something black and stretchy that oddly covered all of her torso except for her breasts. A voice intoned the evils of the decadent Kylaran empire . . . while the image changed. The animated graphic figure now was tortured by faceless figures with whips; then, limbs spread beyond the view of the screen, she was entered from behind by a man. The soundtrack in the background featured a woman's cries and screams as the voice listed the kinds of service that were commonly expected of caitan, the elite Kylaran sex slaves.

Merin laughed. "This is obviously a piece of propaganda. But is it condemning the Kylar? Or promoting their way of life?"

Kobi mouthed the word: *cai-tan.* "Those sound like cries of ecstasy to me. Look." He pointed out her face, enhancing the image with the control board and enlarging it. "Is she grimacing in pain or smiling?"

Merin squinted. "The resolution of the data's not good enough. I can't tell."

The clip ended with the image again of the woman kneeling,

 Cecilia Tan

rotating slowly to show her reddened buttocks, her full breasts, the metallic cuffs at her wrists, and the collar around her neck. The screen went dark.

"Where did you get this?" Merin looked at the throwaway with the code written on it.

"A guy at the Velderet wrote it down for me." Kobi shrugged. "Do you think it's contraband?"

Merin considered that. "Maybe not. If it purports to be a piece of propaganda against the Kylar . . . the legislators really haven't dealt with this issue before." It was illegal to create or distribute dramas depicting "inequality" except for certain educational programs about the Gerrish. No one had *wanted* to create such things before, either. She was deep in thought about these things when Kobi touched her on the arm.

She felt the dampness of his fingers and smiled. "You horny bastard."

"Please, Merin, I . . . "

She held up a hand. "Are caitan allowed to beg for favors?"

He got down on the floor and bowed his head.

"You had better beg well."

"Please, mistress, I'm so hungry, I could die."

"Hmph, well, we can't have you dying now, can we. I paid good money for you." Merin struggled to keep a straight face. So it wasn't the most eloquent improvising she'd ever done.

"Please, mistress," Kobi said again. "I am so full of need."

Oh, Kobi, you always are, she thought. Merin was hot, too, she realized, between watching the propaganda and now seeing Kobi's face flushing with desire. *Still, that's no reason to rush,* she thought. "Then touch yourself."

Kobi flashed a look at her and she raised an eyebrow. He slipped back into character and slid his pants off. He wet his hand with his tongue and began stroking. Merin had never watched a man touch himself before. She was fascinated by the way he curved his fingers to catch the lip of head. She wriggled out of her own clothes while he pulled and stroked. His hand was beginning to shake.

"Don't you dare come unless I say," she said, pulling his hand away from his cock as he gave a little whimper. She motioned for him to lie down and then straddled him, stroking herself and teasing him with the sight and scent of her cunt. Then she settled onto his erection. She'd been on top before, but she'd never ridden a man like this. He jerked and shuddered under her trying hard not to come, but in the end he couldn't stop himself. Then again, neither could she.

"Oh mistress, let me take care of that mess," he said quickly, and they switched places. He put his head between her legs and lapped up his own seedless come as it leaked from her, and then kept lapping until Merin clapped her thighs so tight around his ears he could hardly hear how loud her screams and moans of orgasm were.

A little bit later, he asked, "So, do you think it's true?"

"About the Kylar in the propaganda?" She shrugged. "Who cares? What matters now is who is putting this data out and why. And if others like us are seeing it, how it is affecting them . . ." She put a hand on his shoulder. The time had come to tell him about her idea. "I'm sure now we're not the only ones. About the Velderet . . . "

Under Merin's instruction, Kobi made an appointment to fulfill his monthly quota of sexual satisfaction in one of the Velderet's cyber suites. "Pick a time when there will be lots of other people there," Merin had said. "Your chances will be better." He eased up to the console and began the registration procedure.

"Hello, Kobi," the programmed computer voice said to him as the words appeared on the screen. It asked him whether he wanted his previous preference file loaded or if he'd like to choose a new set.

"New set," he said, and the registry questionnaire came up in front of him.

The first questions were very basic. Age? Gender? Body type? and so on, as the system tried to determine his ideal partner. He specified a slightly older individual with physical strength rated high, no gender selected. Then it became more specific about sexual tastes, asking him to rate the desirability of certain acts, both performing them and receiving them: Massage? Ear licking? Cunnilingus? Fellatio? Anal penetration? Hundreds of sexual and sensual activities. He tried hard to draw an erotic map that showed his underlying motive—to be the erotic plaything of a domineering partner—something the computer wouldn't sense, but perhaps the human being it matched him up with . . . Merin's idea had been to try to work the system to match Kobi up with a partner who might also have the same idea as he did. "We know we're not the only ones, now," she insisted. "What better way to find the others?" One couldn't request of the system any encounter that had any element of dominance in it. But perhaps the person it matched him with, perhaps he could say to him or her "Let's reenact the Kylaran Desire . . . "

He marked HIGH PREFERABILITY for all the acts that required him to be penetrated in some way, and designated himself PASSIVE. Then it came down to the personality and mood selections. ROMANTIC did not seem the right choice, although being swept away to a distant, exotic world by a tall dark Kylar was about as romantic as he could imagine. He also rejected the categories of NURTURING, and INEXPERIENCED, among others, and settled for PASSIONATE. He checked COMPLEX rather than STRAIGHTFORWARD but specified ANONYMOUS. All that setting really meant that he wasn't interested in meeting a relationship partner through this encounter, so names did not have to be exchanged.

Last, he selected LINK ONLY. By meeting his potential partner through cybersex and not in person, he could not only choose from anyone linked up at sex houses all over the world, he would risk no physical damage if he found what he was looking for.

"How would you like to appear?" the computerized voice prompted him.

"Oh." He had almost forgotten Merin's facsimile. Since he would be projected into the computer's mind, he could change his appearance if he wished. "Please use my usual nude body," he said, knowing it was on file. His naked figure appeared on the screen. "But clothe it in this." He fed the paper into a scan slot. The computer filled in a dark outfit that fit snug over his shoulders and around his waist. Merin had designed a male equivalent to what they had seen the caitan wear in the propaganda clip. "Hair in a topknot," he added, remembering the way the woman in the clip had hers piled atop her head.

"Material of clothing?" the computer reminded him.

"Something stretchy," Kobi said, realizing he did not know what to say.

"Choose from the following." A list of fabrics and materials both natural and synthetic scrolled down the screen. He had never used this option for anything before. The cybersex he'd experienced had just been in the nude. His eyes stopped on the word LEATHER.

"That material will limit mobility and make sexual activities difficult or uncomfortable," the system advised him. "Please choose something with greater elasticity."

"List from least elastic to most."

The list flickered as the words rearranged themselves. He scanned to the bottom. There was something he hadn't seen before: ULTRA-STRETCH RUBBER.

The Kobi on the screen was suddenly clad in something shiny and tight. The computer showed the figure doing jumping jacks and the material stretching accordingly. "Within acceptable limits," the computer said. "Please lie down and await connection."

Kobi stripped out of his clothes and lay down on the bed in the suite. He had to ask the computer for further instructions on how to attach the tiny leads to his skin at various points on his head and neck. Cybersex wasn't something Kobi had done very often. In fact, the only times he had done it were once when he had a broken arm and shoulder and could barely move and once when he had been sick with a bad flu that he didn't want anyone else to catch. It hadn't been as satisfying as meeting a real live person, flesh to flesh, he had told himself then, but maybe being sick or injured had dampened his response. Cybersex had originally been designed for those with physical disabilities for whom ordinary sex was difficult or impossible, but there was no reason any person couldn't use it. Many people these days seemed to prefer it. In fact, with enough excess currency, one could even buy the right connectors and hook into the sex house network from home.

Kobi lay back in the warm room and waited for a connection to come through. *I hope this works,* he thought.

Merin scanned over the many brightly colored facsimiles spread across the living room floor. "Sensual fashions" were particularly disappointing this season. Mostly androgynous, baggy things, very soft on the skin of course, and easy to remove, but very little looked particularly enticing. She doodled with some more ideas similar to the thing she had come up with for Kobi. It was good to stay in practice with design. Once her three-year tenure in the legislature was up, she could go back to attire design. Most of what she had done was not fashion, but utilitarian, designing better clothes for certain types of laborers, hospital workers, construction . . . She tried to imagine, if this was how a slave was dressed, how would a master be attired? What would the needs of a master's clothes be? The clip hadn't shown anything useful. Her pen ranged over the control board as she searched for something else that might inspire her. She passed out of the fashion sector and into a branch on historical costume, and checked the heading ANCIENT MILITARY UNIFORMS.

To Kobi it seemed that the light in the room changed, but as he looked down and saw himself clad in the black Ultra-stretch suit, he knew that he was seeing the room in the cyber network. He could feel the Ultra-stretch now, too, tight and slick, not like cloth at all. He wiggled a bit and loved the feel of it on his skin. What would it feel like without body hair?

A chime sounded and the room warped as a naked, male figure appeared. He had short sandy hair and looked to be about five years older than Kobi, probably breeding age if he swung both ways. "Hi," he said.

"Hi." Kobi resisted the urge to get down and kneel. There was no way to know what this guy's reaction might be to that. Kobi stayed on the bed as the man approached and looked at him, like a doctor looking over a patient. Kobi tried to imagine he was a prospective slave buyer, examining the merchandise before trying it out himself. *I better try to feel out this guy's true preferences,* Kobi thought. "I have a very talented mouth and ass," he said, watching for a reaction. No change. Time to initiate something. "And I'm ready for you whenever you are." There, that was almost like something a slave would say.

The guy ran his hand over the Ultra-stretch and Kobi shivered, back in his mental game of slave for sale. He turned over onto his stomach and waved his ass in the air.

"Well, here," the guy said. "If you suck me off some I'll be hard enough to fuck you, okay?"

Kobi pretended that was an order and went at the flaccid penis with gusto. *What will happen to me if he doesn't get hard?* Kobi thought. He imagined being punished for failing to do his duty, but he couldn't really imagine what the punishment would be, only that there would be some. He moaned around the cock in his mouth. The guy was getting hard. He didn't wait long before pulling away from Kobi's mouth and positioning himself at the end of the bed. Kobi rocked back on all fours. *Oh, perfect,* Kobi thought, *just like in the clip when the caitan gets fucked . . .*

"You ready?" the guy said, spreading Kobi's asscheeks with one hand and guiding his cock with the other. *Maybe cybersex had some advantages,* Kobi thought. *No lube necessary.*

Kobi nodded, pretending that he really had no choice. His master was just toying with him, asking like that. As he was when he later asked, "This okay?" when he changed to a faster rhythm and, "You getting close?" a bit later on. Kobi didn't answer either time—it would have broken the dream too much.

The truth was, he was getting close, and he wasn't able to hold it. Not like a good slave would have. And the guy didn't seem to care much either, as he slicked himself in and out of Kobi as fast as he could, straining toward his own orgasm.

That's it, Kobi thought suddenly, *he's using me for his own pleasure! Oh yes. By the red moon . . .* And he moaned a little as he thought about that.

"Are you okay? Am I hurting you?" the guy asked. "Do you want me to stop?"

Some people are just too nice, Kobi thought. *It's like he's forgotten we're cybersexing and he can't really hurt me.* He shook his head as he clenched his butt tight and sent the guy over the edge into orgasm.

Later, Kobi sat in the dimly lit lounge, playing over the encounter in his mind. *If the guy had kept his mouth shut,* Kobi thought, *would it have worked better?* The truth was, the guy just wasn't into it the same way. *Then again,* Kobi thought, *I never did ask him specifically or give any direct hints.* Maybe

Merin will come up with a more direct way to get the message across . . .

His eyes stopped their roaming as he spotted Mica coming into the lounge. Mica made his way through the softly sculpted tiers and scattered pillows to where Kobi sat. Kobi indicated a soft pillow next to him, but Mica did not sit.

"Here," he said, and handed Kobi a scrap of paper. Then he walked back out the way he had come.

It was another code. *Another propaganda clip?* Kobi folded the paper in half and stood up. It was time to go home and find out.

$\mathcal{T}$he Seamy Side

VI

I haven't written much erotic fiction that centers around sex work or topics of illegal, secretive, or so-called immoral sexual practices in the real world. I think this is because the secret and the forbidden are not really what float my boat. I like porn. I've enjoyed my commercial transactions with the sex industry (no, I won't detail what they are), but they haven't turned me on *because* they are illicit. Still, perhaps it is inevitable that the theme of sex work appears in my writing somewhere. "Crooked Kwan" was written for *Noirotica,* an anthology of erotic crime stories. I'm opposed to thinking of sex as a crime and never really warmed to film noir, so I had difficulty finding an entry into that genre; that is, until I got hooked on the Hong Kong gangster films of John Woo. The idea of crime as commerce and sex as commerce melded into the story "Crooked Kwan."

"Porn Flicks" and "Rock Steady," on the other hand, look at porn movies from the point of view of the consumer. How do these video fantasies intersect with real-world sex, especially my narrators', who are both atypical consumers of porn? As for the parallels between porn stars and rock musicians in "Rock Steady," I assure you, that is a figment of your imagination.

Johnny Kwan tried to lie still in the dark, but the bed moved like a ship at rough seas as his partner rocked above him. He felt the droplets of her sweat hit his chest, *tap tap,* but no coolness, just wet upon wet. Overhead a fan turned: He knew by the creak of it since he could neither see it in the dark nor feel any breeze. All that he could see was the shining outline of her damp cheek, her damp shoulder, her damp breast, in the light from the street that came in the open window. A flash of her blond hair, limp with sweat. The fan creaked, the bed springs protested, and the sounds of traffic and street Chinese crowded into his ears. His partner braced herself against him with her hands on his shoulders and added her voice to the orchestra, an inarticulate moan as she moved to new heights of pleasure. Johnny Kwan did not move, except to clench his jaw. Even when she sighed she had a foreign sound to her voice, something in the vowels that could be British or American but was certainly not Hongkongese. *Two months,* Johnny thought, *two months until the gates close, and nothing to be done about it.* Holding still wasn't working. She began to say things in her low brassy tone that he didn't understand, and he could not stop what was coming any more than he could stop the British from giving up the place. He bucked once, twice, and came into her, his dark hands sliding across her white breasts in the window light as he sank down deeper and deeper into darkness.

He heard the metallic sound of the pullchain on the fan; she was fumbling in the dark for the light. She snapped on the wall switch and Johnny winced in the yellowy brightness. Her hands searched his jacket pocket for something. She stood up with two cigarettes and a lighter in her hands, put both smokes into her mouth, and lit them with a single puff. He took one.

"You good," he said, not smiling. One only smiles when one wants to placate someone bigger than oneself. "Your name?"

The blonde did smile, but she was a girl, a Westerner, and a whore, and they smiled for all sorts of reasons. She spoke some soft syllables and he had to put his hand to his ear for her to repeat them. "Sherrie," she said with exaggerated *r*'s. She sat in a wooden chair by the window and crossed her legs.

Johnny nodded his head. Madame Lun always did good business with girls like these. Back when Iron Circle was in the protection racket, Madame Lun sometimes let men like Johnny sample the goods. Tonight, there was no Iron Circle anymore, and Johnny was a paying customer. He decided he'd hand over the money after he finished the cigarette.

"You like Hong Kong?" he asked, feeling bold with the thought of that money. In all the confusion, Smiling Willy Lim would never know it was gone and Johnny Kwan had no intention of working for him.

"Yeah sure," she said, her eyes out the window on the traffic.

"You good," he repeated. He tried to make his English words come out slow, like the drawl of confidence that American movie actors always had. Bravado made him say "Madame Lun, I ask her for you again."

Sherrie snorted half a laugh. "Well, it better be soon, honey, because in a few weeks I am outta here. When the Brits go, I go. Madame Lun, too. Gone, sayonara, bye-bye, Chinaman."

Johnny stubbed out his cigarette, not smiling even harder. The implied insult—that because he couldn't leave he was somehow beneath her—would have earned her a slap from most men. *One couldn't expect whores to have respect and one didn't pay them to be kind,* Johnny told himself. *Just pay her and go.* He slid his pants on and buckled the belt. He pulled his cotton T-shirt over his head and picked up his Western-style button-down shirt and jacket. From the inner pocket of the jacket he produced a wad of green—American bills. He tugged a few out of the wad and put them onto the damp bed. But he held out his hand for his lighter before he left the room.

On the street, Johnny Kwan, also known as Crooked Kwan— not because of his trade but because of the way his face never seemed to be on quite straight—looked for a taxi. He had more stops to make tonight as he made his best attempt to spend what was formerly Willy Lim's money. Their former boss, J. Y. Fung, head of the Iron Circle, had bought himself a citizenship to Canada and was already on his way to Vancouver, where he had legitimate businesses and ties to a powerful ancestral clan association in San Francisco. Smiling Lim, conniver that he was, had tried to take over Iron Circle in J.Y.'s wake but the organization split into factions. Small men with small influence were scrabbling for what little hold they could get in the fading light of Hong Kong's sunset, as the island sank into the great, hulking economic morass that was the People's Republic like the sun into the sea. Already there were mainland tongs taking over the drug trade, and anyone with enough money in the bank had bought citizenship somewhere else. Madame Lun was probably one of them. Johnny Kwan wandered down the street through the crowd of people and noodle stands and mah-jongg players, the smell of steaming fish and garbage seeping through his still-damp skin. Iron Circle was rust and he knew it, so he was doing what any sensible person would do: He was on a binge.

Working his way up the hill and up in price, he went next to the House of Jade. They put him in another little room with a glass of water on the table and a fan that almost cooled the room. He could feel the breeze it made, anyhow, even if it felt like all it did was recirculate the heat that had risen back down into the room. There they brought him a bleach-blonde who had white skin but didn't look or sound American, but he took her anyway, holding on to her blond hair as he pushed her mouth down on his hard cock. That way he couldn't hear her talk and couldn't see that her pubic hair wasn't bleached. He let her smoke one of his cigarettes and had to buy more before his next stop.

He took a taxi to the House of the Flowering Lotus, where the sheets were red silk like a wedding dress and stained in a puddle as dark as blood when he sweated on them. They had a genuine blonde white woman, who, like Sherrie, tried to get on top to finish him off as quickly as possible. It wasn't necessary. Crooked Kwan wanted quantity now, and although he stayed on top, he was done without much delay. Then he ordered a clean shirt and decided to fuck her again while he waited for it. She lay back on the bed and spread her legs wide, beckoning him by spreading wide the pink shaven folds of her cunt and fingering herself. *So brazen, only a Western woman would act this way,* he thought. *So this is what a higher price can get you.* He approached her but found he was still soft. She took him in her hands and mouth and made him hard again. Another bonus. In a cheap house if a man couldn't get it up he didn't get his money back, either. He teased her with the now hard pole, rubbing it against her lips and sliding it around everywhere but into her. She cooed and writhed and said, "Oh come on, sugar, fill me up with that sausage." He made her wait even

 Cecilia Tan

longer for it. By the time he was fucking her again, his clean shirt arrived without his noticing. *This is heaven,* he thought, as he buried his face between her white spheres. There was only one place more expensive than House of the Flowering Lotus, and he looked forward to trying there next.

"*Fay dee ah,* quickly!" He banged his gold ring against the dark wood of the table. He had come into the Palace of Summer Clouds and demanded their best white girl. Some silent, demure women in long silk dresses had seated him here, poured him tea, and withdrew. Surely such a high-class place would not keep him waiting so long. He had drunk two cups of tea already. The air was thick with old incense to mask the odor of sweat and other men. "Ai," he muttered. The place would be a communist work camp by the time he got any service.

An older woman bedecked with too much jade and mascara entered the room.

Johnny Kwan tossed some bills onto the table. "*Gwai lo,*" he spat. Someone white. "American, British, Australian, I don't care."

She named him a price, an exorbitant, ridiculous price, Johnny knew, but he was in the charade now and threw more bills down.

She plucked the bills from the table with her lacquered claws and held them up to the light. Satisfied they were genuine, she jerked her head to indicate he should follow her.

She left him in a room full of ornate woodwork and red paper lanterns, jade statuettes and incense, things probably arranged to meet the expectations of some rich *gwai lo* who came here to see what an Oriental brothel was *really* like. Johnny stripped out of his shirt and was glad this place was air-conditioned.

The sound of soft footsteps behind him made him turn. In the dim lantern light he could see she wasn't blond, but she was white. She was dolled up in a satin *chongsam* and had chopsticks in her hair, which just made her look all the more un-Chinese. *"Fay dee ah,"* he said. "Get out your clothes." He slipped off his pants and shoes. She began wriggling out of the dress, fumbling with the cloth buttons.

Too slow, he decided. He pushed her onto the bed and tore the *chongsam* open. She gasped. Her pubic hair was mousy brown, like the hair on her head, and he knelt down to put his face in it. That was enough foreplay for him. Holding her at the edge of the bed, he buried himself deep inside her. In the light he could see the darkness of his pubic hair contrasted with hers and he nodded to himself.

Her eyes were shut and her head was turned away.

"Open your eyes," he said. He didn't remember what color they were, and hoped they were green or blue.

She shook her head. Her brown hair came loose from the chopsticks and spilled out over the brocade of the bed cover.

"Come on." He thrust harder into her as if he could force her eyes open with his cock. "Open."

She grimaced and shook her head again.

Aiyah, I thought this was an expensive place with good whores, he said to himself in street Chinese. She made no sign of understanding him. "You listen," he said as he kept up his rhythm. "You do what I say or your madame will beat you."

She still did not move or open her eyes.

Johnny Kwan shrugged. *Maybe this was a part of the service,* he thought. The extra price he paid must have been for this. *They think I want to rape this white woman, so she plays unco-operative. Good act.* He lifted her up so he could slide farther onto the bed without pulling out of her. He slowed down his stroking and began to caress her soft white breasts. *Let's see what kind of whore she really is,* he thought. *When she starts to go wild with pleasure she will drop this act.*

He leaned over to tease her nipples with his tongue and they

  Cecilia Tan

stood up obediently. He breathed hot in her ear and twirled his fingers around her hard nipples and tugged on them. She still clutched at the bed covers and did not look up. *Well, no matter.* Johnny Kwan slid his fingers along her stomach until he began to burrow in the crease between their bodies. Every time he pulled back he would slide his finger farther down into her cleft, seeking the right spot for her pleasure. She bit her lip as he found it, and he began to stroke it in time with his thrusts.

"Come on, little sister," he said to her, "come to Big Brother Kwan. Open your eyes, little sister, show me eyes."

Still she refused. He buried himself deep in her and slapped her across the face and she gasped with shock. "What the matter with you?"

She began to cry. Johnny Kwan turned her face toward him but did not pull out of her. He crooned. "Hey, hey, little sister. What wrong?" He'd been a drug-runner and a small-time hustler, but he'd never thought of himself as a bully. He stroked her cheek where he'd hit her.

She opened her eyes. They were a kaleidoscope of colors, brown, with flecks of green, red, eyes like Johnny Kwan had never seen before, not on a woman he was in bed with, anyway. The eyes were also full of tears.

He hugged her to him. "Hey, hey, okay, okay," he said as he rocked. He was still fucking her, after all. She wasn't sobbing and the tears stopped.

He held himself above her and made his strokes long and slow. "Okay now?"

She nodded and two American-sounding syllables came from her throat. "Uh huh."

Johnny Kwan tasted her neck again. "Sweet little sister," he breathed. Either she was an even better actress than he imagined, or her little act had gotten out of hand there. Well, she was all right now. He decided to slow down even more, to see if he could make it last longer. Maybe she had a few more surprises for him. "Why you cost so much, little sister?"

She blushed. "I . . . I don't know." Clearly a lie.

"Come on, you got something special? Madame of Summer Clouds wouldn't charge that much for any piece of tail, even *gwai lo* tail." He quoted the price back to her as if that might remind her which service she was to provide.

Her eyes went wide with recognition and her tears started again.

"Well?"

She went limp with resignation. "That old bitch, I can't believe she did that."

That was not what Johnny Kwan expected to hear. "Eh?"

The white girl grimaced. "You and I just paid for her ticket out of Hong Kong, my friend. That was just the amount she needed."

Another bought citizenship, he supposed. If only he'd been stealing this much from Willy Lim all along, he could be in Canada, too, by now. But he wasn't. And what had the girl said? "You, and I?"

The woman rolled her multicolored eyes and sighed. "She told me if I didn't . . . service you, that she'd make sure I lost my papers and couldn't stay. With the new government, I don't think the bribe system will work. So I agreed."

He must be hearing her wrong. She seemed to be implying that she wasn't a regular whore, and she wasn't planning on leaving with everyone else. Crooked Kwan was so puzzled he had to stop fucking for a minute while he thought about it.

"Why you here?" he finally asked.

"I just told you. Because Madame Wing blackmailed me."

"No, no, in Hong Kong."

"Business," she answered. Her mouth was set now, tough, and her voice rasped with sarcasm. "Haven't you heard? The PRC is the world's biggest fastest-growing economy. And Hong Kong is its new doorstep." She lay back with a tired sigh. "Let the old bitch go. I thought she was just trying to humiliate me, but no."

"But, why you? No other white girl?"

She shook her head. "Summer Clouds is where big-time white businessmen come to fuck gorgeous Asian women, not the other way around," she said, slowly as if he must be dim not to know it.

Johnny Kwan repeated his earlier question. "Why you here? Summer Clouds, I mean?"

"To meet big-time white businessmen."

"Ah." Johnny Kwan blinked. Life must look different through multicolor eyes. He still had some money left and could afford to lie low for a while longer. Willy Lim might be dead already in the squabbling, and when the dust cleared, there would be opportunities for Crooked Kwan, who had pledged no damaging allegiances. There would be money flowing through Hong Kong and he could drink from that river as well as any man, PRC or no.

She looked down at where he was still sunk into her and then back up at him. "Are you done?"

He did not smile. No, he decided, he was definitely not done.

The first porn flick I ever watched was with the first woman I ever dated. I know, I know, you'd think to look at me now, in my leathers perched on my bike, that I had been licking pussy all my life. But not so long ago I had just one foot out of the closet and was living a sheltered life. Mona taught me the right way to appreciate porn movies, among other things.

I met her at a bar. Not a dyke bar, just a regular, smoky, loud rock-and-roll club where my friend Derby's band was playing. I first caught sight of Mona in the back of the crowd, talking with some other women who hooted out comments toward the stage from time to time. Derby's band wasn't that popular so the crowd was thin. I wandered by, trying to get a good look without being too obvious. She wore all black, biker boots, with a loop of dog chain hanging from her neck. Now that I think of it, that's how most people in those bars dressed, but something about the way she stood or the look in her eyes tipped me off, I don't know—I wanted to go home with her the minute I saw her. It wouldn't have been the first time. I had been an avowed bisexual for years. That is to say it had been at least six years since I had told my parents I might bring someone of the same gender home for Thanksgiving. But I never had. I'd had my crushes, my flirtations, my passing acquaintances, but eventually I decided I just didn't know how to meet women.

I still hold that the only way to meet women is through Fate. And that night Fate was with me. I went backstage after the show to congratulate Derby and the band on another searing rendition of *The Brady Bunch* theme, and there she was. A friend of hers was a friend of Derby's, too, and that's just the way Fate works. Mona and I talked at the bar until they threw us out and then we ended up at her place.

Mona lived in a one-room studio apartment, which means that the kitchen and the bathroom are only ever a few convenient steps away from the bed. We spent all the next day in that bed, getting up only to answer the various calls of nature and to pay the pizza deliveryman. After the workout she gave me, it was heaven.

At first I hadn't been real keen to reveal that I'd never slept with a woman before. But after I found out that she'd never ridden a motorcycle, nothing was held back. She grinned evilly as she pressed me down into her futon. "I'll be *happy* to teach you everything I know. But you have to promise . . . "

"Promise what?" I was so eager to lose my virginity again it didn't matter to me what I had to promise.

"Promise that you'll do everything I say from now until sunrise."

I promised. She kissed me, her smile wide open, and hugged me. I remember thinking, *Wow, women are so curvy.* And she was, as she put it, "a big girl." I loved the shape of her hips, her jiggly thighs, her mounds of breasts, and couldn't wait to get my hands on them. "Strip for me," she said, lying back against the pillows.

I stood up, my striptease abbreviated by the fact I was wearing a one-piece catsuit and not a lot else. I stood in front of her naked, and turned myself around for her to see.

"Not bad, now come here."

She enveloped me in softness, her hands like silk all over my arms, my back, my breasts. She felt me over like a veterinarian would a cat. "I like your nipples," she said, circling them with her fingers so they stood at attention. "Nice and dark." She slid her hands down over my pubic hair. "Now let's see what you like." She searched over the hood of my clit, so hard it felt like it was burning. As her fingers slid down into the wetness her eyes lit up. I gasped and clutched at her as she slid two fingers deep in me. "Oooh, you like penetration . . ."

She wiped her hand on a bedside towel and pulled my mouth to her breast. She coached me very strictly on nipples. "No teeth to start with," she said. "And don't suck too hard. Now, about your tongue . . ." Near the end I bit her and she gasped. "Hey, you promised."

"I promised to do what you said, but not to not do what you didn't."

"Smart ass. For that you get the Het Chick Torture. Stay right where you are." She stood up on the mattress and clicked on the television set in the alcove at the foot of the bed.

"What's the 'Het Chick Torture'?" My stomach filled with butterflies.

"You'll see." She put a tape in the VCR. "Here are the rules. We're going to watch a het porn flick. Every time a man gets his cock sucked, you have to lick me. Every time a woman gets something in her cunt, you get something in yours. Every time someone comes, you have to come."

If I had to tell you the plot of the film today, I couldn't, but somehow it involved several men and women in various combinations in various rooms of a house. Maybe there was no plot and it just involved the same actors and actresses over and over. I was surprised; the film was much more comical than I had thought it would be. I had always heard, of course, that porn videos were dark, evil, misogynistic affairs of a seedy underworld. But then again I had always heard that lesbians were women who really wanted to be men, and we know how well that story holds up. So much for stereotypes and assumptions. This movie was silly; in one scene a guy getting sucked off by the pool fell into the water when he came.

And the women in this thing, I had to admit, weren't as bad as I had feared. Sure they all had bigger tits than their waists would suggest, but I decided I liked a lot of tits, especially Mona's. In fact, I decided that from their necks to their ankles, all the women in the film were damn hot. If only they'd lose the stupid shoes, the makeup, and the Farrah Fawcett hair. They looked like they were enjoying themselves, anyway.

In the first sex scene the blonde and her boyfriend did it in about ten different positions, none of which I had ever seen before, much less tried in the privacy of my own home. And they had no attention span, constantly switching from one position to another, with her sucking him in between. I started keeping my head near Mona's crotch since at unexpected moments the actress would suddenly start gobbling. I would bury my face in Mona's pubic hair, my tongue beginning to learn the way between her folds better each time. With my face there I couldn't watch the screen, and Mona had to say "Fingers," when it came time to put her fingers inside me. Then for a long time the couple fucked on the floor of their living room and I floated away while Mona pumped me and tickled my G-spot. We both laughed when the guy's roommate came in, and with a shrug of his shoulders, threw off his clothes and joined in. The actress began sucking him without climbing off of the other guy. "Put your own fingers in," Mona said, while pushing my head down between her knees.

I moaned while I licked her. I was close and it was hard not to make myself come. But I knew if I was going to come once for every orgasm in the film I had better save them up. Lucky for me while my head was down there the first guy came all over the actress's back. "Come now," Mona said, while luxuriating under my tongue. My nostrils filled with her salty smell; I came muffled by her muff.

The next big scene involved the women in the bathroom. Mona pulled me up next to her, telling me, "Watch this, you may learn something." The two women rubbed each other's breasts, sucked each other, fingered each other. Mona put her fingers inside me whenever one of the actresses did it to the other one, and told me to do it myself whenever they were doing themselves. Like the male/female couple, they switched positions and activities faster than a cable TV junkie switches channels. Now they were cunt to cunt, bumping and grinding against each other. "Will we do that?" I asked. "Maybe later, if you're good," she said, kissing me on the top of the head. Now they were sixty-nine, side by side. "That?" I asked. "Definitely," she answered. Both women came simultaneously and she made me come twice in a row, not letting me pause between to catch my breath or reset my clit.

"But why is the music so cheesy?" I asked later, during the big orgy scene in which every actor and actress was involved, and the cutting from one shot to another was getting fast and furious. I had come about seven or eight times by then. I was on top of her, my head between her legs, pausing in my licking to talk. She paused hers to say, "Who knows? If you wrote *good* soundtracks, would you sell them to porn flicks?"

"Ah," I agreed, letting my tongue fly. By the time the credits rolled we had forgotten the game and were just licking and fingering and sucking each other as much as we could.

Two days later I got a membership at the local video store. And I took Mona for her first motorcycle ride. Neither of us has ever been the same since.

 Cecilia Tan

I'd been playing bass with Sardonyx two months when I started to lust after Alan. Okay, no, you're right, that's a lie. I lusted after him the very first time I saw the band play live, at the Shake-n-Bake (what a dive) when they opened for Glimmer Twitch. Sadie, my ex-girlfriend, was "singing" for Glimmer at the time (more like howling and peeling off her clothes from time to time), and she'd begged me to come to the show. Not sure why, but she put me on the highly touted guest list (which at Shake-n-Bake means you only pay two dollars instead of the regular five-dollar cover—whoopee). So what the fuck, I went, I hung around backstage, and when Sardonyx went on, I went to see them out of sheer boredom.

They were hot. At the time they were all men. Alan thrashed his guitar and sang like a wild man, sometimes into the microphone, sometimes not. His coppery blond hair was just long enough to cover his eyes. Short, stocky Midge sat behind the drum kit like he was some kind of kick drum himself, steady and solid. Then there was the bass player, an asshole named George. *Chill out, girl,* I thought when I found myself clapping and hollering between songs. But I wanted more, more; they were so hot, so tight, it was the kind of rock I liked, with a heavy move in the bass line and buzzsaw guitar. Call me a postpunk purist.

When they came off the stage I had walked up to Alan and told him I thought it was a good show. He'd tossed me one of those condescending looks, you know, like I was a groupie but not fuckable material. *Well, fuck you, too,* is what I was thinking, but deep in the pit of my stomach I still wanted him between my legs. I put it out of my mind.

Two weeks later Sadie called to say that George had gotten so pissed drunk (again) at a gig that they'd tossed him out of the group and were looking for someone new. *Okay, fine,* I thought, *I'll audition, I'll see His-High-and-Mightiness again, what the fuck.* It'll probably just be the waste of an evening, but it wasn't like I had a lot else to do. I still had four months of unemployment coming to me after the layoff and couldn't spend every waking hour job hunting, could I? (Regardless of what I had to make the unemployment office believe . . .)

And bang, I got the gig. Alan didn't seem to remember me at all, just had some vague notion I was a friend of a friend of someone's and so he should be nice to me. We dove into rehearsals and getting me up to speed since Sardonyx had a pretty full schedule that summer.

Two months later, though, it started to get serious. We were doing a show at Randy's Lounge (don't laugh, it's a cheesy name, but it's actually one of the coolest places to play) and there was this electric tension in the room. We were rocking and I had almost forgotten to be nervous. See, I'd been in a couple of bands here and there, but never really played out very much, and suddenly I'm doing four or five shows a month and I'm petrified the other guys will figure out I'm not a "real" musician. Anyway, picture this: I'm laying down the beat, thick and heavy with Midge pumping the kick drum, and I slowly wake up to the realization that I'm humping the bass with every note, my thighs are humming, and I'm wet. And there's Alan, creeping toward me as he solos, grinding his hips while the notes soar . . .

At the time the thought I had was: *Maybe I need to get laid more than I need a job?* Well, I suppose I'm in the right line of work for getting laid, eh? Well, not exactly. When the set was over and the gear was packed, Alan and Midge had their pick of groupies—I wouldn't have minded taking one of those sweet chickadees home myself. Even Carl, Midge's cousin and our official roadie, got hit on. I got nothing much but a couple of leers from the unshaven, beer-bellied soundman. And it struck me (not for the first time) that there are some things that are cosmically unfair about being female.

That night I had a dream. There we were, on the stage, the same pumping rhythm throbbing in the background, and Alan was taking one step after another toward me. Suddenly I was naked except for my bass (a burnt cherry Rickenbacker and one of the few things I blew a couple of paychecks on back when I was employed in the real world), and lying on my back on the top of an amp, the thud from it making the throbbing in my clit stronger. Alan's pointing his guitar toward me now, and the head slides in up to the nut . . . *Wait,* I think, *is that a guitar or his anatomy?* and who named them that, anyway? . . . but it doesn't matter, in the dream, something is sliding up my cunt, filling me up, and it feels so good, so good. My hands keep playing, *thump, thump, thump,* but my legs are spread wide for him and I never want it to end.

Of course, I wake up, the dream dissolves, and I end up jamming my fingers into my panties and trying to picture someone else, Keanu Reeves, Winona Ryder, anybody other than Alan, but my brain keeps looping back to him and I think: *Shit, this is serious.*

Because you know all the twisted shit that can happen when people in the same band start sleeping together. It's like when housemates start doing it, or coworkers, or maybe it's the most like incest (I can't speak from personal experience on that one), where the people involved have all kinds of messy interconnections and there's more at stake than STDs. It's okay when people who are already sleeping together start a band (Wings? well, maybe that's not a great example) or move in together (that's called marriage). But when you're already in a band . . . it's the whole shitting where you sleep thing, I guess.

Two days later at rehearsal, I got to hear all about Midge's and Alan's masculine exploits. Whenever we took a break, we'd sit out on the concrete loading dock of the building where our cinder-block-and-acoustic-foam practice space was and smoke and yack. They'd gotten used to me being around and didn't try to couch their language or anything anymore. In the beginning Midge'd say "Fuck" and then he'd apologize to me, or Alan would trail off before finishing a sentence. Maybe that one time I'd grabbed my head and whined "Ooohh! my virgin eeeears!" they got the hint that they did not have to excuse their French. Even to Carl, now I was just like one of the guys. So I got to listen to every Technicolor detail of their amorous adventures. *Oh man,* I thought, *wouldn't it just be the greatest if I did bag one of those groupies, take her home, and rock her world?* But well, I probably still wouldn't be crude enough to tell these guys about it, shock value or no. It was one of the reasons Sadie had dumped me—she claimed I was too repressed, didn't know how to relax around sex. And well I'd countered: Maybe if I ever got some I'd get used to it. That had shut her up. Sadie could be mighty frigid even when she wasn't too depressed to feel anything at all.

Anyway. Much as the thought of taking home a groupie was entertaining, there was still the gnawing attraction I had for Alan. Okay, maybe Sadie was partly right, since there's a fine line between repressed and suppressed. I decided the wisest course was to shut off the hormones and ignore my libido. I had enough things to worry about, didn't I? We were working on a new tune Midge had written and he wanted to do this very funky rhythm-section thing. Now, while we worked out the parts, I felt Alan's eyes on me. *I will not flub this, I will not flub this* . . . But I still hadn't nailed the part by the end of the night and I went home feeling rather empty. I thought about calling Sadie—hearing about how fucked up her own life was often cheered me right up—but the twisted way her mind worked she'd probably be in bed with Alan before the week was out. Instead I lay on my futon in the dark, staring at the stripes from the blinds on the ceiling and running my fingers over the fretboard of the Rickenbacker.

You're kidding yourself you can keep this gig, I thought. *You could save yourself a lot of trouble if you went back to job hunting, quit the band, and then you could fuck Alan's brains out with a clear conscience.* But despite the seeming logic in that conclusion, I knew it wouldn't work out so neatly. I mean, if I quit Sardonyx, Alan'd probably never want to speak to me again, much less sleep with me. And then what? Well, I guess I'd have even more time for job hunting. It all seemed pretty pointless no matter how I looked at it.

You know, the subconscious doesn't stop rolling because the rest of the brain got its knickers in a twist. I fell asleep and had another one of those dreams. In this one, I'm in a very dark enclosed space and there's this kind of constant low-level hum . . . my mind starts weaving explanations—this is a tour bus I'm sleeping in—and suddenly I'm huddled next to somebody. My brain conveniently fills in Alan. He's pressed against me and his breath is warm as his fingers dig through the covers and clothes to slide across my stomach. Two fingers are pushing their way down into my panties, down between the folds of my slit, down into the crease that became instantly wet as soon as I felt where those fingers were going. He slips them inside me and begins fucking me like that, all the while his mouth near my ear, the dark closeness of the space all around, I'm suffocating deliciously in sensation. This is what dreams are like.

The next morning I think to myself: *That's two heavy pene-*

tration dreams in a row. Maybe I should buy myself a dildo?
No, wait: I remind myself that I've decided to forget about sex
and I push it to the back of my mind.

If I were an accountant or a chef or a postal worker (or a cler-
ical worker, which is what I was before the layoff) this plan
might have worked. Ignore your lust and the waiter/mail car-
rier/cute guy in the next cubicle you have the hots for will
eventually fade to the background. But in rock and roll, everything you do is sex. Every song you sing is about sex (or death,
or both), every move you make is sex. The words *rock and roll*
even mean, literally, in the old slang they came from, "sex."
This lust I had for Alan was sort of always there, and the
dreams came pretty often for the next month or so.

Toward the end of the summer Warren, our sleazoid booking agent, set up a bunch of dates for us to play some bars and
rock clubs in upstate New York. Midge, being a drummer with
a lot of shit to lug around, had a van, so we three piled into it
with all our gear and took off for Syracuse. Or was it Albany?
Van like that, two people sit up front and one in the back. I lay
down in the back and slept most of the way to where we were
going for that first gig.

Let me tell you something about booking agents: They don't
give a fuck. They aren't the ones who have to put up with their
great planning jobs ("Oh come on, it isn't that far to Rochester."
"Yeah, from Canada!"); their money-saving ideas ("It's good
weather for camping"); or their lameness when dealing with
club managers ("Nah, they don't need much. How much ya
got?"). Warren had set us up in a bunch of college towns while
school was out of session and the club owners hadn't lifted a finger to promote the shows. That first night we played for twenty
people and then slept at a campground where the running
water wasn't running. Midge had brought a little dome tent,
barely big enough for two, then insisted that Alan and I sleep in
it. He wanted to spend the night in the van, paranoid that it

Cecilia Tan

and/or our gear might get ripped off by grizzly bears hungry to start a power trio. Alan just shrugged and crawled into the tent. I crawled in after him and pretended to go to sleep. Lying there next to him, I couldn't quite get comfortable (okay, that's an understatement). We were both sweaty from the show, the ground was lumpy and uneven under me, the round tent was the wrong shape for anyone to sleep in much less the gangly length of Alan, and he had curled into a ball, leaving me a crescent-moon-shaped sliver to lie in. So I lay there for a long time, breathing in the sweet scent of his sweat, curled around him but trying really, really hard not to touch him. In my mind, I played fantasies that only made it worse: He was faking it, too, and would suddenly roll over and confess his own suppressed lust for my gorgeous body; or, he would wake up from an erotic dream and, too horny to go back to sleep, would beg me to help him . . . It was another one of those cosmically unfair situations. Playing a show, even a kind of lame one like that night, is always like a kind of foreplay. It gets the juices pumping. Does anybody really not get that connection? Famous rock stars don't fuck only because pussy gets thrown at them. They're primed for it. So, end result? I spent most of the night wallowing in a pool of hormones and frustration. Weird thing is, the next day, I swear he got friendlier—more familiar, putting his hand on my shoulder, shit like that. And onstage, he seemed to spend more time in my orbit, playing back against back, sharing my mike.

Not that the ten people who showed up to see us cared all that much. The club refused to pay us. I talked Midge into letting us rotate who slept in the van, and he and Alan took the tent. After the third show, where there was a sizable (okay, thirty-five people) but openly hostile crowd, we got paid fifty dollars, and the owner tried to claim that our mike stands and cords were his. Midge and I were all for packing it in, canceling the other three dates, and going home where we could sleep in our own beds, have hot showers, things like that. But Alan wouldn't hear of it. "Oh, come *on*," he said. "Why did we bother to come out here? This is good for us." Apparently the adulation of even a minuscule number of people was enough for Alan. I was surprised a little by this fact. Camping out hadn't made for any groupie liaisons and I'd thought the lack of nookie would have made him more cranky than any of us. But he rallied us to persevere. The next date was Ithaca.

We arrived to find the bar where we were scheduled to play closed. Not closed permanently, just CLOSED WEDNESDAYS, as the sign on the door read.

"Is it Wednesday?" Alan said, standing there with his hands on his hips. "Is it fucking Wednesday?"

"It is," I assured him, "Wednesday."

"This is just fucking great." He kicked the door with an unsatisfying thump. "Now what?"

Midge folded his arms. "I say we find a liquor store, go to a motel with hot running water, and get rip-roaring drunk."

It seemed like the rock-and-roll thing to do. I suggested one modification to the plan once we were back in the van: that we find and pay for the motel first before we spent all our money on booze. In the end we had about thirty dollars we could blow and still have money for gas. We stocked up on hard cider, Pete's Wicked, Southern Comfort, and Mad Dog.

You can guess what happened next, right? I mean, I wouldn't have bothered to go through all this buildup if there wasn't some payoff, yes? We got drunk first, of course, which is everyone's excuse for the fuck they might regret or want to pretend to forget. Alan and I on one bed, Midge on the other, we drank and watched cable TV, Alan flipping between MTV and a slick, high-budget porn movie where hairless-pussied starlets were being fucked in a fountain. Sometimes it was hard to tell which channel was which. I was fascinated by the porn, though. I hadn't actually slept with a man for two years or so and I'd forgotten what a naked, erect penis looked like.

 194   *Cecilia Tan*

At one point I realized Alan was looking at me.

"What?"

He gave a little smirk. "You're so . . . into this. Your eyes are bugging out of your head."

I probably blushed but I tried not to. "Give me a break," I said. "Not everyone's such a pervert that this stuff is commonplace." My eyes returned to the screen where yet another erection was being revealed in all its glory as an actor doffed his briefs. *And straight men watch this?* I thought to myself. *Amazing.* "So tell me," I said, "why do guys always lie about their penis size?"

Alan snorted. "Guys don't always lie. Sometimes they exaggerate."

"Okay, but when they say 'eight inches' where do they measure from?"

Midge laughed.

Alan thought about it for a moment. "Well, from the base."

"Yeah, but what do you mean by base? Is that on top of it? Or do they inflate the figures by counting from the balls or what? It's still a lie."

"You know," Alan said seriously, "I don't think there's been a lot of development of a scientific method of dick measure."

"Well, where do *you* measure from?" I was definitely drunk or I'd never have said anything like that. Would I?

Alan scooted close to the TV and pointed with his finger to the actor humping on the screen. His finger moved back and forth as the guy's hips thrust back and forth with almost blurring speed. "See, from here."

"No. There's too much movement."

Alan frowned. "Look, it isn't that hard to figure out. If you really want to get technical about it, every guy should have to give more than one number. Length from the top, length from the base of the balls . . . "

"Don't forget width," I said. "How about total volume?"

"Yeah, whatever. I mean, I'm six inches measuring from the top, which is like nine inches from the underside, you know? So I could just say 'nine inches' and not qualify that and who's going to know? That's what guys do."

"No way are you nine inches," I said.

"Yes I am."

"No, you're not," I challenged. "You're just lying like all the rest of them."

He stood up. "Okay, all right. I'm sick of women making male-bashing statements like 'Guys always lie about their dick size.'" And he began unzipping his jeans. I didn't think he'd really do it, but he showed no signs of stopping. I felt like I should say something to stop him, but I didn't really want him to stop.

Midge snickered but didn't say anything.

Alan pushed down his briefs to reveal a beautiful erection. I don't know how else to describe it. Neatly circumcised, his cock curved upward at a graceful angle and had a certain symmetry about it. The sight of it made my mouth water and my loins ache. I thought about all the dreams where his fingers, his guitar, or unseen appendages fucked me in the dark. Now I could see the tool for the job and I wanted it.

"See?" he said. He measured off the length on the top with his fingers. "On top, this long. On the bottom . . ." he reached between his legs, "this long." And held his hands up for comparison.

Midge eyed him critically. "Well, that's not quite nine inches."

"But it's close. This isn't an accurate measurement, asshole."

All right, I'd had enough. I'd tortured myself long enough. And I was drunk enough. I reached a hand to the shaft pointing toward me and gripped it gently in my fingers. It felt sweet hard, rigid but velvety, and I tugged him closer to me. "Mind if I borrow it for a while?"

Alan was staring down at me now like I was a total stranger.

Which, in a way, I suppose I was. His gaze flickered from my face to his cock sheathed in my hand. Then he turned to look at Midge.

Midge got up. "Three's a crowd," he said, and went out into the hallway.

As soon as the door closed, Alan took my hand off his cock and pushed me slowly but firmly back onto the bed. He climbed on top of me, his cock pressing hard against my pubis, and said. "Okay, you want me? I only do it one way."

"What do you mean?"

"I mean, I only do it like this. You lie where you are and let me do the shopping. That's the way I like it, that's the way we're going to play it, okay?"

"Okay," I said, not sure why he was so particular about this. But what the hey, I'd had lovers who liked to pretend they were dogs while they fucked. This was no big deal.

He started by stripping off my clothes. When I tried to help he held me still with one hand and pulled at the clothes with the other until I gave up and let him strip me. Then he lifted my knees and spread my thighs wide.

"Oh, Sandra, you've got a nice, dripping pussy here." He ran his hands down my thighs but did not touch my cunt. I thrust my hips up a little at him, wanting to feel what his fingers would really feel like down there, but he tsked and let my legs drop. "First things first." He lay down the length of me, still wearing his T-shirt, and kissed me on the lips. After a few tentative kisses, he let his tongue out and explored around the inside of my mouth. After a few minutes of that, while he continued French-kissing me, one of his hands strayed to my breasts.

I figured it out. It reminded me uncannily of my first real sexual experience with a boy when I was sixteen, on a school ski trip. I had lain there while he undressed me and did all the work, starting at first base and working his way along until eventually he had his fingers up my cunt. At that point I dared to touch his penis and he had come, which dampened his spirit of exploration and we had stopped there and never spoke to each other again. I wondered if Alan had started out with this pattern, too, and just never deviated from it? He was so earnest about it, this routine. I imagined him using it on groupie after groupie . . . it probably worked like a charm.

He fondled my breasts for a long time, first with one hand, then he stopped kissing me and used two hands while he looked lovingly at what he was holding. He kneaded them like soft dough and then flicked his thumbs over my nipples until they hardened and I gasped. "Ah, that's good," he murmured as he began to suck on the hard buds. While he sucked, his fingers began to stray again, this time to my cunt.

I spread my legs for him and he stroked back and forth with the palm of his hand, dragging it over my clit and labia, the whole pubic area. I suppose that way he figured he couldn't miss. And he began to talk more. "Oh yeah, baby, nice and wet for me, nice and hot for me." He narrowed his hand to one finger sawing at my slit, then crooked the end of it into my hole. He ran his finger around in a circle and I moaned. "You want my cock, don't you."

"Yes."

He got up on his knees but kept fingering me. "Look at me. Look at it."

As I do believe I mentioned, it was easy to worship this cock. It was redder now, and I wanted to touch it, to lick it, to help me get ready for having it inside me. His eyes told me to stay down.

His finger made deeper circles. "You're tight, so tight, Sandra. Are you sure you can take this?"

I didn't know if that was a rhetorical question or a real one so I stayed still and didn't answer.

"You sure you want this?"

Okay, that was a real one. "Yes."

"All of it?"

"Yes."

"All six or nine inches of it?"

Quit paraphrasing Robert Plant and put it in me, I thought. "Yes."

He pulled his finger out and smeared the cockhead with my vaginal fluid. Then he got off the bed for a moment and I thought: *Oh, how thoughtful.* He was putting on a condom. One less thing for me to worry about.

He returned to kneeling between my legs. If anything, his cock looked bigger now that he'd manipulated the rubber into place. He pressed the head against my cunt and rubbed it back and forth there, over my clit, smearing my juices around. Then he sank in about a half an inch. "Okay, Sandra, convince me."

"What?"

"I said, 'convince me.' This is what I say to every girl I fuck. I don't go any further than this until I hear it from you that you want me to. That you are absolutely sure you want to go through with this. That there is no doubt in your mind that you do not want me to stop right now and forget about the whole thing."

I put a hand on his chest and stroked him, marveling at how he could hold himself up like that. Was it just that I was drunk, or was he kind of twisted? He'd wanted me to lie there and not even move while he had his way with me, until now, when he was insisting he wouldn't go any further unless I convinced him to. "Is this some kind of anti-date-rape strategy?" I asked.

His voice returned to normal for a moment. "Exactly. You think I don't worry about whether some chick I pick up at a show is going to try to hit me with a lawsuit in the morning? I ain't giving her STDs, my sperm, or an excuse to complain." Now his arms started to shake a little and he dropped back into his husky seducer voice. "So if you want it, now's your chance."

"I want it."

"But do you really want it? Or are you just horny?"

"I really want it."

"You want this long pole of man meat inside you?"

"Yes!"

"Deep inside, grinding around, sliding in and out, pinning you to the bed, no mercy until I'm satisfied?"

"Yes! Yes!" I tried to pull him down onto me. He held off for a second, but I wrapped my legs around him and pulled myself another inch onto him. He let his weight drop then and as I sank back into the mattress he sank into me. True to his word, he began to grind. It was a tight fit, but I didn't mind.

"Oh, Sandra," he said. "I never imagined you had such a hot little cunt. Oh, I would have been fucking you since day one if I knew you were this good."

I didn't answer that.

"Yeah, mmm. I always thought you were a dyke, because of Sadie, you know? Are you a dyke? Did I convert you?"

I pursed my lips. "No, you didn't convert me. I slept with men before. Just not . . ." I sucked in my breath as he doubled his speed, "not in a long time."

He pressed my knees up toward my chest and began slicking in and out fast, slapping our bodies together on the springy bed. "Oh yeah, you like that don't you."

My voice was kind of quavery as I said, "As a matter of fact, I do. If you keep it up, I'll probably even come from it."

"Oh, baby, you'll come. Don't worry, you'll come."

He was right about that. I didn't even have to sneak a hand down to twiddle my clit. The angle and the rhythm and the speed and the duration all worked together such that some time later, after we were both completely soaked in sweat and I began to wonder if he really could keep it up long enough . . . I began to scream. I mean really screech. The orgasm had been building for so long, and my breathing had gotten so hard, screaming just seemed like the natural thing to do. And somewhere in the midst of all the noise I was making, he came, too.

I blanked out for a while then, blissed out, lying there in a wet, happy heap. I forgot who we were, where we were. It wasn't until he got up to throw the condom away and said, "I wonder where Midge got to?" that I remembered: *Oh shit, I just slept with a bandmate.*

Alan seemed to remember it, too. He came back and sat down. "This isn't going to turn into a psychodrama, is it?"

"I hope not." We eyed each other, wary now.

"You gotta make a choice, Sandra," he told me. "Now you've had a taste of it. You gotta decide if you are going to be a cock worshiper or if you're going to be on the other side."

"What do you mean?"

"I mean, you're either a groupie or you're on the stage. Can't be both. If you're a groupie, I can't respect you anymore, can't work with you anymore."

You are really twisted, I thought, but what he was saying kind of made some sense. "You mean, after tonight, you'll still respect me in the morning?"

"Hell yeah," he said. "After all, we're both drunk."

"Right," I said. "Okay. Where are we playing tomorrow? Rochester? We better get some sleep, bud. That's a long drive."

He nodded. He climbed into the other bed (Midge never did come back—he'd fallen asleep in the van), and that was the end of that. I didn't have any more dreams about him, he never propositioned me, and Midge never mentioned it. I still don't get laid anywhere near as often as they do, but what the fuck, it's a living.

The Other Half Lives

VII

I mentioned earlier that I considered myself somewhere between female-identified and male-identified. That's maybe a fancy way to say I'm a tomboy who never grew up, and that I have been attracted to, and attractive to, people of all genders and identifications. There's also the fact that in fiction I can be anyone, and I won't limit myself to one erotic milieu. These three stories are set within the gay male subculture. "Jean-Michel & Juno" is a period piece, from the days back when *The Advocate* was the only gay-oriented publication I could get my hands on, and when Greenwich Village was the one place I had ever been where I had seen people openly out. "Blood Ties" and "Whipmaster" come forward in time and in my life to the sub-subculture I currently spend much of my time in, the gay male leather scene. There have been plenty of scholarly books and political articles written about the compunction of women to write with gay male voices, both pro and con, and I have never decided for myself what to think about them. I writes what I writes, characters come alive for me, and the stories emerge. On the one hand, I must argue that if every narrator in every story were *me*, the stories would be dulled by sameness. Now that I think about it, every narrator *is* me. But I am not always the same.

Jean-Michel rolls over in bed. The maneuver must be done with care, as the bed is so narrow he has fallen out more than once. Jean-Michel yawns and stretches, as best he can, feeling languid and warm. His partner has long since gone, but he basks in the afterglow, brushing the hairs on his stomach with his fingertips while he remembers the evening in greater detail. He picks up the red telephone by his head and dials his sister.

"Hello?"

"Bon jour."

"Mee-shay," she says. "I am just on my way out. How are you?"

"Fine. I am still in bed."

"Lazy. You had a date last night, didn't you."

He smiles, pressing his hand against his stomach. "Let me tell you about it. I met her in the hospital."

"Did you get the bandages off your foot?"

"Yes, yes, the cast is off. Now be quiet and let me tell." He closes his eyes, draws a deep breath, and speaks. "Her skin was white as pearl, white but with a glow underneath, and her hair was black like the feathers of a raven. She spoke so quietly to me, and touched me so gently, I just knew I had to bring her home with me."

"She was your nurse?"

"Yes. She took to me like a fish to the sea, drink-

ing me in. She slept here last night. I am exhausted!" Jean-Michel rolls over with the telephone, hugging the dark blue sheets.

"You are a liar. Tell me what was *his* name, really."

He replies, "Sherrie," but the pause has been long enough that Amanda knows it is a bluff.

"Why do you even bother to lie to me, Mee-shay. You do not delude me. You delude yourself." She moves the phone from one ear to the other. "You listen to me. Mother would turn over in her grave if she could see you now. I kept your secret only because I thought the news would kill her . . . "

Jean-Michel puts the pillow over his head, reducing Amanda's voice to a tinny squeak. When he hears a moment of silence he sits up and talks to the receiver. "Tell me why we came to this country."

"You are an idiot. I have to go to meet a client now. You go back to your fantasies and—" Before she can say more, Jean-Michel has hung up.

He stands in the narrow space between his bed and desk. The desk has had many coats of paint in its lifetime, the latest one white, the color of paper. A late-model Selectric typewriter sits next to a plastic cup full of pens and pencils and other elongated objects that have found a home there—markers, crayons, chopsticks, things of unknown use and origin. When Jean-Michel touches the wall above the desk with his hand, he can reach the wall the bed is against with his good foot. From the wardrobe next to the desk he takes a robe and hobbles to the kitchen to make some tea.

He picks up the sturdy cane they gave him at the hospital. Just two or three weeks with the cane, they said, and you should be walking fine again. He smiles into the mirror, leaning on the cane with his head at a rakish angle. The ankle is still stiff from the injury and the time spent in plaster, but the cane looks good. He has put on loose canvas pants and a white shirt

 Cecilia Tan

with long sleeves. He twirls the cane. He lunges with it. He glances to see if it is raining and decides to take the cane for a spin.

He browses through the racks at the large newsstand on the corner. Many people are standing in the aisles, reading science magazines, literary journals, comic books, newspapers from far-away places. While he appreciates the owner's leniency, it makes it difficult to see the racks. He looks for *The Advocate*. He has never read it before; he has never dared to buy it. But it is time to look for new markets to write for, and he justifies his decision to buy it that way. He spots one copy on the rack one aisle over.

From between two overcoats, a small plain hand reaches for the only copy there. Curious, he traces the arm back to the face. At first he thinks it is a boy, with short black hair, coarse like an Oriental's and cut bluntly. But as the rest of the body steps between the businessmen, Jean-Michel knows it is a girl. A woman, rather, wearing oversize canvas pants like his and an open suit jacket. He wonders if she is a student at New York University. She catches him looking at her, then, and winks.

She starts toward him. He notices she is also carrying *The Village Voice,* and another magazine under it. "Did you want this?" she says, holding up the magazine with a beefy, bare-chested blond leering from its cover. He cannot answer. He is too conscious of the people filling the aisle, of the man at the cash register looking down over him, of the volume of her voice.

As she comes closer it softens. "If you really want it I'll give it to you." She smirks. "But if you're just interested in the pictures, *Playgirl* is much better this month."

He opens his mouth but still hasn't thought of something to say. He can't. She laughs. "Don't be embarrassed. I'll buy it for you if you want."

"No, that's all right." He eyes the door. "I'm a writer and I was curious—"

"Okay, okay, I won't hassle you about it. I can always borrow a copy." She jerks her head toward the high counter where a clerk is perched looking for shoplifters. Magazines in hand, she works her way through the crowd and Jean-Michel follows. Her eyes barely see over the tall countertop when she is on tiptoe. She must be just over five feet tall, he thinks. She pays for all of the magazines, takes them in a bag, and then beckons for him to come outside.

"Here you go." She takes her purchases from the bag and hands it to him with *The Advocate* inside. She pats the bag. "Since you are still sensitive about that sort of thing . . . "

"Thank you." He cannot take his eyes away from hers. She has an uncanny stare. "How much do I owe you?"

"Oh, don't worry about it." She makes a loose-wristed motion. "But if you really feel indebted you could take me to lunch."

Her smile is open and friendly. Intrigued, he nods. "Very well, lunch it is. What do you eat?"

"Anything. What is your name?"

"Jean-Michel."

"That is very beautiful." She falls silent a moment before speaking again. "I am Juno." She offers him her arm, and they walk in search of lunch, a bit slowly because of the cane.

Juno takes him to a place called Phebe's in the East Village, where she seems to know all of the waitresses and waiters. "Quite a few of them are gay, you know," she says, sipping a straight club soda through a stir stick.

"That's very interesting." He cannot figure what she is driving at.

She crosses over to his side of the table and they look at the magazines together. He has never seen the inside of a *Playgirl*

before. Where do they find all these dark-skinned men with blue eyes? Jean-Michel wonders aloud. She points out that they could be colored contact lenses.

"But it's nice to fantasize, isn't it?"

"Yes." Briefly he wonders what Amanda would say if she saw him lunching with a woman and poring over glossy photos of naked men. Juno picks out Mr. March as her favorite. He can feel the strain of an erection stirring in his groin.

Juno tells him about her friends. The waitress who serves them is named Judy, and she is also a poet. She helps out at the WOW Café, a performance space for women just around the corner. The bartender's name is Russell, but he is engaged to another man, Juno says, so Jean-Michel shouldn't even think about him. He has to laugh. She says the things that he will not. She asks him very few questions, almost, he thinks, as if she already knew all about him.

"When I was a child," she says, "my mother used to put a *pink* bow in my hair and take me for walks in the park. And people would bend down to the stroller and say, 'Oh, what a cute little boy!' As an infant, of course, I didn't notice it much. Later I grew to like it. I always kept my hair short, since it would mat into terrible knots and I would scream and scream while my mom tried to brush them out. Ugh, thank God for creme rinse!"

She has him smiling and laughing all through the meal. "Men's clothes fit me better, too. Except for shoes, of course. If it weren't for my feet, I'd say I would have made a pretty good boy. Eh?"

He nods.

She cocks her head. "Jean-Michel, do you think I would have been a good-looking boy?"

"You would have been a very sexy boy, Juno."

She smiles, quiet for a moment. Then, she sits back, and smirks. "I bet Mr. March is gay." Before he knows it, the subject has changed. She smooths his light-brown waves of hair with her small hand. In the front there are streaks of blond from the sun. She tugs lightly on his forelock and it covers his left eye. "Have you always had your hair this way?"

"I have been letting it grow since we came to America."

"We?" For a moment her eyes are guarded.

"My sister and I. We came a few months ago. She is living uptown with her American fiancé." He feels goosebumps as she moves her hand up the nape of his neck, combing the hair out of his collar with her fingertips.

"If you want to get it cut, I can recommend some places to you." Her voice is the quietest it has been all afternoon. "Or, I can do it myself." He cannot take his eyes away from hers. He is frozen. He wants to protest, but can't help but think he must be imagining this come on. He tries to think back to when it began, to prove to himself it is just his imagination. But it is hard to think of anything other than the wad of flesh in his canvas pants and the round face of a boy in front of him.

"So, how did you hurt your foot?" She is spooning gourmet ice cream into her mouth, pausing only to chew the almonds.

He chuckles. "Moving in to my apartment. There is a step which is higher than the others, and I tripped on it and fell down the stairs. That was before the elevator was fixed." He points east with the cane. "The cast was just removed yesterday over at Beth Israel." From where they are seated in the park, the round shape of the hospital building is not visible.

Juno shoos away pigeons with her foot. "Does it hurt?"

"No. It would if I twisted it, though."

A smirk lifts her cheeks. "Want to go uptown, then?"

Jean-Michel thinks for a moment. "Where, uptown?"

"Anywhere!"

She takes him first to Thirty-fourth Street on the subway. She speaks Spanish to the vendors selling toy birds, sunglasses, hats. She buys a cabbie hat. She shows him the vast outside of Macy's and swears she has never bought anything in it. She puts a token in his hand and they ride the bus farther up, to Trump Tower, where pieces of chocolate are sold for more than the price of their entire lunch. He offers to buy some for her, but she insists that the chocolate is better at another place she knows, and cheaper, too. She talks a carriage driver she knows into taking them through Central Park.

After dark, they take the bus back down to the East Village. Jean-Michel has some trouble maneuvering with the cane at first, trying to hang on to a pole and it at the same time, but a few blocks later more seats become free and he sits. Juno is silent in the bus, not meeting the eyes of the other passengers.

Jean-Michel worries a bit. In the hours he has known her, she has never been so quiet or withdrawn. He follows her off the bus at St. Mark's Place and walks with her a block east before speaking. "Juno? Do you feel all right?"

She stops walking, faces him. "I don't know what to do."

"What do you mean?"

She chews her bottom lip. "I—" She looks around the street.

"Do you want to go home? Do you want to tell me something?"

"Yes. Yes, please." She jerks her chin forward, indicating he should lead the way.

He walks her to his apartment. They ride the cage elevator in silence. He wishes he had a secondhand sofa to sit her on, but there is no furniture yet but his bed and his desk. He puts her at the edge of the bed and leans the cane and himself against the desk gently, as if to make a loud sound might frighten her away. "Please tell me what's wrong."

She looks at him. He feels her appraisal of his figure, her eyes lingering over his hips, his hands, his chest, before she looks into his eyes. "Jean-Michel," she begins. "I'm confused. I'm mixed up. I don't know what I want."

He waits for her to say more, encouraging her by squatting down in front of her. His ankle makes a small sound, but holds.

"You are a very nice person," she says. "You could be my friend."

"I am your friend." He cannot figure what she is driving at.

"Yes, you are my friend. I am your friend, too." She reaches with both hands toward him. She holds his head behind his ears. "But— " She drops her hands and closes her eyes.

Jean-Michel thinks of the restaurant and feels something in the pit of his stomach move, a dull throbbing down below. "Juno," he says, hoping she will open her eyes again, "I have been with women before in my life. I think you are very . . . "

She stiffens, clenching her eyes. "No. You don't understand."

"Are you afraid that if I love you, that I will not like you?" The palms of his hands grow hot and he wants to touch her.

"Yes. And no." She fixes her gaze in the middle of his chest. "I want to be friends. That's true." She lets out another slow breath. "And I want you." Another breath. "But I want you to . . ." She whispers the rest and he cannot hear it. She rolls over onto her side, the bed creaking as she moves.

"Juno?" He moves to the floor to sit by her head. He grasps her hand. "Tell me?"

She pulls his ear to her mouth. "I want to be your boy." Unable to move, she does not let go.

Her fear paralyzes him for only a moment. Then he kisses her ear, wets it with his tongue. She begins to uncurl, peers at him, questioning.

"And I thought I had a difficult time, sometimes," he says, smoothing her hair back from her face. He sits back on his heels and his erection shifts.

She moves onto the floor next to him, straightens the flannel hat on her head. "Do you want me?"

He pauses for a moment, while some overly sensible part of

his brain tries to stop him on principle. "Yes." He touches her lips with his fingers. "Don't be ashamed. I'm not." I am not, he tells himself. He tastes the back of her neck and the desire to throw her down on her stomach grows.

"Don't be afraid to hurt me," she whispers.

He reaches around her waist from behind and slips the wide pants off her narrow hips. He holds her close and feels her heart beating like a hummingbird's. "Come here." The jacket and shirt slip off, too, and he tosses them with his own shirt up onto the bed. The skin of her back is smooth as he runs his hands down from her shoulders to her buttocks. "Relax. Relax." Her back, her narrow fine back, reminds him of Jean-Pierre, when they were both fourteen and summered together with their families. He tells her so with a whisper into her ear. "He had hair like yours, black and feathery, and his grandmama would never let him out into the sun, so we spent hours and hours in the attic of her summerhouse . . ." He presses her against the carpet in the small space between the bed and the desk and the hat falls away. As he presses his bare skin to hers, he kneads her shoulders. The tip of his penis has pushed out of his waistband.

"We would sit in the attic and make ourselves hard. And I would always let him when he would want to come inside me." He runs his hands down that back again, holding her hips. She lets out a small gasp. "But when it would be my turn to come in him, he would sometimes get scared." He strokes her hairless buttocks. "And I would whisper to him 'Jean-Pierre, Jean-Pierre, do not be afraid. It is only fair that you do your manly duty.'" She shivers, when she feels his naked legs against hers. "And though he would moan and whimper, he would never fight me."

A terrific shudder wracks her small body as she anticipates his entry. "Don't wait," she whispers. Her voice is low and hoarse. "Take me."

He wonders if there is another woman like this in the world, with a lonely boy trapped inside. "As you give yourself to me," he says, and pushes against her tailbone. The tip is becoming slick and he spits into his hand and helps it along. He spreads her buttocks and uses the tip of his tongue to moisten the way. And then he presses the head against the tightness there, and presses, holding her firm by the hips, and presses, until the flesh begins to give, and he nearly falls forward into her.

She claws at the carpet and opens her mouth but makes no sound.

"*Oui,* my darling boy," he says, his voice coming rough through his own fast breaths, as he feels like his whole body is sinking as he penetrates her, "*oui,* my sweet one." He moves his grip to her shoulders as he moves in and out of her. "Jean-Pierre always said that it hurt, but I suspect that he liked it that way best."

"I am sure," she gasps a bit as she speaks, "that he did." She presses her face to the carpet and closes her eyes, but not too tight. As his rhythm builds she twitches a bit, and seems lost in it.

He is beginning to lose himself, too. It is only when his ankle begins to throb that he thinks perhaps he must end this. "Jean-Pierre," he whispers, "Jean-Pierre, do you remember how you used to make it so tight . . . ?"

"I do."

And then there is nothing to hold him back from a final frenzied set of thrusts. He spends himself with a guttural cry as he presses his cheek to the smoothness of her back.

A minute or so later, he helps her into the bed and they lie together, soaking up each other's sweat. "What else can I do for you?" he asks, trying to think of an adequate way to reciprocate.

"Nothing," she murmurs, a wide satisfied smile on her face. "I'm full."

 Cecilia Tan

"Amanda?" He presses the receiver to his ear with his shoulder.

"Yes, Miche' is that you? How are you?"

"I'm fine. I met someone I think you would like to meet."

Amanda snorts. "Don't tell me, let me guess. She has black hair and fair skin."

"You are right so far."

"Come, now, Jean-Michel, when are you going to get tired of— "

"Her name is Juno. She is right here." She puts her hand over her mouth, trying to keep from laughing aloud. Jean-Michel continues: "Would you like to know more about her?"

"Yes, yes, for the sake of your future as a romance novel writer. Tell me about this ravishing beauty."

He looks her over with a critical eye. "Well, first of all, she is very short. Five feet and five inches. And she wears no makeup. Her bright eyes and smiling lips need none. On her hands are no rings, just short round trimmed nails, and smooth skin. As you said before, her hair is black, and is shorter than mine."

"Delightful." Amanda applauds. "So, this is your ideal lover? She sounds like a boy."

"Thank you," says Juno into the receiver, ready to burst from contained laughter. "Let's do lunch sometime." That sets him to laughing, and together they hang up the phone.

Tim listened to his leather creak as he settled back against the bar and took a better look at the men around him. This was one of those nights when he could taste the smoke of the cigar several feet away, smell the sweat and musky cologne of the man with his back to him, see each face clearly in the dim haze of the bar. The bottle was cool and damp in his hand, though he'd lost interest in the beer inside it. Every pore was open and aching for someone, something . . .

He hated nights like this sometimes, when he was alone or he let himself feel sick about it. Too much like some nights in his childhood in the mountains, when he'd sneak out of his bed and run through the dark woods because he felt like he'd go crazy if he didn't, straining to reach something, touch something that was so needed but so far away. He'd always ended up crying alone in his bed, silently, so his father wouldn't hear. His father would have made some kind of religious pronouncement about it, Tim was sure, and sent him to the monastery up the road for "cleansing." But now Tim thought he knew what it was he needed, what it was he had wanted all along: adulthood, and the satisfaction that it brought, to be among other men like him, to touch and connect and be with someone else. Even if it was just to suck or get sucked off by a nameless

216   *Cecilia Tan*

stranger in a dark alley—some nights that was enough, but not tonight. Tonight was one of the strong nights, he felt the tug and need deep in his gut and knew he wanted more: sex and power and pain.

The bar was beginning to fill up with men, the black leather creaking all around him. Somewhere here there had to be a man who could handle Tim, or so Tim hoped. Some topman who could cage him and control him and fuck him silly all at once. More than once he thought he saw a tall dark fellow with a sleek ponytail looking at him, but every time he tried to make eye contact the man had his head bent toward the surly blond boy next to him. *Wasting my time,* Tim thought. *He's already got one like me.*

Some hours later though, Tim found himself still in the bar, frustration making him edgy and desperation turning him sour. He'd thought maybe that guy Mark would have been ready for another go. But he'd just laughed and walked away with a wave of his hand before Tim even had a chance to say hello. *Wimp,* Tim thought. *And I'd thought he had balls.* Maybe it was getting to be time to move on to a new city again, even though nothing terribly bad had happened here yet . . .

The blond boy was looking at him. Tim stared back in curiosity. The dark top was nowhere in sight now and the boy looked a little lost. His hair curled slightly in front and his chest was well shaped under his black harness. The boy started making his way through the crowd toward Tim. Tim met him halfway, by the pool table. The hard clack of one ball against another seemed to echo in his skull as Tim asked, "Why are you staring at me?"

The boy seemed younger now, younger even than Tim. "Because I, um, I saw you looking at me before . . . "

Tim pursed his lips as he listened to the boy's words and gleaned their underlying meaning: Fuck me, fuck me hard, I don't care if you're a top or a bottom, you're meaner and more experienced than me and no other top would have me . . . Tim filled his chest with air, feeling as if his role of unwanted bottom had been lifted from him by this unexpected meeting. *Maybe this time nothing will go wrong,* he thought. It was easy to get the boy to agree to take him to his place so Tim wouldn't have to explain his own lack of furniture, sex toys, or belongings. If the boy started thinking of Tim as the anonymous drifter he really was, he might back out. And now Tim wanted a piece of him.

The boy's place, a converted South End industrial loft, was as well equipped as any dungeon or tack room Tim had seen in the three years since he'd discovered the leather scene. He rubbed his own erection through his jeans with his leather-covered palm in anticipation.

"Put these on," he said, thrusting a set of leather cuffs at the boy. "Strip your clothes off first."

The boy's face turned surly, as it had been early in the evening. *No wonder his other top took off. Tired of this rebellious crap.* Tim, on the other hand, was beginning to wonder what it was like to break the will of such a bottom. What sort of methods could be justified? But the boy didn't provoke him further. Surly as his eyes were, he stripped down to nothing and put the cuffs on his ankles and wrists.

With all his weight behind his shoulder, Tim knocked the boy to the floor. The boy looked up, shocked, maybe just a tinge of fear in his eyes. *Good.* Tim was much stronger than his size revealed. It had kept him alive on the streets many times in the years he had been vagabonding from city to city. *Now let this pampered, prissy boy have a taste of that.*

He chained the boy's wrist cuffs together and hung them over the hook of a whipping post. Tim started snaking the belt out of the loops of his jeans. Yeah, some kind of Bad Boy/Daddy kind of thing . . . ? He'd never done anything like that but he knew some guys got off on it. His own father had been a vegan and a pacifist; he'd never owned a leather belt much less ever threatened Tim with it. Tim chuckled as he snapped the leather in the air and watched the boy flinch. His father had always said that eating red meat would make him a violent person. *Well, tonight I had a hamburger,* he thought as he let the belt fly. It raised a welt on the boy's left buttock and a cry from the boy's throat. *What would Dad think of me now?* With the rhythm of his arm swinging the belt and the regular wails from the boy, his thoughts drifted. His father had always talked crazy about some things; eating meat, sex, and violence were his top three. He'd been in bad shape near the end there, with raging fevers and delirium, his fears turned into twisted paranoia. Maybe it had always been paranoia, bad enough that after the accident that had killed Tim's mother, he'd moved away from the city and become a hermit with his toddler son. Tim just hadn't known it was paranoia until he'd gone out into the world.

He laughed to himself—maybe the old man had been right about sex and meat and violence all being one: The boy's back looked like hamburger now, with bright red places and mottled spots and bumps, and Tim wanted to fuck him. Tim tossed away the belt and shed his clothes, pressing his sweat-cooled skin against the hot, welted flesh. His nails dug into the boy's chest as he pressed his hardness against the boy's buttocks, and his teeth grazed the boy's shoulder. He felt the boy stiffen as he teased him. *Let him think I won't put on a condom. Does that excite you, boy? To know you're helpless if that's what I want?*

The boy struggled to get away, but he was bound. Tim felt his lips part and the sweetly salty flesh of the boy's neck against his tongue. He began to suck, his teeth hard in his mouth, his erection hard against the boy's opening, his nails hard on the boy's skin . . . he was dimly aware that he had begun to shudder.

And then something sweeter than anything he had ever tasted began to flow into him, through his mouth and down into the empty place in his guts where he felt the longing, into his loins and out to the tips of his extremities. What he needed . . . he tingled and surged and sucked harder and wondered why the boy was screaming what he was.

"Jeezuschrist, he's got me!"

So sweet. Tim felt as if he were slipping away into ecstasy, like that moment of orgasm, stretching on and on. Running through the woods on a cold, moonlit night, rarefied air burning in his lungs and his mind a million miles away . . . he could see the woods, feel the air. So long ago, and yet it seemed so real . . . another time, in the wind and the rain, the rain and branches lashing at his face as he made his way through the trees, racing the storm. The day of the visitors, the day his father had had visitors . . .

The boy was screaming now, and what he said made him wish he could stop and ask him how he knew . . .

"Argent! Argent!"

He could not stop, could not pull away from the life in his mouth or the flesh in his hands, not until a hand grabbed him by the throat and forced him away.

Tim gasped as he felt the hardness of the floor impact his back. Where the fingers had touched his throat felt like fire, and everything seemed to glow around him. He looked up at the newcomer who was ablaze, or so his eyes told him, but even through the glow and flickering he recognized the dark top from the bar. *It can't be,* Tim thought desperately, *it can't be Argent . . . some kind of a hallucination, the memory . . .*

This man did resemble the strange man who had come to visit his father when he was ill, his hair sleek and straight, his eyebrows thin and arched, but that was almost ten years ago and this man seemed even younger.

"Timothy Delancey?" asked the dark man, who appeared impossibly tall now.

Oh god, Tim thought, *he knows who I am—he's a fed, tracked me across state lines, set me up with this . . . oh, fuck . . .* "Look, it was an accident, okay?" That kid in Chicago had practically killed himself already, and that one in Columbus had been a mistake . . . Tim had been sticking to bigger cities ever since then. Tim struggled to get up, to get to the door, but the man was on him now, holding him, keeping him from moving. His still-heightened senses felt the roughness of his clothes against his own bare skin, the rustle of it too loud as they struggled. Tim's head was buried in his own arms when the man said:

"Tim, don't you remember me?"

Tim stopped struggling while his mind raced to catch up. *This can't be . . .* "Ar- Argent?"

"Remember an evening full of rain and wind? The hurricane. I came in a red Jeep looking for your father. You were twelve years old . . . "

Another voice. "Jeezus, Argent, I'm bleeding up here . . . "

"Shut up!" Argent hissed. Then in a quieter voice he went on. "I've been looking for you since that night, Tim. We've almost caught up to you a couple of times . . . "

Tim coughed as Argent let him go and he unfolded halfway. Nothing was making sense. Why would they have been tracking him that long ago? He hadn't done anything yet. Had Argent been there that night in Columbus? In Chicago? "I didn't mean to kill them . . . "

Argent and the boy exchanged looks. Argent let the boy's arms down from the post and then knelt by Tim's side. "We know. We're here to help."

Tim saw the boy roll his eyes as he put a hand to the wound at his neck. Tim stabbed a finger toward him. "You got a problem?"

The boy snorted. "I ain't the one with the problem, boy."

Tim was on his feet, his hands reaching out to push the boy

down again, put him in his place. "Who you calling 'boy'?" But before he could reach, Argent was between them.

Argent's eyes went as cold as ice as he glared at the boy. "Luke," he said in a too quiet voice, "why don't you go make us some tea."

Tim took a step back then as his mind wheeled. That was what Argent had said that night, as his father had sat and refused to listen to what Argent had to say and as Tim had listened in secret from the top of the second-floor stairs. Argent had sent Luke to make some tea.

This was the same Argent, the same Luke, only Tim was twenty now, not twelve, and Argent had hardly aged a day, and Luke looked younger than Tim remembered. "How . . . ?"

Argent pulled his leather trench coat over Tim's shoulders. "I promise to explain everything. But you must trust me now—we don't have much time. How many times have you drunk human blood?"

Tim looked into Argent's dark eyes and watched the glowing halo like a corona around them. The chances of Argent being a cop seemed very remote now. "Twice before."

"Jeezuschrist," said Luke as he set down cups and saucers a few yards away on a cement table. "Third time's the charm."

"Then we're just in time," said Argent. "We're just in time." Argent gestured and Luke brought him one of the teacups. Tim watched in frozen fascination as the dark man flicked open a small knife, made a slit in his wrist, and squeezed red into the cup. He then handed the cup to Tim. Tim stared at the pattern of white lilies embossed around the edge of the cup.

"What am I supposed to . . ." but even as he was saying the words, he knew the answer, and lifted the cup to his lips.

"Drink," Argent said. He folded his legs under him, and sat on the floor. "Drink."

Tim poured the red fluid down his throat, slurping at the cup. Then he staggered.

 Cecilia Tan

"I suggest you sit, also."

Tim sat down hard, the cup slipping from his fingers as he pressed the heels of his hands to his eyes. The glow that had suffused Argent seemed to flare up behind his eyelids. He heard the cup shatter in a faraway place and Argent's voice—"Is it the visions?"—from even farther away.

As the glow faded, images flowed and melded, the trees parted and the roadway shone wet and slick in the oncoming headlights of a car. A Jeep, pulling up to Tim, the window rolling down, and Argent's face inside.

Eight years ago, twelve-year-old Timothy Delancey climbed into the back of the Jeep, wet and shivering and desperate to know who this man was who knew his father's name, who wore a coat made of oiled leather and a tailored suit, who smelled like something pungent and sweet—an emissary from the outside world. Luke was there, too, in a similar suit, blond and surly.

Tim saw himself hidden at the top of the stairs, out of sight and straining to hear, listening to his father and Argent talk in riddles. They'd gone on for hours about things Tim could not understand well enough to remember, his father's breath getting more weak and watery every time he spoke.

Then Argent had brought the subject around to Tim himself. "Does the boy know what he is?"

What am I?

"You're wrong, he won't be that way."

"How can you be sure?"

"His mother was pure." *Pure what? Vegan pacifist?* Tim had never known his mother. He hoped they'd speak more about her, but they did not.

"Surely he needs his father's love?"

"Never. I'd never give it to him." Tim felt a chill. His father did love him, didn't he?

"If you don't, someone else will."

"You stay away from him, you pervert."

Argent's chuckle had been cold. "Oh, is that what you call us now? Very good."

"Yes, because you're sick, preying on ... "

"Ah, ah ... I prefer the term *flirting* ... " Now the chill crept up Tim's back.

"You *are* sick. You get anywhere near him and I'll ... " *Was Argent dangerous?*

"You'll what? Spout pacifist literature at me?"

"You can't touch him so long as I live."

"Which, from the looks of things, won't be long. John, that's why I'm here."

"You won't take Timothy away from me ... "

"Calm down. I have no intention of taking him anywhere. I want him to grow up strong and healthy, just as you do. But you aren't going to live out the year."

"I'm stronger than I look ... "

"Come on, John. We both know what it is that's killing you. If you want to live long enough to see Tim grow up, let me help you."

Tim. No one had ever called him Tim before.

"I don't see how you can help me."

"Kiss me, John. Kiss me and ... " Tim began to back away from the stairs. He wanted to know, but he did not want to hear any more.

"No!" His father had begun coughing, struggling for breath.

"Kiss me the way you did long ago. Let my love heal you."

"Never again! Get away from me, you monster!"

The sound of a struggle. The sound of a cup shattering ... the last thing he heard before he was out his bedroom window and into the lashing wind and rain of the hurricane outside.

Tim found himself curled up, Argent's leather coat under him and Argent kneeling over him. He remembered looking at

Argent in the bar, wanting and hoping that he might be the one . . . Argent's voice low in his ear: "What did you see? Tell me."

Tim felt the click in his mind as elements of his memory filtered into his present situation. He was naked and prostrate in front of this tall dark man, a man who, he realized, he'd always associated with what was dark, forbidden, lustful, and dangerous. All from that one night's eavesdropping. The taste of blood was still on his lips and his lust raged back through his loins. He shivered as Argent's hand came to rest on his shoulder. He wanted Argent to . . . to something. The smell of leather was in his nostrils and his skin ached where he longed to be slapped and hurt. Tim never begged or asked for favors. He affected a surly look like Luke's. "Make me."

Argent squeezed his shoulder hard. "Don't play games with me, Tim. Tell me what you saw."

"Nothing, I didn't see nothing." He would not look into Argent's eyes.

He could see Luke's boots, standing behind Argent. Luke's voice: "Are you sure this is him? Maybe he's just some kinky junkie, thinks this is a part of the scene."

"Tim, it's Argent. Remember me?"

Tim remembered coming back to the cabin dazed and dripping to find his sick father, Argent, and Luke gone. A few days later he had found his father's body near the house and buried it, and waited, but Argent had not returned. Tim shivered again as Argent's hand brushed his back. Maybe he could make Argent angry enough to whip him.

"Tell me what you saw, Tim."

"Make me." Tim repeated.

Argent shook his head and looked at Luke. Luke walked to the other side of the room and came back. Out of the corner of his eye, Tim could see Luke hand something over.

Tim's own belt. He watched as Argent doubled it over and

tightened his grip on the end. "I came here to teach you discipline, Tim, but I didn't think it would have to be like this."

Tim felt the first stroke of the belt across his back like an explosion inside his head, the pain setting off fireworks. Argent had that luminous look again, and Tim shut his eyes against the brightness that seemed to be growing. Another stroke, and another. Tim struggled against the pain; even as he felt it surge through him like lightning, energizing him, he fought it, until it overtook him and he succumbed, letting the pain drive everything away from him, anguish, distress, disturbing thoughts . . . everything except for Argent, the source of it, the one thing left . . . it was almost as sweet as drinking his blood from a cup, and left Tim feeling a kind of thirst again.

Argent stopped and left Tim gasping. He looped the belt casually over Tim's shoulders. "Are you ready to tell me, now?"

"Yes . . ." Tim croaked, his eyes still clenched.

"What did you see?"

"I saw you . . ." How could he explain this? "I saw you, in a Jeep, in the rain . . ." He hugged himself and drew a shuddering breath. He couldn't say any more, shame coloring his face and making him feel nauseous inside. How could he tell Argent that he'd been listening to that conversation?

Luke snorted. "That's as much as you told him, Argent. He's faking. The sonofabitch is just trying to get a kinky thrill out of us by playing along."

Argent shook his head. "Well, if it's a kinky thrill he's after, he's going to get it."

Tim looked up to see Argent slide his jacket from his shoulders and begin to unbutton his crisp white shirt. It was hard not to want him, his lean, sculpted body, as he stripped down to nothing.

Argent sat down again, cross-legged, and took the little knife out of his jacket pocket. He held it against his manhood and Tim gasped. The red trickle, though, looked so . . .

Argent grabbed him by the hair and forced his head down onto the hardness there.

Tim let the erection slide deep in as he began to drown in the sweetness again and lose himself in the images that swam before his eyes.

Like some kind of crazy dream, he could see his father across a low table, but somehow he could also see, through his father's eyes, Argent on the other side of the table. His father looked younger than Tim had ever seen him; Argent looked the same as ever. On the table, two small soup bowls, some chopsticks, stray grains of rice. Candles burned about the room and Tim felt the weight of ritual in the air. Argent cut himself and let the blood flow from his hand into one of the bowls, and he began to speak.

"This is the only time we will ever speak of the blood or of the magic or of what we are, in such terms. You must learn the way to speak of such things, so you will be able to pass among us and so we may work together, all without fear of discovery."

He could feel Argent's flesh inside him as he seemed to taste Argent's blood in the bowl, as his father took the bowl and drank from it.

"To speak of the bite is forbidden. To speak of the blood is forbidden. To speak of the hunt is forbidden. To speak of the kill is forbidden."

Tim heard his father's voice repeating these words, and felt as if he were mouthing them, his mouth full of Argent.

And then the trickle became a spurt, and another, and he swallowed eagerly as Argent came.

When Tim opened his eyes, Argent's were closed, and there was sweat on his brow. Luke stood a few yards behind, his face stony as he watched.

"Luke," Argent said. "Let me kiss you."

Luke did not move; his eyes flicked from Tim to Argent and back. Tim returned the stare.

Argent opened his eyes then. "Luke! I said I need you. Now."

Luke stepped forward with precise steps and knelt, hands crossed in front of him. Argent pulled him out of that careful stance, as he pulled the wound Tim had made earlier to his mouth.

Now it was Tim's turn to stare. When Argent pulled his mouth away, blood ran down his chin. He and Luke both seemed to glow. Luke sullenly put a hand over his neck again and sat back.

Argent's eyes burned at Tim. "Now tell me what you saw."

Tim shivered even though his skin felt as if it was burning. Some kind of fever. His eyes locked with Luke's. There was some kind of challenge in Luke's eyes and Tim was eager to meet it. He could not describe the crazy dream. "The blood . . ." he managed, trying to remember the words Argent had said, trying to repeat them. Had he not just taken an oath that said he would not speak of the blood? No, not him, his father, in the dream . . .

Tim looked at the two men across from him and narrowed his eyes. Argent got to his feet, his cock limp but long. "You're going to have to do better than that," he said, his voice dangerous and low.

"Yes, sir."

Luke yawned. "I'm telling you, this one's a waste of time. Remember that guy we tried in Buffalo?"

Argent gritted his teeth but did not take his eyes off Tim. "Third times the charm. This should be causing his memories to bloom, but if he's been particularly out of things . . . "

Luke got up and stretched, walked to where Tim's leather jacket had fallen. "Come on, Argent. Timothy Delancey had brown hair."

"Hair can be bleached. If this really is Timothy Delancey, then he's even more perfect than any of the others. John might have even done us a favor, isolating the boy that way . . . "

Tim wanted to back away, but he couldn't take his eyes off of Argent's beautiful, cruel body. The beating had subdued the rebellion in him and now he wanted Argent to push him, wanted to be taken. His breath came in shallow gasps ... Argent smelled pungent and sweet and Tim felt small and young. *But can I trust him?* He reminded himself that Argent had possibly killed his father.

Luke snorted. "I hate to burst your bubble but his driver's license says his name is 'Roger Wilcox.'"

Argent turned to face Luke, took a few steps toward him. "What? Let me see that."

The cobra's eyes are off the bird, Tim thought as he backed silently toward the door. Before Argent could turn around, Tim was down the stairs and into the alley.

Argent stared at the space Tim had occupied on the floor moments before. "Damn."

Luke stood next to him. "I'm telling you, once this kid figured out what our game was, he played along. He's just some hustler. Once he was found out, he split."

Argent shook his head. "But I was so sure this time." He went to the window and looked onto the quiet street. Luke came up behind him and laid his head on Argent's bare shoulder. Argent stroked his hair. "Get him back."

"What?"

"Go out there and get him back. I want to test your skills. If you have truly taken to the discipline, you will find him, and bring him back to me without finishing him. If he's not Timothy Delancey, well, then you can have him when I'm done with him." Argent began to dress.

"Are you going out, too?"

"To flirt, to cruise." Argent said. "I need to score."

Luke narrowed his eyes. "That little creep didn't take that much out of you."

"No, but I'm going to need all my strength to prove or dis-prove who he is. And if I'm right, he's in a very dangerous position now. So get going!"

Tim felt like he couldn't walk in a straight line. He made it through the alley and across the next street. There wasn't far he could go, naked like this. He huddled into the barred steps of the closed subway station where no one going by on the street would see him. He could fake like he'd been mugged, except he didn't like the idea of going to the police for help, even if it was unlikely that anyone had tied him to those two deaths.

If only he hadn't left his wallet and jacket behind. That driver's license had been helpful. He'd stolen the wallet off a trick in Providence because of the likeness. With his hair bleached, Tim could pass for the man in the photograph. Now he'd have to start over again.

Or, he could go back to those two and ask for help. Now that he was away from them, Tim tried to think clearly. He'd run because it was his rule: Run when things get too weird. It had kept him alive when he was twelve, and he was still alive today. Argent was definitely weird. All his talk of kissing and love didn't seem as strange to Tim now as it had when he was twelve, but the drinking blood and talk of a plan . . . there was just too much he didn't understand. Had Argent and his father been secret lovers before Tim's mother came along? Or . . . he replayed the conversation in the cabin in his mind. Was Argent his real father? Had John kidnapped him and hidden him away in a cabin to escape detection? He couldn't make all the facts he knew fit together, but couldn't just pick and choose the ones he liked.

Tim laughed and his voice sounded too loud around him. Pretty far-fetched. It was an attractive idea, a nice fantasy to keep him warm nights, imagining Argent was his father, beating him with a leather belt.

 230   *Cecilia Tan*

"There you are. Boy, you didn't get far." Luke looked down at the grimy nude form at the bottom of the steps.

"Get away from me," Tim said, as he came into a defensive crouch.

"Look, we didn't mean to scare you. If you want to come back upstairs, I've still got your clothes." Luke came down the steps, his arms spread wide. Tim tried to hear Luke's real message under his words—he wanted Tim out of his hair, badly. "Argent's gone out for a while. It's okay, really." Luke's smile showed white teeth in the streetlight.

"I just want my clothes back, and then I'll go."

"Okay."

"Bring them here."

Luke shook his head. "Bad idea. If the transit cops find you here, or worse, the Boston police, your ass will be fried." Luke took his own jacket off. "Here, put this on, and come with me, quickly."

Tim took the jacket from the outstretched hand and wrapped it around his shoulders. Luke turned to go up the steps and he followed. *Okay, I'll just get my stuff, and then I'll go. It was stupid to run out here, anyway. I should have just told them I wasn't really Tim Delancey, and they'd have let me go. I'd never see them again.*

They reached the vestibule of the loft and Luke opened the door. Tim peered in. "See, Argent's gone. Here's your stuff."

Tim took three steps into the apartment and Luke slammed the door and bolted it. As Tim turned to see his escape cut off, Luke body-checked him and Tim fell to the floor. Luke was on top of him before he could get back on his feet.

"You little shit, I owe you for this one. You've really got him in a tizzy, haven't you."

"I don't know what you're—"

"Shut up." Luke trapped Tim's hips by straddling him and backhanded him across the face. "You thought you were really hot shit, didn't you, first getting off on topping me, then as soon as the top came along, trying to bottom to him. Well, you don't know what you've gotten yourself into, boy. Time for the payback." Luke bent Tim's head back and lowered his face toward Tim's throat.

Tim put his hands on Luke's chin, trying to keep him back. "Hey . . . you're the one who brought me home. Argent— "

"Leave Argent out of this, Roger. He's deluded, yeah, but he's mine. He's so into his quest for the perfect . . . man, that he's convinced himself that you're some kid we've been chasing for ten years. So sad. Well, usually, he takes care of this part. But this time, it's going to be me."

Luke twisted one of Tim's arms and tried to bite Tim's wrist. Tim pulled his hands away and tried to hit Luke in the face. Luke caught his hands and held them together, trying again to bend toward Tim's neck.

Why does Argent think I'm the perfect man? "But I am Timothy Delancey," he said then. *Luke wouldn't hurt me if he knew Argent wanted me, would he?*

"Yeah, right." Luke sneered. "Well, I'm going to tell you a little secret, Roger. If you were Timothy Delancey, you'd be able to break this hold. You'd be able to do a lot more than lie there like a sack of junkie shit. Because Timothy Delancey, if he's even still alive, is a vampire."

Tim froze. *Okay, okay, okay,* he thought, while he struggled with Luke, who was still trying to get his teeth sunk into his neck. His mind rearranged all the pieces and tried to make them fit again. *There's two possibilities here. One is, these bozos are totally fucking nuts, and it's this kind of crazy shit that my father tried to escape from. Two is, he's telling the truth, and I'm a vampire.* Luke's mouth inched closer. If they were nuts, how could they know that was his real name? And, if Luke was right, that Tim the vampire could get out of this, then that's who he must be. He strained against Luke again and held him off. "I am Timothy Delancey," he repeated.

"I don't care," Luke said. "I want you dead either way. It's the only way Argent and I will ever have any peace. He doesn't need you, and he'll see that."

"You don't have to kill me. I'll go away. You'll never see me again."

Luke laughed. "If you are Timothy Delancey, then I want you double dead. If you're not, then I just want you to feed my own strength. Argent never lets me have enough. It's always discipline, discipline, discipline. And he never lets me kiss—drink—from him. But you've just had a taste of him, so if I have a taste of you . . ." He plunged suddenly toward Tim's throat.

Tim blocked his neck with the only thing he had left, his own head. Luke's teeth caught him on the cheek while Tim bit Luke on the chin. *Argent's blood,* he thought, trying to think of the sensations he had as Argent's blood had flowed into him. He felt a surge of strength in his midsection, which flowed out to his limbs . . .

. . . and he threw Luke off of him.

Luke snarled with rage and flew at him again. Tim rolled with him onto the floor, trying to come out on top. They threw fists in each other's faces and came away bruised and separated. Tim bent his knees and waited for Luke to charge again.

This time, he let Luke bear him down, but he thrust his wrist into Luke's open mouth. Even as he felt Luke's teeth sink into his flesh, he had Luke's shoulder by the other arm and pulled his own mouth back to the wound he had made so long ago tonight.

Luke tried to pull away, but he was locked in the loop now, unable to stop feeding from Tim's wrist, even as Tim was draining him faster from the pulsing flow at his neck. Tim let his eyes close and let himself sink into that ecstasy once again.

* * *

A long time later, or so it seemed, Tim pried Luke's dead jaw off his wrist, and rolled the body to the side. He sat up and drew a deep breath.

A key clicked in the lock at the door. Tim pulled his legs up to hide his nakedness somewhat and waited for Argent to come in.

Argent's gaze flowed over the scene and he shook his head once. He took slow steps toward Tim, his boot heels tolling out a steady count. He went to one knee, took Tim's damaged wrist in his hand, looked at it, and let it fall. "Tim."

"Yes."

"I told him not to . . . ah well." Argent looked into Tim's eyes. "How do you feel?"

"A little dizzy. And everything is still all shimmery."

"It will be like that for a while."

Tim hesitated a moment before saying, "You killed my mother, didn't you."

Argent sat down on the floor next to Luke's body and said, "No."

"You killed her, and Father fled from you, but you tracked us down in the boonies and killed him, too."

"No, no, no." Argent said. "To hell with the ritual. Let me start at the beginning. Do you know what you are?"

"A vampire."

"Yes. Now I'm going to tell you what that means. It isn't quite what you think. There's . . . power, in the blood. Call it magic, call it sacrifice, call it an unexplained scientific phenomenon. Doesn't matter. When one human drinks another human's blood, power transfers. When one human drinks enough other human blood, it builds up. You become more powerful. You discover you can do things beyond normal abilities. You are faster, stronger, your senses are sharper, your reflexes faster. And you don't age as fast. Drink enough, and you stop aging altogether. But if you stop drinking then, you begin to have problems. You degenerate. That's what happened to your father. And he was alive the last time I saw him, shaking his fist at me as I drove away."

Tim stared at Argent, knowing that what he was hearing was somehow true. His father had probably gone out that night looking for Tim, and the strain had been too much. "My father . . ." he said, but couldn't think of quite what to say.

Argent filled the silence. "He stopped drinking blood and tried to escape 'the curse' as he called it, when your mother died." Argent no longer looked at Tim, but into the blank distance between them. "He killed her accidentally while they were making love. She never drank from him, he always drank a little from her. That one time though, in the heat of passion, he could not stop himself. He was . . . horrified, and rightly so. Instead of facing his difficulty, he ran away, with you, swearing that you would never grow up to know the curse. If he had not been so stubborn, if he'd drunk a little from time to time to maintain himself, he might have lived long enough to see you grow up and, who knows, he might have succeeded. Maybe if you never had the taste of meat you might never discover what he had." Argent rubbed his lips together. "I think you had the taint already, being of his seed produced while he was . . . active. And I think your earlier experiences prove it."

The halo around Argent glowed bright as Tim crossed his legs and put his hands on his knees. "But it was you who made my father a vampire."

Argent grimaced. "Not exactly. He had the taste already, but he didn't know what power it had when he started doing it. So many these days . . . " Argent's jaw was set in a determined line as he shook his head slowly from side to side. "In the old days, people were not so foolish and feared magic. There were taboos against drinking blood or eating flesh. But now . . ." His eyes went to the wall of hanging S/M gear and he shrugged. "I tried to give your father the discipline necessary to contain the power, to use it wisely, but when he lost control with your

mother . . . he fled as much from failure as from horror."
Argent kicked at Luke's corpse. "And here is another failure."
Then Argent's eyes seemed to focus on Tim for the first time
since he had come in.

"And you want to try it on me, next," Tim concluded. The
perfect man.

"Yes."

"What do you—I—have to do?"

"It involves intense physical and mental discipline. It
involves invoking passions and controlling them."

Tim's eyes drifted to the array of bondage and S/M gear
across the room and back to Argent's slim, strong, glowing form.

"If our power is to do any good for mankind, we must be able
to control our appetites, and choose to wield it wisely. That has
been my function throughout the ages, training those like you,
until they could go on to train others. There are always those
humans willing to risk everything to gain power, to misuse it.
I'm hoping, Tim, that you'll join me."

Tim thought about life with Argent, and his memory of
Argent strapping him across the back returned. He thought
about bowing to Argent's will, until his own will was shaped
and formed and he could stand on his own. "I'll go with you on
one condition." he said, a last piece of curiosity burning him.
"You explain to me what you and my father talked about that
day. Were you two lovers?"

Argent's smile was wan, his eyes betraying complex emotions. "I always wanted him, but no, we were not lovers. I was
still trying to find the right paradigm for my disciplinary practices in the current age and he did not want me. As for what we
spoke of, the kiss, love, flirting, and cruising . . ." He broke off
with a soft chuckle. "Maybe the ritual has its place after all.
After this night, we will never again speak aloud of the blood,
or hunting for prey, or drinking. It is too dangerous. In the
olden days, when people were more superstitious, we adapted

 Cecilia Tan

the language so we could speak to one another of our common activity without detection even if we were overheard. In those days, men hunted for their meat, and so all our euphemisms and metaphors were of food. That rubric ceased to work in the modern age and we had to find something else. Hence, the bite has become the kiss, the blood, love, and to kill . . . "

". . . To go all the way," Tim finished. "But can't that also get confusing?"

"What do you mean?"

"If one of us is your lover."

Argent licked his lip.

Tim wanted to curl up instinctively under that predatory look, but something in him also wanted to present his body to this man like a gift. He wondered if Argent could do the same trick he could, to hear what someone was really after no matter what they were actually saying. He'd always thought he was just smart, but maybe it was part of the magic. His tongue tumbled over the words "I mean, I want to be sure, if I ask you to fuck me, that you know I want you to . . . fuck me, and not . . ."

Argent stood up in one fluid motion. "I'll know." He stripped out of his clothes and herded Tim toward the heavy wrist restraints that Luke had worn earlier that night. As he strapped Tim's hands into them he said, "After all, that's the key difference, isn't it? You won't make the same mistake your father made."

Tim shivered as he felt the belt brush his bare back. He would not beg, he thought, or ask for favors, but nor would he goad Argent into things. Luke had whined about not getting enough, but somehow, Tim was certain, Luke had gotten exactly what he deserved. *I will be better than Luke, better than my father, better than all of them,* he thought, as the belt lashed at him like tree branches in a storm, like dark wind-driven rain.

Author's Note: A few thoughts on why I wrote this story in tribute to John Preston.

John Preston and I only ever met once, briefly, less than a year before his death, and I gave him a copy of my book of self-published S/M erotica, *Telepaths Don't Need Safewords*. He probably would not have recognized my name—though maybe he would, I will never have the chance to know now. This does not matter. The things that matter are the things we had in common: both "pornographers" (his word and mine) on a disenfranchised fringe, both writing fiction about dominance, both concerned with things like mentorship, discipline, and fantasy. In my most deep-seated, archetypal fantasies, John Preston was the mentor that I, as a pornographer of this kind, never had. And in sitting down to write this tribute, I found I could not write an essay or reminiscence about him or his writing or his funeral. I could only express what he meant to me through this kind of fiction that we both shared. In the story, my sadomasochistic creativity is replaced by the symbols of my sadomasochistic libido—the pen becomes a whip, and my unfulfilled longing for a masculine, disciplined, experienced mentor becomes embodied in the character of the whipmaster. But a mere fantasy in which all is exactly as it should be is interesting to no one but the author, and the snarls and difficulties of real life compel me as strongly as any libidinous image. And so in come the troubles, some shadowing real life, others not. This is a piece of fiction. Like any fiction, it is a creation of the hopes and desires and visions of the author. I don't know what John Preston would have thought of it. I can only hope that the values I think he espoused will be in some way embodied here, and that how sorely I miss him will also.

I moved to New England just in time for the winter, just in time to get settled and start hibernating in a town where I knew no one and didn't relish slogging through the mixed precipitation to find them. There was one thing I hoped to find, now that I was single, and well away from the gossipy, backbiting, conformist queer culture I had known in Pennsylvania, unfettered by antisex feminists, leatherphobic lesbians, clingy, monogamous significant others . . . I was free and alone, and I started looking for a whipmaster. The personal ads did not seem promising—there was no section for "Sadists Wanted." So I put up a sign in the one bar I thought would attract the right clientele, and waited.

It was a long wait. I had a couple of calls from guys who sounded like they were calling from the pay phone in the bar, looking for a quick screw. Most of them hung up when they heard the answering machine. I went to a couple of meetings for local social groups, but felt like most everyone knew one another already and I didn't stick around long after the meetings broke up. Around February I was starting to kick myself and wonder if maybe I should give up on this fantasy when a phone message came to my machine. "This is a message for Roe. I have received word that you are in need of some instruction. If I find you a suitable student I may be willing to tutor you." His voice, so staid and reserved, encouraged me maybe he was what I was looking for, and made me tremble at the thought that I might not measure up to his standards, one in particular. He left details of when and where I should meet him—the next evening, at the bar.

That night his voice entered my dreams as I slipped into fitful sleep. I woke up restless, jittery with anxiety. I slid a hand to my crotch hoping to tire myself as I turned over visions of long black coils of leather striking out. The beauty of their dance, the precision of their discipline, the smell of the oiled leather between my fingers, these things I knew. But the vision could not go beyond that—I did not know what he looked like, and worse, if he would take me at all. The fantasy felt empty, false—I lacked the vision to see what would or could come next.

I spent the whole next day preparing to meet him, thinking on the ball of energy in my belly, and strutting back and forth in my apartment in torn jeans, an undershirt. I spent a long time looking at my arms in the mirror, my shoulders. I had been doing push-ups, chin-ups, curls—it was something to do on cold winter nights—and I was happy with how beefy my triceps had become. My chest was still a problem and probably always would be. A leather jacket fastened at the bottom but not zipped made it look almost right. I coiled my best whip with care and attached it to my belt loop. On the left. Our rendezvous was still four hours away.

I decided it was best to be early and went to the bar at eight P.M. instead of nine. Outside, two men were leaning against the wall, one lighting a cigarette and the other talking in a low voice, his breath fogging in the air. They both watched as I swung open the unmarked door to the place and went in. It wasn't the first time I'd been there, but I was not what you would call part of their regular clientele. No one gave me any particular looks as I made my way past the pool tables to the backroom, and whether this was a good or bad sign I did not know. I passed the bulletin board where my "classified" note still stood:

Wanted: A Whipmaster's Expertise

There is only so much one can learn from oneself. I crave to learn from a practiced expert. Let me prove myself worthy of your instruction.

Roe

The other details of that night do not matter—they blur into all the other nights I'd spent in dark smoky bars alone. What does matter are the memories I have like snapshots, sound bites, that play in my mind sometimes. How he took me by the hair and said, "You must be the boy I'm looking for." I struggled a bit—oddly, I felt as though the struggle was the sign he wanted that I was willing to play along. He forced me through the bar to the far side of the room. Men were looking at us, I heard the hush as we caught their attention. John's voice was loud. "Where did you get this?" With his free hand he pushed my leather jacket from my shoulders, pulling the sleeves until it slipped off my back to the floor. "My boys earn their leather. *Do you understand?*" It was not just a simple question. In it I heard the unspoken *Are you with me?*

"Yes sir." The answer slipped out as easy and natural as could be.

He tore the undershirt from my back then, and I suppressed the urge to cover my tits. I kept my head down, my eyes down, not wanting to see the looks of shock or disdain from the circle that was gathering. "Be proud, boy," he said in my ear. "Your skin is what I want." His hand turned me by my bare shoulder to face him. "So," he said, "you want to learn the secrets of the whip." He had two whips at his belt. "Tell me why."

"Yes sir." No easy answer came this time. A jumble of images flashed in my mind, of penitence, of gladiators, of an old-movie childhood, of a fist, of power . . . "I want a slave of my own," I

Black Feathers 241

said. "I want to be able to deal the ultimate discipline, I want to master the tool . . . "

"Bullshit," he said, and took me by the hair at my neck again. "Tell me about *that* whip." He pointed with his chin to the one I had looped at my hip.

"I made it myself, from a book on whipmaking. I keep it through my belt loop so it takes some time to draw."

He smiled, then, a rare, terrifying smile. "Very good. A whip is not a tool of random violence. Its use is deliberate, calculated, focused. To use it is itself a form of discipline. It is never to be used without thought and care, without weighing the costs of bringing it to life." His words were like a gospel I had waited all my life to hear.

"Now tell me what it feels like." He pulled me closer and I felt his breath on my neck as he spoke.

I hesitated. "It . . . it feels like the wrath of God."

His eyes searched mine. "You've never felt it, have you?"

I mouthed the word *No,* as it seemed all my energy and substance ran out at that moment, no voice, no will, no power . . . my knees were buckling. My body knew even before I did what was to come. He sat down on a stack of beer cases and pulled me down with him, my bare back like a blank slate in his lap. He ran his fingers over my shoulders, down to my hip bones. "I told you I wanted you for your skin."

"Yes sir."

"If you are to learn the secrets of the lash, you must start here. Do you understand?"

"Yes sir."

"If you say no, or if you tell me to stop, I will. But only once."

"Yes sir."

"That rule is good now, and is good ever. If you ever call for a stop, it will be your only chance. Lose your nerve, break your spirit, whatever, if you ever beg me to stop, it will be the end. Do you understand?"

 Cecilia Tan

"Yes sir."

He whistled then, a sharp taxi-hailing whistle, and another man came up to us. He was a classically beefy blond, in black jeans and a heavy motorcycle jacket. John positioned him so that I was pressed face against his back, his leather cool against my cheek, and the man held my hands in front of his stomach. His grip was strong. John walked away from us with measured steps, the heavy tap of his boot heels like a drum tolling, a countdown. Then a long pause, and I knew he was uncoiling the long whip, taking his time, deliberating, and I knew that this was the moment I had been seeking, the moment of truth. The skin on my back felt electric with anticipation, hungry and eager as my heart pounded and one small part of my brain questioned whether I could go through with this or not.

The blow came and I did not cry out. My scream was paralyzed inside me as every cell in my body joined the frantic scramble to process the pain, to absorb the line of fire burning across my back, the lingering ache deep inside me.

Then John was there. "How did that feel?"

I smiled. "Like the wrath of God."

He gave a little nod then, as if he'd made a decision. "Fair enough." He pulled me free of the muscle man and pointed at the wall. My little classified note. He motioned for us to stand back and several other men stepped away for good measure. The whip whirred in the air as it flew and with a quiet crack, shredded the paper into oblivion.

He coiled the whip with slow circles and tucked it away before he turned back to us. "Gary," he said to the man who had held me, "meet my new boy." Gary gave a curt nod to me, and walked away.

I had passed the first test, but now, as my training began, I realized that I had to pass my own test every time I picked up a whip or stood under the lash. We settled in to a routine where I came to his house on the outskirts of town every Saturday for instruction. I was eager to learn, but reluctant to make a mistake or to show how poor my skill was. You would think that it would be easy, to have a master to force one through what one is shy of doing. Perhaps that was the strongest part of John's mastery. He never *forced* me to do anything. If I did not want to do something, I always had my choice—walk away and never come back. So I persevered. It began with caring for his leathers, learning the difference between mink oil and neat's-foot oil and hard fat, between cow leather and deerskin, latigo and oak, and learning to cut leather strips as straight as a ruler and as long as a car. I braided and unbraided and rebraided a new whip until it was perfect enough for him, or until my fingers were too stiff to continue. He let me handle some of the short whips, no more than four feet long, with soft falls that would do no damage if they flew stray. And I bared my skin when he requested it and learned lessons of pain and ecstasy, fear and surrender.

It was a sunny April day when he told me the time had come for me to earn my leather. "If you're ever going to use this," he said, holding the coils of the newest whip we had made, a finely braided four-foot signal whip, "you'll need the armor."

"What do I have to do?"

The tiny curve of his lip twitched, which I knew by now counted for a smile. "You've already done a lot, don't you think?"

It sounded like a trick question so I kept quiet.

"Tonight's a special night at the bar. There'll be ... challenges." I could tell from the way he said it that he'd say no more about it. We hadn't been back to the bar since that first night we'd met.

When we arrived in the backroom he instructed me to strip to the waist and put on a kidney belt. Now my suspicions about

Cecilia Tan

what kind of challenge I would be facing were confirmed. I noticed a number of other boys there, prancing about shirtless, too. Not one was without a collar. My fingers brushed my throat and John must have seen me looking. "Do you want one?"

I hesitated. Unless the answer was an unconditional yes, I always had trouble speaking. Again he gave his little smile. "That's because a collar's not for you. You are not a slave. Do you understand?"

"Yes sir."

He exchanged words out of earshot with some other men, masters, tops, and then whistled for attention. Even among tops he was in command. He issued a challenge then, to them, to pit their boys against me for ten lashes. There were immediately some takers, and I knew it had all been set up beforehand. John selected the first boy and beckoned for me.

They put us up against the back wall, hip to hip, and the boy gave me a comradely smile. I sneaked a look back to see John going through his little ritual of uncoiling. Then came a single crack, the signal that it was about to begin. I drew a deep breath and tensed for the blow. The whip sliced through the air and I twitched expectantly—but the first blow fell on my companion who howled out the pain. I felt weightless for that moment, like a ghost with no substance, as if the whip had passed through me to strike him, so strange it was not to have it connect. But then, the second one came down on me, and made me whole and real again. It was a hard blow, and I wished I had something to bite on as the pain raced up and down my back as if I did not have enough skin to contain it. The first one was still hurting when the next one came, landing just below the first, multiplying the agony. The third came just below that. Like notches in a tree, I realized. Both my companion and I lasted through all ten. Then he was replaced with another one. Again, a single crack in the air. And then the blows began

Black Feathers

to fall, creeping slowly down my back on one side. I stopped breathing when the whip would connect, then gasped for air in the respite. *I can do this,* I told myself, *this is just as we've done it before, only this time everyone is watching.* Just last week I had taken twenty-five strokes on each side, and felt as if I could take more. How many boys were there, five? That would be fifty? My math was disrupted by the next blow. I had lost count of how many I'd had. *It couldn't be too many more,* I told myself, *could it?*

It was. Boy after boy was put into place beside me and it dawned on me that John had only just started on the left side of me. I had those long-distance-runner thoughts going through my head: *Just past halfway, that's good, keep breathing, breathe, if you've made it this far you can go this far again* . . . trying to ignore the fact that each blow that fell seemed to multiply the pain of the others and I felt as if every pore in my skin was screaming just as I was screaming, not stopping between blows anymore . . . until the blows did stop.

It took a few moments for me to realize that someone else was being put in place next to me, but that something was happening behind us. I turned to see Gary and John with their heads together. Several others were murmuring behind them. Gary spoke up, then. "This test is bogus, old man! You're letting the bitch off too easy."

John's face was red with the effort of the whipping and with controlling his temper. "What do you mean."

"If my boy's going up against her, I want to be the one to dish it out." There was some noise of assent from the background. "If you want her to prove her 'worth,'" at which point he snorted, "let someone else have a crack at her. It's only fair."

John was grinding his teeth. "And you think it should be you."

"My boy's the last in line, why not me?" He was already brandishing the whip.

John looked into the faces of the others. "Very well."

I looked away. Gary was snaking the whip in front of him like a rodeo trickster. His boy would not meet my eye so I closed them and waited. I knew from the fire on my skin that there was no inch of it untouched on my back.

This time the salutatory crack came right across my shoulders in a long slash that sent me up against the wall. His boy merely flinched a little and grunted. The second came directly on top of the first, like Robin Hood splitting the fucking arrow. I thought, *Dear God, let him hit me somewhere else . . .* The third snaked around my ribs to lash me in the tit and I knew without looking that it would well up in a black bruise. I couldn't look, I couldn't do anything but scream. Gary's boy still hadn't done much more than say "Uh." *The bastard,* I thought, *is doing exactly what he accused John of doing, taking it easy on his own bottom . . .* he lashed me across the buttocks and it felt as if I wasn't even wearing jeans. My mind was idly wandering, wondering about the tensile strength of denim, of skin . . . he got me in the soft flesh under my arm, high on my shoulders near my neck. Too damn accurate . . . I remembered that first night in the bar when he'd held me for that very first blow. Had there been bitterness in his tone? Looking back on it now it seemed that there was something passing between him and John that I hadn't been able to read . . . still couldn't. Then three blows in a row fell in the same spot across my shoulders, and suddenly I wondered about the students John had had before me, and why Gary wasn't still his student now. Some part of my brain was thinking this over while the rest was overloading on the pain. *Hang on,* I thought, *this is ten coming up now!* And the tenth blows fell, one on me, one on his boy who cried out this time. I was about to take my arms down and move when I heard the whip crack and Gary roared, "Stay where you are!"

The whip began to fall at twice the speed. The other boy was screaming now, but I was beyond screaming. I kept my eyes and my jaw clenched tight and just prayed for it to be over. Now that the blows were coming faster, I stopped thinking about each one, and tried to sink down into the endorphin haze that had been built up over the evening. I doubted I had any skin left on my back. *John will stop this if it goes on too long,* I thought. Gary's blows were beginning to miss their marks. He caught me once on the spine, and once missed so all I felt was the air of the lash in motion. The boy started sobbing. John had brought me to tears with the whip, too, on other nights. But now I was not crying; now I was on fire, and with each deep breath I breathed fire, power welling up in me like a flaming torch. Gary was growling now as he threw the whip again and again, and his boy sounded like a wounded animal.

Suddenly the boy started crying out. "Please! Please! No more! Stop, oh, stop, enough!" He was still saying things to that effect as he slumped to the floor. When no one moved to help him, I knelt down and cradled his head on my knees. That got Gary to move. He pushed me aside. "Are you all right?" His voice sounded small and ridiculous. The boy curled into a fetal position.

John leaned down to Gary. "I told you, you never did know when to stop." Gary tried to return a bitter look, but his eyes sidled away.

John took me by the arm then and walked me around the room. Each man we stopped in front of admired my back, and a couple of the boys shook my hand. Some said, "Welcome," and some said, "Congratulations." When we had gone all the way around, Gary and his boy were gone. John sat me on a barstool to let my shaky legs recover and talked with some of the men. In my daze, I don't recall anything they said.

The next moment that was clear and real, we had just stepped out of the bar onto the sidewalk, into the streetlamp glow and

 248   *Cecilia Tan*

noise of taxis, and Gary was there, leaning against a black-and-red motorcycle. The smile on his face was plastered with sarcasm. "So, John, we don't see much of you anymore. How've you been?" He came forward as if to put his arm around John's shoulders.

John took a step back. "You're a disgrace . . . "

Gary wasn't listening. "You know how we worry about your health."

"Get away from me." John's slow boil was beginning to steam, his face reddening.

Gary actually laughed. "Old man, you gave up the right to give me orders when you cut me loose, remember? I was such a bad slave, too. Never obedient. Not like this one . . . "

"Be quiet," John was saying, but now Gary had turned to me.

"He's going to leave you, you know. You don't have what he needs. He doesn't need your little tits, sister, and he's going to be gone soon . . . "

"Shut up!" John's hand flashed toward Gary's cheek, but Gary knocked it away.

"Uh uh, you gave that up, too, didn't you, when you put me out!" The calculated coolness of his voice was beginning to crack. "And for what! For this little cu—" Thereafter his comments degenerated into mere profanity. John hailed a cab. Gary was still ranting on the sidewalk as we pulled away.

That night, as John rubbed some Chinese salve on my welts, he apologized for losing his temper. "As you can see, that boy can be mighty trying."

I said nothing.

"I know you're thinking about the things he said. You'd be a fool not to."

This time I nodded. I wanted to forget all the things Gary said, and just feel John's fingers on my skin and remember each loving touch of the whip. For that's what they were, now I was sure, having felt the difference between his strokes and Gary's. Loving. I folded my arms across my breasts and said nothing.

John snorted, and lifted up my arm to slather some medicine on the welt that snaked under my arm and over my breast. "There are two things I love a boy for," he said. "Your skin, and your heart. And that is all. And Gary, well, is just a prick." He gave a little laugh. "Most of all your heart. That is where obedience, loyalty, honesty, and self-worth reside. That is where all that I teach you goes. Not your arm or your eye." He pulled me back to lean against him and said softly, "Do you understand?"

"Yes sir."

"I suppose I should explain some of what he said." He sat back and looked at my glistening skin. I did not turn around. "You've probably guessed that Gary was formerly a boy of mine. The exact details do not matter. He wanted me to teach him to throw a whip and I kept telling him no. He wasn't mature enough for it. But then, I did start to teach him. A mistake. He does not take criticism well and wouldn't listen. Eventually he became so unmanageable that I told him to get out."

All that I had guessed. What else had Gary said? Something about John's health? My neck muscles froze as a thought occurred to me and I kept myself from turning to look at him. My voice was gravelly as I asked, "What made you change your mind, and start to teach him?"

The long silence before he answered confirmed my hunch before he said, "I learned a while ago that I have cancer."

"How long . . . ?" I blurted out before I could stop myself.

"Don't know." He stood up. "You can sleep on the floor in the workshop if you like. Or I'll call you a cab."

When I didn't move or answer he continued. "Pillows, sheets, in the linen closet." I went to retrieve them.

As I lay in my makeshift bed, waiting for sleep, my mind sifted over the evening's events again and again. An ugly thought reared up: *There's nothing special or worthy about you—he's only teaching you because he's desperate to find someone before he dies and anyone other than Gary would do, even a girl like you . . .* I tried to quash it. He had been genuinely proud of me, hadn't he? I remembered my earlier thought, about how John's whip had felt. Loving. Eventually I fell asleep and that stopped me from arguing with myself.

In the morning my whole back and shoulders were stiff, not to mention Technicolor. John recommended a hot shower and I took one. When I came out, clothes were laid out for me, my heavy boots, new jeans, a black undershirt, some deerskin gloves, and a leather jacket so new I could smell it from across the room. As I put it all on, I found a pair of safety goggles in the breast pocket. I fished them out. While I was wondering if I should put them on, I heard a noise like a cap gun firing in the backyard. John was out cracking, calling me to join him.

That day he started me on a six-foot bullwhip, showing me how the stiffness in the handle gave me just a few more inches' margin of error, and how the reach was actually longer than six feet, including the cracker. He could hit individual leaves off of the linden tree in the yard with it. He also showed me a scar on his chin that was years old, now just a thin white line that looked as if he might have done it shaving. He assured me he hadn't.

By the end of that day I could hardly move my arm, but I could hit the pillow on the picnic table more than half the time.

I kept wondering when we were going to go to the bar again, but as I found out, John didn't go there very much except for a few club meetings. "Bars are for drinking in," he told me.

"Which is fine if drinking is what you want to do." So most weekends I would go directly to his house, and care for his whips, and learn to repair them, and practice with the pillow, and on Saturday nights he would whip me and let me sleep in the workshop that smelled of mink oil and dye and leather. He served up the whip as a main course that he garnished with a touch of flogging, rabbit fur, mist from a spray bottle.

One night we went to another master's house for a new boy's initiation into the group. John gave me a quirt to carry, just two and a half feet long, even including the fall, with a slightly stiff handle, very easy to aim and use, and very hard to do any accidental damage with.

The master's name was Henry and he insisted that we have some cheese and crackers while we waited for the others to arrive. A few men I recognized from the bar were there, already seated on a leather couch that creaked against their leather pants and jackets as they rocked forward to pick up a cracker or turn toward a conversation. One of them I recognized: Gary's boy, but Gary did not seem to be anywhere around. He smiled when we sat down in chairs across from him.

"I don't think we were formally introduced," he said, holding out a hand to me. "Andrew."

"Roe." It was my last name but I liked it better than my first. We shook.

"John." They shook, too, and I saw John's eyes roving in appraisal, though I could not discern whether there was approval in them or not.

Two more men came to the door, Henry let them in, and then we were ready to begin. Henry led us all down into the basement. His boy was already blindfolded and adrift on the quiet music while he waited on a soft padded whipping bench—a kind of sawhorse with attachment points for his wrist and ankle cuffs. We stood in a loose semicircle while Henry explained the rules. I saw the boy's ears perk up as he heard his fate being discussed.

"You each must introduce yourselves to Michael by name before you begin." He indicated the bound bottom with a sweep of his hand. "You can each deliver a maximum of ten strokes to his back or ass. He really likes it on the ass," he said with a mischievous lilt and we laughed a little. There were ten men in the circle and me. I wasn't clear yet whether I was going to participate or not and looked at John. But John was looking at Andrew at the moment. "The final rule," Henry said as he stepped away from the bottom "is that I get last licks."

The assembled crew held paddles, riding crops, whips, heavy floggers—the two men who had come in last were rifling through their heavy toy bag, evaluating what they had brought and vetoing each other's choices. One of them eventually stepped into line clutching a hair brush, the other a plain leather belt with a chrome buckle. I watched him swing it and slap it into his own palm several times. He was short and somewhat heavyset, and I watched the belt end land squarely in that palm a few times before I realized that something about those hands was attracting my eye.

She was a woman. Or at least biologically speaking she was, or had been recently. I felt as if a new spin had just been put on reality. *Should I say hello?* I wondered, I mean, a special hello—a double-X chromosome hello? And why did I feel even more reluctant to talk to her/him? I decided to wait and see if we were introduced, cringing at the thought that Henry, the perfect host, might catch us by the hors d'oeuvres spread and say, "You two have a lot in common! I bet you have lots to talk about!" *Just be yourself, Roe,* I told myself. I'd been a dyke for years before I figured out that I always felt creepy in "woman-space"—like some kind of secret invader, a sleeper agent. I didn't dislike being female; I didn't dislike women, either, but I always felt as if their expectations of me were all wrong, especially dykes in all-women circles. It just rubbed me the wrong way. Not to mention the fact that the only people I'd ever met who tried to oppress me for my sexuality—my leather sexuality, that is—were lesbians supposedly fighting for their rights to love as they wished. *Get a grip,* Roe, I thought, *this person isn't one of them or she wouldn't be at this party. The guys accept her; get used to it.*

I was so preoccupied with this train of thought that I didn't even pay attention to the first men or the boy's yelps and cries. Then John was stepping forward and uncoiling a four-foot whip (anything longer wouldn't have fit in Henry's basement) and I snapped back to attention. I'd never seen him use it on someone who was lying down, where the striking surface was horizontal rather than vertical. I watched as he swung his arm over his head and the whip moved slowly out through the air until—*crack*—the tip exploded right on Michael's near cheek. What was different? It seemed that something was, but only watching for ten strokes, five on each cheek, I couldn't quite discern what he did differently. The wrist?

And then the man with the hairbrush got up to take his turn, joking before he began that it was high time Michael got what he deserved after working so long in a hair salon. Michael laughed a little, even as he braced himself for the blows. The hairbrush looked so innocuous to me, I was surprised how loud it was and how loud Michael was in response. How much could it hurt compared to the whip? Of course, the hairbrush was being laid on top of the whip welts, so perhaps it hurt a good deal more than it would have otherwise.

Then came the woman. I heard her introduce herself to Michael as Uncle Bulldog. "Bull for short," she said, and most people laughed. She was good with the belt, using more of it with each stroke until on the last couple she was holding it right by the buckle and laying it on with her full arm in motion. Michael said, "Ow!"

The only people left who hadn't delivered any blows were Andrew, myself, and Henry. Henry gestured at Andrew, who took a half step back, shaking his hands. "Come on, Andy," Henry said. "Just this once." But Andrew declined.

Henry turned to me. "Roe?"

John was somehow behind me then. He must have been there for a while. "Go on," he said, giving me a small nudge. "That's why you have the quirt."

"Yes sir," I said, and stepped up to Michael. "Michael, my name's Roe."

"Hi, Roe," he said, sounding a little drunk on endorphins. "I'd shake hands but . . . "

A little more wordplay came out of my mouth as if some divine playwright was prompting me. "Don't worry, little puppy, I'll teach you to shake." And I snapped the quirt between my gloved hands so it was arrow straight. His head twitched at the sound it made. I was aware of the men at the periphery snapping to attention at the sound, too. "Ready, puppy?"

He clenched his buttocks, which I took as a definite yes, and I brought the quirt down across them. He howled, very doglike, which gave me such glee I did an undignified hop to his other side to see if the fall of the quirt had wrapped around his hip. It hadn't. I hit him again, this time from the other side, and he howled again. I patted him on the head and he gave out some high-pitched dog whimpers. "Good puppy." I gave him a few more, and then patted him again. He nuzzled my gloved hand, then bit the edge of the glove and growled playfully, shaking it back and forth. I whacked him across the shoulders then, and he let go, yelping. I used up the last few strokes all in a row on his butt and stood by him waiting for his howling and yelping to die down. I patted him and scratched behind his ears. "Good puppy?" He panted happily, tongue lolling, and wagged his "tail" vigorously. I gave him a last pat on the head and stepped back.

Henry was looking at me with a huge smile on his face. "Well, that certainly gives me some ideas!" he whispered as he went past me. Time for last licks, there was no one else in line.

After all those different implements, his choice showed a lot of class and intimacy. He used only his hands on Michael's ass, and he went way beyond ten smacks, taking Michael up to gasping, shaking, and thrashing in his bondage, and back down until Michael was just grunting limply under each blow. Henry then lay his body along Michael's red ass and Michael sighed and the rest of us broke into spontaneous applause.

Once Michael felt up to walking again, Henry and John helped him upstairs and some of the other men tried out the bench. I wondered if now I was going to be introduced to Uncle Bulldog and wondered if I could say that without laughing and still couldn't decide if he or she was more appropriate. As we neared the top of the stairs, John faltered, stumbling the last step into the living room.

"Well, Henry," he said, shaking hands with our host. "I think I'd better call it a night."

"Thanks, John," Michael said, looking sleepy as he wrapped a blanket around himself. He kissed John on the cheek. "Thanks, Roe," he said to me, and held out a hand to shake, a gesture that we both appreciated.

John asked me to drive, holding out the keys while he rubbed his eyes with the other hand. He sat with his eyes covered for a few miles and said nothing. When we were nearing his house he said, "No no, your place," and then lapsed back into silence. I did as he asked. If he didn't want me sleeping in his workroom I certainly wasn't going to insist. I thought about asking him if I should leave him off at his place and take a cab, but I turned the car toward the center of town and didn't question him.

 Cecilia Tan

As I was getting out of the car and he came around to take the driver's seat, he stopped in front of me and looked me in the eye. "You did a good job tonight."

"Thank you."

"Be on time next weekend. And don't forget to practice."

"I won't."

He gave me an affectionate cuff on the top of the head and smiled just a bit. Then he got into the car and drove away.

I did practice. The next couple of months I spent a lot of time in the basement of my apartment building, as the bullwhip was too big to swing in my apartment. As I got better, I discovered to my delight that I was able to pick off large cockroaches as they would scuttle across the floor. I wondered what John was going to say when I told him I'd been able to blast roaches, and wasn't sure whether he'd be more proud of my skill or disgusted at my choice of target. It felt slightly sacrilegious somehow. You can be sure I cleaned the cracker very well after that. I was practicing so much it was going to be time to replace that one soon anyway. *Maybe this weekend,* I thought.

Saturday morning came and I took my usual public transit route out to his place. It was a crisp fall morning, probably one of the last warm days we'd see before the chill of November really set in. I expected he would be out in the lawn already, shredding brightly colored leaves off the trees. But the house was quiet when I went up the walk and the leaves hadn't been raked. I rang the bell and waited.

When there was no answer after several minutes, I rang it again, listening to be sure it actually sounded inside the house. Then I tried the door. It was open.

I didn't stop to wonder if this was some game he was playing with me. I ran straight up to his bedroom and looked in.

He was asleep on the bed, facedown as if he had fallen there and not moved all night. I could see his back rising and falling under the thin blanket. I backed away, trying to decide if I should wake him.

I decided not to. I started a pot of coffee brewing in the kitchen and went down to the workroom to change that cracker. When that was done, I looked in on him again. He was still sleeping, but now he had rolled to his side and was snoring. I went into the backyard.

The maple tree was afire with crimson leaves and dropped spinning seeds into the air with each gust of late-October wind. I started stretching out my arm, my back, loosening up muscles grown tight with the close work of changing the cracker. This one had no fray in the end and sliced through the air like a shark fin through water, quick and leaving no trace. Soon I was cracking that thing, feeling as if I could cut the thin sunlight with it. I wondered if I could pick the leaves off the trees now, the way I had seen him do so many months ago, wondered if I dared try it.

I discovered that not only could I hit the leaves I wanted, I could often use the same one several times as I sheared it away bit by bit, as long as the wind wasn't blowing. When a gust did come up, sending laves and spinners into the air, I found I could keep my eye on one leaf and nail it as it floated toward the ground. Soon I was waiting for the next gust to try it again, keeping the whip moving in even circles over my head.

I heard the bang of a windowsill being thrust open. "Not bad," he said, his voice a little hoarse and just loud enough for me to hear. Then he ducked back in, and the window closed.

I drew the whip in and tried not to hurry into the house.

I found him sitting in the kitchen with a cup of cold coffee and an old gray bathrobe wrapped around him. I had never noticed before just how thin he was. He stood up slowly when he saw me and moved into the living room, where he settled himself into a big chair. I sat on the couch.

"You've made excellent progress, Roe."

"Thank you." The sound of my name goosed me a little. He'd never used it before.

"I think you are ready to think about trying that"—his eyes flicked toward the whip still coiled in my hand—"on a person."

Are you sure? I wanted to ask, but I knew better than to interrupt.

"I was planning to test you today. You've shown you would have passed it."

But I want to be tested, I thought. This seemed like letting me off too easy and I was uncomfortable with that.

"So you might want to keep your eyes open for someone to put at the other end. Don't try anything just yet, though," he added, wrinkling his chin, "there's still some things about people you could learn." He had to pause to cough, then covered his eyes with his hands in what was becoming a familiar gesture. "There's so much more you can learn . . ." and again he was coughing. This time it took him longer to stop. "Too much." I saw a dark emotion in his eyes, something like sadness and regret.

After all this time my first thought still was that I had failed him in some way, but as I came to understand later, he was most sorry for the fact that a lifetime's wisdom and knowledge is not passed on in anything short of another lifetime. That afternoon we sat and talked in his living room for hours. I fetched us water and sandwiches when he asked, although he ate only a bite or two, and he told me things about his life.

For a while he was silent, his eyes steely on the back of his hand. "You've been the best student I've ever had," he said. "I wanted to tell you that while you were under the lash. But I'm too groggy to swing a whip right now, and I am not fool enough to put off saying some of these things." He was not looking at me as he spoke, but now focusing on the air in front of him. "When people die, they always leave things unfinished, but that doesn't stop us from trying like mad to finish them."

It seemed like my best chance to ask what I had always wanted to know. "Why did you decide to teach me?"

His lip moved a bit before he began to speak. "Gary was a failure, you know that. So, I needed someone that I didn't want sex from, or who wouldn't want it from me. I wanted someone loyal, diligent, mature, and undistracted. I wanted, myself, to be undistracted. Also, knowing that I"—he paused for a sip of water—"might leave things unfinished, I did not want to leave behind a blubbering dependent slave. And considering that I might have to rush, I had to choose someone who . . . "—he paused again, as if testing the words like pebbles in his mouth, rolled back and forth—"had an admirable sense of self-restraint and wisdom to begin with. You seemed to fit the bill. Does that answer your question?"

I nodded, feeling oddly exposed in the truth of his answer, now that my buffer layer of doubts and delusions was stripped away.

"There's a contest tonight at the bar. I think you ought to go."

"What kind of contest?" I was picturing one of those leather-man beauty pageants.

"A skill competition. They do it every year. I don't think I'll be going. You go on, I think you'll do well."

That night, after dinner, he felt good enough to put the flood-lights on in the yard and show me a few tricks. "These are going to take you some time to master, but in a couple of months or years you probably can." I was particularly impressed with the way he could toss the whip out and make it crack, then wrap tight around a pole, or my outstretched arm. Soon he was tired and went inside to lie down. I helped him out of his boots.

"You know," he said as he lifted one bent leg into the bed, "there were some things very handy about having a slave."

"If you need a hand, I could come around more."

He started to say no, but I stopped him. "Not to be your servant, John, to be your friend."

He held out an arm to me and I let him pull me into a bony hug. "You go on, now," he said. "The contest starts at nine o'clock. I suppose I could stand to have you come around a couple times a week to help sort out the workroom."

"All right."

So it was settled that I started visiting on Tuesday and Thursday evenings, and spending Friday through Sunday with him. That night I went down to the bar and walked away with fifty bucks for being able to hit a cigarette out of Andrew's mouth without touching him. Afterward he and I talked a little. I told him about the cockroaches and answered his curiosity about crackers and different types of whips and things. I got his number and decided to invite him to have dinner with me and John some time very soon, and discuss the state of his skin.

The Near Future

VIII

Time marches on, and I like to try to imagine what life will be like in a decade or two. This is true, of course, both in what I write about and in what I try to imagine I will be writing a decade from now. Here are my two most recent stories. Like "Three of Cups," which was written at about the same time, they seem to point to a certain amount of unrest in me. The protagonists in all three stories venture out searching for something—in all three cases they find sex and something other than what they sought. If I had to do a quickie, pop-psychological diagnosis I'd have to say this: When I'm alone, I fantasize about everlasting love and finding the perfect mate. So, what does one fantasize about when one *has* everlasting love and the perfect mate? At the moment my psyche seems to say that prickly stories with huge loose ends are the way to go. Right now I like writing endings that seem like beginnings, that make me wonder *What next?*

I'll leave any grand conclusions about this body of work for someone else to write. I'm already onto more things, more stories, more deadlines, more daydreams.

Call it the weather (which was a steady millennial rain), call it the postproject blues (or burnout, more like), call it *whatever*, but for weeks I'd been home, restless but without the energy to do much, no interest in dinner with friends or concerts or much of anything. This is the life of a technolinguist, I told myself. A few months of neuron-burning, sleepless intensity, interfacing and trying to keep up with a project, and then a few months of dullness and checking my bank balance. Cleaning my office. Playing video games. Every night I sank into bed with the vibrator and thought nothing more of it.

At least, that was the way it was for the first week or so. Then it began to sink in that maybe I really ought to go out and get laid. Such an expression, *get laid*, but apropos—I wanted to be laid down, pressed flat under another human being's body, cruelly literal but true. It had been a couple of years since I'd had time to maintain or look for a regular relationship. I mean, even I can admit that I'm not the most fun to be around when I'm talking like a machine and I can't tell anymore whether the blue in the sky is real or optic nerve burnout. I didn't think of what other complications might have kept me unattached, of course not—I'm into cognitive intelligence, not psychology.

It sank in one night when I was, literally, twiddling my thumbs and thinking about the motor mechanism of habitual motion. I looked at the liquid silver display morphing the seconds on my wall. Only nine P.M. I could suit up, head down to the Market, and try my luck. As soon as I thought of it, energy came to me and I ran to the bedroom to brush my hair and make myself presentable.

Communications is my business, it's true. The communion between human and machine becomes more intertwined every day. We need it now, our economies and political outcomes and resource allocation and transportation—computers handle it all, and humans need to work harder and harder to keep up. Yeah so anyway, I was muttering to myself all the way there to make sure I remembered how to actually talk to people. Please, thanks, how you doing? The rush of air around my helmet meant I could hear myself only subvocally.

At the Market, the music never stops, but in some parts of the club it's louder than others. I like the loud part, which is also the darkest part, usually. But if I was going to meet anyone, that was a sucky place to wait. Just in case, I made myself an Illumiprint card that read: I JUST WANT SOMEBODY TO TREAT ME ROUGH, FUCK ME SILLY, AND KEEP MY SAFETY THE TOP PRIORITY in glowing green letters when stroked. The card was in the back pocket of my jeans. I caught a glimpse of myself in the mirrored side of the bar's cash register. Disaster, probably, I told myself. I hadn't been able to decide butch or femme, and ended up in just a T-shirt and jeans, my riding boots unglamorously scuffed. Well, I actually rode a two-wheeler, unlike most of the posers in here. Well, whatever. I checked my signals to make sure they were in place: The black ribbon around my throat officially pegged me a bottom, the red one looking for sex. To me the red one was redundant—what was the point if they didn't fuck you? Some people swore No Sex, so you had to know somehow. I always said those people should have worn a Band-Aid or surgical mask or something, but the system wasn't exactly designed by semantic experts. Before my time, you know.

Bill, the one bartender I knew, was too busy to talk. There wasn't anyone else there I recognized. No matter how little time has gone by between when you last visited a place and the current time, if it feels like a long time has gone by, you can be sure there has been some disconcerting piece of renovation done since the last time. The reverse is also true, that the renovation itself can make you feel as if you haven't been there in forever. I struck a pose near a new-looking holographic fountain and waited.

The waiting's the boring part so I won't tell you much about it other than that my thoughts were high on the statistical list of what ninety percent of the other people in that place were thinking: What if I don't meet anyone? What if I meet some psycho? What if I embarrass myself? What if s/he wants to get serious? Just because I know the stats doesn't make me any less common in that respect. Anyway, to cut to the chase.

When "he" came along, I was almost convinced that I should give up and leave. He had his hair cut short, peach-fuzz short, and somehow the way that it revealed the hardness of his head was sexy, as if he was one giant erection. He walked up to me, flicked his eyes toward my ribbons, and said "Does that say it all?"

I palmed the card to him and he looked at it, chuckled to himself. "I don't know . . ."

"Don't know what?" I burst out. "What do you want me to do?" He had dark eyes, dark skin, but I couldn't guess where he was from. He couldn't have been any older than me.

He rummaged in his leather jacket for a second and jutted his chin toward the back of the bar. I turned to take a step in that direction but didn't want to take my eyes off him.

His hand on my shoulder propelled me into the men's room. (It was somehow less objectionable, even in this day and age, for a woman to be caught in the men's room than the other way around.) He pushed me into a stall, sat me down on the lid of the toilet, and told me to push my jeans down.

I did. Underneath I was wearing a G-string because I liked how it sawed at my clit. He propped my heels against his hips and spread my knees. From his inner pocket he took something small and plastic with wires that ended in small pads—my mind was already giving me two descriptions for it: The common me would have seen it as an old-time transistor radio with headphones, the technolinguist me wondered what the electrodes were for and whether he was going to read my brain waves here in this muffled-dance-floor-scuffed-paint-sex-club bathroom stall. He squirted a small bit of jelly onto my clit from a tube and stuck the pads on either side of it. Then he pressed one small plastic piece against my clit while he held the other in his hand.

The plastic piece began to vibrate and my hips jumped. A weak vibration compared to what I had at home, but enough to make my breath quicken at first.

He stared down at me with his dark eyes, patiently it seemed, yet I wondered if I saw a hint of anger there. He moved the vibrator in a circle and I moaned and thrust myself against it harder.

"Does it always take you this long?" he said after a while, and I wondered how much battery power he had.

"No, not always," I said, my teeth a little gritted. "It's just . . . "

His eyes went back to the little box in his hand. "If you don't peg these meters, I'm not taking you home, understand?"

I nodded. I was aroused, of that there was no doubt, and I felt wetness drip down my open cunt to my ass. I looked back up at that hard cock of a head and wished he were doing it already.

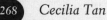

"Are you holding back?" he asked then.

"No! No, I swear. It's just . . . I've been using a vibrator every night this week and it's got me a little desensitized . . . "

He snorted and went back to watching the meters. I was dying to have a look at the readings. My hips shook and my teeth ground but I was no closer to coming. Damn it! Why would I have to get one of these types? Why'd he have to pick the one test I might not pass today? I squeezed my eyes shut, trying to will myself to come. I imagined him inside me, thrusting in, no mercy, no stopping, and yet in complete control . . .

I whimpered out loud and broke my own reverie. He was looking down at my face now, a little bit of pity and a little bit of anger on his. "I don't . . ." he began.

You know I'm desperate when I interrupt, one method of verbal interface that always annoys me when other people do it to me. "Please, sir, just a little longer. I . . . I want you so much. I wish you could just fuck me, stick your hard cock in me, sir, please, anything, sir, please . . ." I stopped myself before I said anything else stupid. I'd called him "sir," hadn't I? Inside I cursed myself for manifesting old, stupid habits, things I thought I was done with.

But if I was really done with them, I wouldn't be cruising a place like this for rough sex, for sex without mercy, would I?

His look mutated to a catlike bemusement, a little hungry, a little distant. "What are you really looking for?"

"Nothing, just a good fuck, dammit, even if I have to beg to get it, understand?"

"Oh, I understand," he said, and began to shake the vibrator with his hand, "Peg these meters for me, sweetie, come on, do it for me, honey."

The come started at the tip of my clit like fire, and ran over the skin of my cunt like live acid, shaking me and making me howl, but it was all on the surface and my vag was gasping like a fish. That's what I get for abusing that stupid vibrator.

He ripped the device from me and I gasped even though it didn't hurt. He was smiling. "It was good enough," he said. "Pull up your pants and follow me."

At his loft the back of my mind noticed things like his Ikaru rig and charts of hardcopy on the wall. The thought went through my mind—he's some kind of project technologist, too, maybe a hardware engineer. We "soft"ware types, cogno/comm types like me especially, we're almost more like guinea pigs than we are like scientists. But I wasn't really thinking about talking shop with this guy; I was following him behind a paper screen to a low futon bed, where he pushed me down and, one hand on the back of my neck, started undressing himself with the other. He stepped back to finish and when he stood completely naked in front of me it seemed somehow that in nakedness there is power, and my clothes denoted me the poor, weak one. (No, I can never shut off the symbology filter, so just get used to it.) He leaned down to me, one hand tugging the thin ribbons around my neck while the other slipped inside my jeans, down into the wet place, and I prayed silently to myself that he would put his fingers in me—he did. One, then two, the knuckles widening me as he maneuvered the second one in, and my eyes closed and my mouth opened like I was giving thanks to the saints.

Then his hand was at my throat and that little question (What if I go home with a psycho?) flitted by, but he was growling in my ear, "You like that? Is this what you like?" and me answering, "Yes yes yes . . . "

The hand at my throat threw me back and he tugged my jeans down around my ankles. He stood with his knees touching mine and indicated his bobbing cock with his hands. "Sit up."

I did.

"Come here and breathe on me."

I knew what he meant, and I opened my mouth around the helmeted head of his cock. He was good and thick, heavy with veins and angry red.

 Cecilia Tan

"Go on," he prompted. I hesitated. I've never been good at sucking cock, and given this guy's penchant for tests and shit I worried what he'd do (or not do) if I weren't good.

"Come on, if you want it, you better." I hesitated a second longer and then he pulled my head forward by the hair until my tongue made contact.

So then I sucked him, trying hard to please him. By the same token I was worried that he'd come and then what would I do . . . I varied what I did, slurping him up and twisting my neck so he could dig into the soft flesh of my cheek with the tip when he thrust, nibbling the edges and flicking my tongue, until, finally, he said, "Enough. Get your fucking boots off."

I got the fucking boots off, or nonfucking boots, in this case, and my pants, and my G-string, and he pulled the T-shirt over my head and laid me back on the bed. "I'd tie you," he said, "but that makes it harder to fuck." I love that word, *fuck,* when it refers to what it really means. It's an old word, older than Modern English, even older than England itself, and yet it always sounds so current, so *now.* As in, Fuck me *now.*

He slid on a form-fit condom and it made his cock appear even bigger. Then I realized it had leads of some kind and he snaked them out and stuck them to my clit. Hardware technologist? I thought again. Or did he buy this stuff somewhere? I don't keep up on new sex toy technologies. Then he was inside me, the first thrust pushing for an awkward moment against me until it slid in, and suddenly I was clinging to him with all my limbs. His whole body was hard and rigid with well-toned muscle, in motion it felt like it rippled, as I imagined his cock rippling inside me. Maybe it was. Who knows what his doodad could do. His thingamajig. His apparatus. But that makes it sound like I'm referring to his anatomy, not to his device. See?

I was losing myself in the sensation, almost not believing that I actually found what I was looking for. His thrusts got harder; my hands roamed over his shaven head; he slowed down and made each one long and deep; I clawed at his back as if I could push him deeper.

A little bit later, as he held himself above me with his arms, going in with short jerks, he said, "Do you go there often?"

My breath was short and it seemed an odd time for a verbal exchange, but I participated. "Aren't you supposed to ask that before you take me home?"

He ground in hard, painful in the way that I like. "Answer me."

"I used to, I guess." I said, realizing I still think of myself as a regular even though none of the old crowd is there anymore, and I'd been there, what, once, twice this year? Only when I've been desperate. And before that there was Sasha. "You?"

He shrugged and switched to grinding his hips in a circle. "Not that often. Not enough women there. I mean, worth meeting."

I tensed, the relationship question surfacing briefly as I read the potential implications of his words. He was onto his next question already. "Rough you up, fuck you, but safely, huh?"

I nodded, my breath coming in time with his strokes.

"Why'd you call me 'sir' back in the bar? I don't see any discipline chain on you." He moved his head, a redundancy in the communication as he made a false show of looking for my hidden/nonexistent chain.

I tried to shrug but it came out like a spasm. "Don't know. Just feeling you out, I guess."

"Good. Because I don't need no stray pets around here, you know what I mean? I can't take care of a slave. Too much responsibility."

"Oh yeah," I agreed, "too much. I'm not into that kind of thing anyway," I said, but I knew from the tone of my voice and the way he looked at me that the lie was obvious. "I mean, not anymore," I amended.

He shut his eyes suddenly and doubled his pace. "Good," he said again. "'Long's we understand . . . each other."

 Cecilia Tan

And then he began to come. I knew it not just from the way he clenched and strained in his throat, but because the sensation was channeled through his condom device (which I'd forgotten about) into me, and in a millisecond I was coming, too. Right from the center, deep rooted in me, the orgasm squeezed my guts and then exploded outward through my bones.

He disengaged and peeled off the gadget, let it fall on the floor as he slumped next to me. "That's how I make sure my partner always gets off," he said. "The anxiety of worrying about it was enough to keep me from cruising before. I mean, there's only so much . . . bah, you know what I mean."

I did. For a lover, a girlfriend, a wife, you could take your time and figure out her favorite things and invest more emotional energy in her orgasm. But with a one-night trick? "Thoughtful of you," I answered, unable to move a muscle other than my mouth, or so it seemed.

"Nah, just practical." He sat up then and I was amazed that he could. He was looking at me and I realized this was an honest-to-God postcoital chat.

"So," I said, against my better judgment, "why do you think a slave's too much to handle?"

"Tried once," he said, his face impassive. "Fucked it up. You?"

"Tried once," I said. "Was the one who got fucked up "

We both nodded like: That's what I thought.

"Well anyway," he said. "You want something to eat? Drink?"

I propped myself on an elbow. "Nah, got to get back to work."

"You do?"

I shrugged. I didn't really have to start the next project until next week. But I didn't have anything better to do, and I didn't want . . . something. "I'm in software," I explained. "It's never finished."

"Hardware neither," he answered, but got up from the bed. He fished for something in his discarded jeans. "Here, my card. Give me a call in a couple of weeks if you want to do this again. Don't bother with the Market. Buncha sleazeballs there."

"Yeah." I took the card and watched his shadow on the other side of the screen.

"Shower?"

"Yeah, okay." We got into the spray not looking at each other. I did not scrub his back and he did not scrub mine. I got dressed and felt very tired. I slipped his card into my back pocket.

"Hey," he said, as I shrugged on my jacket. "What's your name?"

I opened my mouth but nothing came out. Names meant things, depending on what you meant by "name." In the owner-slave world, it meant something specific. He didn't mean it that way, but I couldn't seem to answer it any other way. "Don't have one," I said then, cursing myself (and Sasha) as I did. "If I did, I wouldn't be here."

He looked at me sidelong and wrapped a towel around his waist. "I thought you were over all that shit."

"Nope," I said. "Never said that."

"Okay then." He took a step forward, his nipples standing out against his hard chest. "I'll give you a name to use with me." But *that's all*, his eyes said. "If," he added, "you think you really will call me."

"I don't know." I bit my lip.

He held up his hands. "Hey, you're the one playing the game, not me."

He was right. I was the one insisting on this stupid thing. I could just tell him my real name and we could be friends and that would be that. He might even know me from the nets. "Lucin," I said then, "not short for Lucinda."

He smiled. "Terence. Not long for Terry." We shook hands, which felt ridiculous. "But I was going to call you something like Cocksucker."

We both blushed and laughed a little to hear it out loud. "You're being sarcastic, right?"

"Not exactly," he said, shifting from one foot to the other. "I mean, you *did*."

"Yeah, but I suck at sucking."

"Not me you didn't."

"Really?"

"Yes, all right, Cock Worshiper."

"That's closer," I said.

"Cock Martyr," he went on, "Cock Saint."

"Now you're pushing it."

"So are you," he said, still smiling. His hand reached for me and even though I stepped back, his long hard fingers still clutched my lapel. "I just want to give you something appropriate, you know." His voice softened with practiced menace and I had one brief moment of curiosity about what he must have been like as a master, flashes wondering what went wrong, before I put it out of my mind to listen to what he said. "Something that would tell you for sure what I think of you, who you are, what's expected, and what the limit is." It was embarrassing to hear him explain the things I already knew, and not be able to tell him that I knew but that it didn't help, that I was still brain damaged when it came to certain issues. "So I thought Cocksucker might fit. If it doesn't, you can walk out of here and name yourself or find someone else who'll do it for you." He let go of me with a self-righteous shrug. "*I'm* just looking for a good screw from time to time."

I held up my hands in apology, not surrender. "You're right. I'm jerking you around. I'm sorry. It was such a terribly nice good screw, too."

"So get out of here why don't you?" He was smiling again and his eyes looked sleepy. "Quit angsting and get some rest."

"Thanks."

"Don't mention it."

I had to walk back to the Market to pick up my two-wheeler, and then there was the ride home in dark wind and deserted streets. For once the only chatter I could hear was from a loose valve; even street signs seemed mute. I didn't have to decide whether I would call him again yet. Next time I emerged from a project maybe. Maybe next time.

Under my direction, Michael, the agency's driver, took me into West Hollywood, where all the best used-clothing shops seem to have ended up.

"What are we looking for today?" he asked as he swung the white electric convertible onto the boulevard. The top was up, of course—even a few minutes of sun exposure would likely lose me some jobs to a severely burned nose, not to mention skin cancer at an early age. Whether I could get the full use out of the convertible or not, it was a much cuter car than the old gas-guzzling limos. I think the anticombustion laws were as good for auto aesthetics as for the air quality.

I stretched in the soft bucket seat. "Oh, I dunno. Maybe something to get me in the mood for this new shoot Charles set up."

"What sort of mood is that?" Michael loved to chat, one of the reasons all the girls love him at the agency.

"Good question." Reaching from the back seat, I tweaked the brim of his official chauffeur hat. "Some rock band wants me to do this big thing, it'll be some video footage, plus still shots for album art, plus who knows what else."

"So, what kind of thing are we talking about? More neo-hippie, love-bead stuff?"

"No, that's out again. These guys want me to

pose on a motorcycle. Some kind of Ms. James Dean–*Wild One* thing."

"Wasn't that Brando in *The Wild One?*"

"Whatever." I watched the palm trees lined up like an honor guard along the side of the road and suppressed the urge to wave to passersby. "It's big money. It's almost a retro-eighties, tits-and-leather kind of video."

He nodded, the dark curls of his lashes flickering for a moment as he glanced at me. "I can't picture it."

"What?" So my tits aren't the size of Dollywood.

"You, on a motorcycle." He craned his neck as he made a turn across two lanes of traffic.

"Me either. I guess I've done weirder things." Although at the time I couldn't think of any outstanding ones. Well, there was that one time with the MGM lion—I decided against bringing it up. "You can let me out here."

"Right here?"

"Sure. Meet me at three-thirty by the skin salon." I had a foot out of the car before he'd come completely to a stop. In fact, maybe Michael never did bring the car to a full stop. I shut the door and he was away before I'd even turned around.

The first shop I went in had nothing interesting. Some kind of retro-eighties, Spandex-and-Day-Glo stuff, but when I asked about used leather the frizz-headed woman behind the counter just shrugged and said, "You can't buy leather no more." Well, duh, that's why I was looking for it in a *used*-clothing shop. Well, it's not as if I needed to find any. On the motorcycle shoot the place would be crawling with wardrobe experts and costume designers and tailors, and no doubt they'd have something for me to wear that would look even more like real leather than real leather would. But when the next three shops in a row were duds, I began to think it was a conspiracy against me. I mean, I lived twenty years without ever wanting to own any, and now that I'm finally looking for some, there's none.

In the dressing room of the fourth shop I called Charles. He was busy, as always, but never too busy for me. "About the motorcycle shoot," I said. "Are you sure about this?" I cradled the phone between my ear and shoulder as I worked the red miniskirt off the hanger. "I'm starting to think it could be kind of tacky, you know. I mean, leather, all that. Not PC." I stepped out of the red heels Janice had left behind when she moved out. It had been so handy having a roommate with the same shoe size. "Doesn't it?"

"No, no, Selia, I told you before. It'll be good exposure for you."

"Ha." I considered myself lucky to have Charles for an agent. My previous agent called "good exposure" a porno spread. He was long gone, now that fame was in my pocket. I've always considered there were two ways to do things— the low way and the high way—and Charles always chose the high. That didn't mean I wouldn't give him a hard time just to make sure. "I've got all the exposure I need, Charles."

Charles knew when to pour on the hard sell. "You think the cover of *Cosmo* is going to last? This album will be selling for years to come, and with the video and all the tie-ins, your face will be everywhere. T-shirts, posters, advertising, you name it." Charles put in a dramatic pause. "It's a quantum leap, Sel."

"Yeah, but this *Wild One* concept? What am I, Ms. James Dean?"

"Uh, I think it was Brando . . . "

"Whatever." It's not my face they'll be looking at, I thought as I slipped the skirt on and stepped back into the shoes. The mirror hung just crooked enough to be arty rather than accidental. The shoes and the miniskirt weren't quite the same shade of red, but I doubted anyone would care. "If you're sure . . . "

"I'm sure. Besides, the contracts are already signed."

"Right."

I folded the phone down, set it on beeper mode in case my

parents tried to call, and tucked it back into my purse. I pulled on my oversize plaid jacket (God, I can't wait for that to go out of style again), pushed my sunglasses up my nose, and looked into the mirror once more. I saw a twenty-year-old who was too skinny, too flat-chested, with oily skin and dry hair. By now I knew what the rest of the world saw: a supermodel with a perfectly straight nose, matched eyes, and parochial-school posture. In a bargain-basement miniskirt and secondhand shoes. I couldn't picture either one of us on a motorcycle, but I bought the skirt anyway. It was such a bargain I couldn't pass it up. You think all supermodels wear are one-of-a-kind designer digs they spend all their hard-earned cash on? Or that they get it for sleeping with the designers? Oh, no. Not a working girl like me. All the designers are gay anyway, and even the superfamous can appreciate a bargain.

On the day of the shoot I arrived at the soundstage with no makeup on, in jeans and a T-shirt. At six-thirty A.M. there are no fans or paparazzi to embarrass myself in front of so I didn't even bother to cover the little zit on my chin. I just showed up with some magazines in my bag for when it got boring, and an apple. At first it felt like any other assignment, but as I was crossing the dark soundstage, I saw a shape in the shadows draped with a tarp, and I remembered why I'd thought this one might be weird. *The motorcycle shoot.*

There hadn't been motorcycles on the American roads since the anticombustion laws, the highway moderation laws, and the safe citizen protection laws had come down heavy in 1999. Sure, there were plenty of electric scooters in a bevy of fashion colors, but nothing that resembled the noisy, macho machines of the past. I'd never even seen a real one.

And now, there was one out in the midst of a big empty space in the dark, like some sleeping animal. I resisted the urge to either walk up to it or to run into the makeup trailer. I would meet my new dance partner soon enough. It couldn't be worse than that shoot I had to do with the MGM lion. Did I mention he had halitosis like you wouldn't believe?

Makeup went pretty quick; I wasn't paying any attention to what they were doing to me. I was thinking about the motorcycle. Everything I knew about motorcycles, I knew from old movies that I hadn't even seen but had only heard of, like *Easy Rider.* Was there also one called *Route 66,* or was that just a song? I knew that in the Sixties the highway police in California had ridden motorcycles even, or maybe that was only the obscure law enforcement branch called Hell's Angels. They didn't teach this kind of stuff in school. Not that I went to school anyway. Then they were done crimping my hair and powdering my nose, and it was time to go out. They put me in a bathrobe since the wardrobers weren't ready yet, and gave me slippers for my feet.

Now all the lights were on, bright and hot, as they prepped cameras, both for filming and photographing. And in the middle of the empty space I expected to see one of those gleaming metal monsters. But all I saw was a bundle of tarp, bound with bungee cords. Someone brought me a chair to sit in, and so I did, while the crew bustled around me.

I'd left my magazines in the makeup trailer so I had nothing to do but sit like a mannequin in some storefront, ever watching. I was about to nod off to sleep when I noticed her, a tech person standing by the tarp. Her back was to me, but I was sure that under the overalls and baseball cap she was female. She wiped her cheek on her sleeve and began unwrapping the cords, backing up toward me, dragging the tarp until we were both staring at the motorcycle.

She stepped forward and ran a cloth over the top and the silvery pipes out the side. No one but me seemed to be paying the slightest attention to her. She crouched down to inspect the spokes of the front wheel and I stood up. She must have heard the scuff of the slippers on the concrete floor as I crossed the empty space between us, because she looked over her shoulder at me. She never took her eyes off me as she turned and stood in one motion. She wiped her hands on the rag while I stood there trying to think of something to say and she said nothing.

"Nice bike," I offered.

She shrugged. "Dragged it out of storage last night." She was a head shorter than I was, and much more round and solid than she'd looked from a distance.

Now that I was standing close, the motorcycle looked much bigger than I thought it should have, as if I'd been expecting a bicycle. The sides were painted in blue and silvery grey with a tapered shape like a teardrop, over which the letters read HARLEY-DAVIDSON. I reached out to touch the paint and realized my palms were sweating.

"Careful you don't scratch the gas tank." She motioned with the rag.

I pulled my fingers back. "Where?"

"This here." She ran the rag over the painted section. "This is the gas tank. If they put you in leather and studs or whatever, don't let your belt buckle scratch this part."

Gas tank. "It can't, I mean, there's no danger of it exploding or anything is there?"

She smiled, but it wasn't at me, and shook her head a little. "Hell, no. This thing hasn't even had gas in it for years. I had to push it here."

She climbed on top then, straddling it like a cowboy in the saddle, and I wondered if that was allowed, somehow. "There is a battery though; they wanted the lights on for this." She pulled a key from an overall pocket and stuck it in above the gas tank. It turned with a click and the headlight came on. "Be careful of this." She pointed to something on the handlebar. "This is the horn."

"Is it a problem?" I asked, wondering if the horn could shock me or something. I felt terribly underdressed all of a sudden, standing next to this oversized machine and this woman in workboots and denim.

"No, just embarrassing if you honk it when you don't mean to. It can startle you."

She stepped off again, and I watched the headlight tip as it shifted under her weight. "Will it, I mean, can it fall over?" I was still thinking of old movies, how whenever an old car would drive off the road, it would explode.

Again, she smiled that little smile. "I doubt it. This bike weighs at least five times what you do. I don't think you'll be able to budge it." I wondered how she estimated my weight, and what she thought of it. She pointed with her foot to a skinny metal arm that rested on the floor. "This is the kickstand."

"And it holds up something that heavy?"

"Obviously." She was wiping her hands again, like they'd gotten greasy, though I couldn't see any. "You'll get used to it," was all she said, and then she began walking away.

"Wait!" I scuffed a pace after her and she turned around. "Will you be around? If I have any, you know, problems with it?"

She just nodded to me and kept walking.

The rock-and-roll wardrobers finally called for me some time later, just as Charles was showing up. "How's it going, Sel?" he asked as two men were measuring me for size.

I tried to smile. "So, when are these rock stars showing up?"

"What am I, their manager?" He shrugged, his unbuttoned leisure jacket exposing the potbelly he was beginning to grow. "I'm going to get some coffee."

One of the wardrobers helped me out of the bathrobe and into a jacket made of heavy black stuff. "Is this real leather?"

He smiled as he adjusted the zippers and buckles. He had thin dark sideburns and thick eyebrows to match. "No, no. We tried to, of course, to get some. I tried to tell them 'Having Selia pose in imitation leather is like having her pose in imitation fur!'"

"Well . . ." In fact, I hadn't posed in any kind of fur, real or otherwise. Selling it was banned before I ever got any ritzy jobs. "It was nice of you to think of me."

He blushed.

"Am I going to get something for under this?"

"Oh, yes. I only do the jacket first because it would take the longest to tailor." He stepped back, tugged on laces running up the sides. "But, it hangs right as is."

He handed me a full bodysuit in sleek black, thin as tissue but opaque and four-way stretch. Once I had that, I put the jacket back on and he and another wardrober began lacing my legs into some kind of leatherette pants that zipped up the inside of my thighs and tightened with laces down the outside. They didn't cover my butt. I thought they were pretty weird until the first wardrober, whose name I hadn't learned, stood back and said, "Ride 'em cowboy," and then it made sense. They were chaps, like the Marlboro man wore before he was banned, too.

The chaps had to come off twice while they tried different boots on me. The cowboy boots looked stupid, and the first pair of black boots were some kind of ultra-shiny stuff that didn't match the leatherette of the rest of the outfit. The nice wardrober prayed to some higher power, his tape measure hanging down from his shoulders like a rosary, and then sent one of his underlings off on an errand. I sat in my designated chair for an hour while he was gone, as I tried to think, what kind of boots did a motorcycler wear? I tried to conjure up a picture, Brando or whomever. Were these guys always shown from the waist up, or what?

 Cecilia Tan

The underling came back with several boxes, all the same thing in different sizes. "Chinese sizing," he explained as he pulled them out in front of me. I could smell them, a salty kind of smell. "I wasn't sure how to convert it so I just bought a couple different ones. Save me another trip."

"Chinese sizing?" I repeated, as he took the wadded paper out of the smallest pair. "Are these smuggled?"

"Chinatown. These are real leather."

"Oh." Things just got weirder again. I knew wardrobers would go to almost any lengths to get the right look, but if he had been caught buying these it would have been two years in jail under California State law and I don't know how many under federal. I had to stand up to get my feet into them. They fit. "Not bad, first try." Now it was back to makeup for a fresher after all the sitting around.

The rock stars were here now, four of them standing in a semicircle looking at the motorcycle and making comments from about four feet back. "Man, it should be one of us on there, not some babe."

"No, the babe on the back."

"Yeah."

None of them got any closer to it or sat on it like the tech woman had.

By noon we were ready for some still shots and the photographer and the creative director walked me out to the motorcycle like it might need wrangling. I put my hand on the handlebar (the one without the horn) like I'd seen the woman do, and tried to swing my leg over the way she had. It almost worked. The chaps made my legs stiff and the boots were heavy, but I didn't fall off or anything. I saw a little look pass between the two guys. Then they went back to yammering about creative effect, attitude, and lights. As always, I ignored this part. Just smile and look pretty is all it ever comes down to in the end.

The machine did feel very solid under me and I relaxed a little. Think about it, Sel, I told myself, if this was the slightest bit dangerous, Charles wouldn't have let you do it. After all, he wasn't the beneficiary of my insurance policy. I felt safer in all the tough leatherette, too. I ran my hands over the smoothness of the chaps. The seat I was on felt like it might be real leather. Then again, I wouldn't know the difference.

Hours went by, as they always do, with flashes and lights and cameras swooping on the ends of computer-controlled arms, as they covered the still shots, the black and white, the color, the film, the video, the digitized HDTV ... I stopped worrying about the thing between my legs. Time made us familiar. When we took a break to freshen my makeup or have a soda, I leaned against it, while the guys in the band skirted around the edges of the light like rats. And then we were filming again and I swung my leg over the seat and felt the machine settle under me. The loudness of the rock-and-roll drowned out all the crew hubbub and the lights made them invisible shadows. My imagination wandered to keep boredom at bay and there I was, riding the beast in a circle of light, machine-made wind blowing back my hair ... was this what it was like, even the slightest bit? To be snaking down the highway with no obligations, no responsibilities, no hangers on? A wild woman, with nowhere to go but all day to get there? I gripped the handlebars and snarled at one camera that flew too close, breaking the dream.

Then, like all image sessions, it was over. The crew was taking down the lights and the wardrobers were waiting anxiously to take back the stuff on my body. There by the folding chairs was the techie woman with her hands in her back pockets, waiting to take the motorcycle back to its shed or garage or wherever it was hidden until some property master called for it again.

"Can I give you a ride to Gianni's?" asked Charles, the keys to his Maserati Series X in his hand. Some kind of reception thing with the band and their management and more free, catered food that I couldn't eat and look the way I do.

"No, don't wait for me," I said, gesturing at all the clothes that still had to come off. "I'll catch up."

And then it was into the clothes I'd packed, something so solidly fashionable it was nondescript. I sent the wardrobers home for that part. One of the band members was hanging around outside the trailer, hoping to make a pass at me, no doubt. I waited until someone else told him he'd miss his limo ride if he didn't get a move on—he could try for me at the party.

Outside, the soundstage was dim and quiet. Someone was whistling and folding up the chairs scattered about. The motorcycle was still there. Perhaps they were going to move it the next morning. I got it into my head to say good-bye to it; then I'd find Michael or page him and get a ride to this reception thing. As I took a step forward, I heard the jingle of keys in rhythm with a heavy booted step. She stepped up to the bike and slotted the key in, swung her leg over, and turned on the light. Her head dipped as she fiddled with something by her leg, and then she rose up and came down hard into the seat. I squinted, trying to see better. Then she repeated the motion and the engine came to life with a sound like an explosion in the emptiness of the hangar.

I took two steps down from the trailer, my hand halfway to my ear. My heels clacked hard against the cement floor but they were drowned out by the throbbing engine sound. I hurried, as if she might fly away, which she might.

"Wait!" I said as I got near, suddenly sure that she would pull out in a screech of tires just as I reached her. "Wait!"

Her head swiveled and she looked at me. Whatever I had been going to say, maybe something about how she'd lied, how there was gas in it, or maybe something else entirely, whatever it was that impelled me to run up to her, now disappeared. She said, her voice cracking a little to be heard, "Need a ride?"

I nodded. I put my hands on her denim-covered shoulders. I swung my leg over the back and settled my butt against the raised seat back. There were pegs for my feet and she settled my hands around her waist.

We couldn't go anywhere, of course. It wasn't legal. This is what I was thinking as my stomach leapt into my throat as the machine lurched forward. She was probably just taking me back to the shed and then I'd call Michael for a ride home or to that stupid party maybe.

I held on to her tighter as we sped up, other gray buildings in the lot blurring by. My jeans pressed tight into my crotch but I was afraid to fidget and upset our balance. What would it be like to fall off this thing? Would I get my skin scraped off? Ew. I held still.

The engine's vibrations were deep, throbbing. There was a *whoosh* as we passed out of the fence that delineated the lot from the scrub desert around it. I sneaked a look around her and saw the black road dividing the twilit ground into two halves. Maybe it was a private road. This was probably where they filmed those millennial remake Westerns. Our speed picked up again and the wind was dry in my face, real wind, not generated by a fan offstage, wind that smelled like tar and wood and long-ago vacations.

I could be at a party right now, getting felt up by some coked-up bass player, paparazzi lenses clicking, the reporters already writing the tabloid headlines in their minds, the same old story, supermodel with Cro-Magnon metalhead. We'd be married in a month and I'd be pregnant as soon as we started fighting, and then it would all fall apart. Come on, I don't have to tell you where I'd rather be. The machine hummed between my legs and something under my bellybutton woke up.

I didn't care if the woman thought I was crazy. Fame will do that to you, you know? And she was probably crazy, too, taking me out here at high speed. I started to hum to myself. I could feel that energy, that throb, right on my button, right inside my stomach, and when I hummed it doubled. If I really wanted to make her think I was crazy, I'd have shoved my hand right into my snatch right there. That really was crazy. There was no way I was letting go of her. Nuh uh.

The wind on my forehead lessened then and I looked up to see what looked like an old gas station up on the right. She slowed and a turn signal blinked (who was she signaling to?), and with a smooth deceleration she pulled under the awning and circled around to the back and into an open garage door. The brakes squeaked as we came to a stop.

The lack of motion made me feel almost dizzy. "Where are we?" I said, the roar of wind still rushing phantomlike in my ears.

"You better get off first," she said over her shoulder.

I swung my leg over and took a step backward. I came to a stop against an old workbench. She clicked off the ignition and held the key in her hand. "You okay?" she said then, squinting at me a little.

There was no one here but the two of us. No press, no shop clerks, no drivers, no handlers, no fans. I had been about to say, "Yeah sure," but my lip trembled a little. Twenty years old and been around the world and until today I'd never worn real leather shoes or ridden an open-air vehicle or smelled gasoline or had my arms around a woman. And now I didn't know what I wanted next. My clit was buzzing the same way my ears were roaring. I stood there like a deer in the proverbial headlights. "Um," I said intelligently. Jesus, I thought, how am I supposed to give her the hint that I'm attracted to her, that I want to have sex with her? It wasn't something I normally had to do, you understand. I spent most of my time fending off interest. I felt like a little girl trying to figure out how to ask if I could go potty.

She sat back against the bike, as comfortable as if she'd

thrown herself down on a secondhand couch. "Like the ride?"

"Yeah. Yeah I liked it a whole lot." The words spilled out in a rush. "Hey, can I ask you something."

"Sure." Outside it was night now and the light from the single bulb overhead was kind to her face. She took off the baseball cap and hung it on one handlebar. Her hair was black underneath it, a little matted but thick, and she looked younger now. "Go ahead."

I was still talking too fast. "I don't want you to think I'm making assumptions just because of the way you look or dress, I mean, I'm not like stupid or anything, and I don't want you to think I'm stereotyping you or anything . . . "

"Yes," she said.

"Excuse me?"

"You're asking if I'm a dyke. Yes. The answer is yes." She squinted in a way that made me think she was hiding a smile. "The real question, though, is, Why do you want to know?"

Okay, Sel, there's two ways to do this, high and low. The low way you grovel or plead and hope she does what you want. The high way, you take charge, you show her you're not a little girl after all. I put my hands on my hips. "That's pretty presumptuous of you."

She shrugged.

I folded my arms over my chest. "But if you must know," let's do this the high way, "I've got an itch and I thought you might want to scratch it."

"Pretty presumptuous of you," she said, but she stood up. One step and she was close enough to touch. She leaned closer, her neck tipped back slightly as I towered over her in my heels. "That might depend on where the itch is."

"It's . . ." I started, but then I gasped as the back of her hand brushed my stomach.

"If it's right here," she said, sliding her hand south, "I think I have just the thing for it."

 Cecilia Tan

I felt something hard but gentle draw a line down to the seam of my jeans, the ignition key in her hand, now pointing at that spot where I could feel it most. We didn't talk after that. I grabbed her hand and pressed it harder there. She ground her fingers into my jeans and I stripped out of my shirt. She buried her face into my soft not-too-large tits and ran one hand down the curve of my ass while the other rubbed my crotch and then began working on my fly.

And to think I'd thought of Quik-seams as just a risque accessory. Once the button clasp came undone, the jeans split into two halves and my cunt was suddenly there, alive and hungry and exposed. She was on tiptoe kissing me then, her arms around me, turning me in a circle like a ballroom dancer, until she settled my ass against that leather saddle. Her lips and tongue made a trail down my breastbone, over my bellybutton, and down to my bush. I braced one hand against the gas tank and one against the back rest, and it was me that exploded.

Then I wasn't sure what to do. I mean, guys, they know when they're finished and they go to sleep or leave or whatever. But I didn't know really what she'd want or how to give it to her. And I could always have more. She shed her jacket onto the floor and pulled me up, placing my hands under her T-shirt. I felt breasts softer and rounder than my own and she moaned when I found her nipples. I gave her a hickey on her neck and she seemed to like that a whole lot.

She moved us to an adjoining room, where there was the secondhand couch I'd pictured in my mind's eye not so long ago. We fell onto it, disrobing further, until what we had was a touchy-feely orgiastic kind of thing going, though there were only two of us. She came rubbing against my leg, riding me like a pony ride, and eventually we were both really tired and decided to stop.

Of course we had to ride the motorcycle back to the lot where her car was, and I got a beep from Michael asking if I needed a ride. The desert night was getting chilly and she put me in an old mechanic's jacket, some kind of sateen with the name BUTCH stitched on it. The ride back seemed shorter even though I got the feeling she was driving slower, to savor it. We switched to her red Honda Bee at the lot, and she dropped me off at home and told me to keep the jacket. It was the same faded red as Janice's old red heels. Maybe I could start a new trend wearing it. It was only ten-thirty; there was still time for me to get to that party. I swapped my jeans for the red mini and dialed Michael's number. The metalheads and tabloid sharks could circle all they wanted. No one was going to get near me tonight—they were all as far away as a memory and just as slight.

"Three of Cups" is original to this collection and debuts here.

"The Nightingale" first appeared in *Once Upon a Time,* edited by Michael Thomas Ford, A Richard Kasak Book, 1996; and was given an Honorable Mention in *Year's Best Fantasy and Horror 1996,* edited by Terri Windling and Ellen Datlow.

"Dragon Cat Flower" first appeared in *Herotica 5,* edited by Marcy Sheiner, Plume, 1998.

"Tale of Christina" first appeared in *Dark Angels: Lesbian Vampire Stories,* edited by Pam Keesey, Cleis Press, 1995.

"Pearl Diver" first appeared in *On a Bed of Rice: Asian American Erotica,* edited by Geraldine Kudaka, Anchor, 1995; and subsequently appeared in *Ms.* magazine (November 1995) and *Best American Erotica 1996,* edited by Susie Bright, Touchstone, 1996.

"In Silver A" first appeared in *Absolute Magnitude* magazine (Fall 1998).

"Cat Scratch Fever" first appeared in the chapbook *Telepaths Don't Need Safewords,* by Cecilia Tan, Circlet Press, 1992.

"Telepaths Don't Need Safewords" first appeared in the chapbook *Telepaths Don't Need Safewords,* by Cecilia Tan, Circlet Press, 1992; and subsequently appeared in *SM Visions: The Best of Circlet Press,* edited by Cecilia Tan, A Richard Kasak Book, 1995.

"The Game" first appeared in *No Other Tribute,* edited by Laura Antoniou, Rosebud, 1995.

"The Velderet, Chapter One," first appeared in *Taste of Latex* magazine (Number 10, March 1995).

"Crooked Kwan" first appeared in *Noirotica,* edited by Thomas S. Roche, Rhinoceros Books, 1996.

"Porn Flicks" first appeared in *Herotica 4,* edited by Marcy Sheiner, Plume, 1996.

"Rock Steady" first appeared in *Backstage Passes,* edited by Amelia G, Rhinoceros Books, 1996.

"Jean-Michel & Juno" first appeared in *Paramour* magazine (Volume 2, Issue 1, October 1994).

"Blood Ties" is original to this collection and debuts here.

"Whipmaster" first appeared in *Looking for Mr. Preston,* edited by Laura Antoniou, A Richard Kasak Book, 1995.

"Rough, Trade" first appeared in *Eros Ex Machina,* edited by M. Christian, Masquerade Books, 1998.

"The High Way" first appeared in *Close Encounters of the Queer Kind,* edited by Stan Leventhal and Richard LaBonte, Masquerade Books, 1998.